THE LAST MAGNOLIA

Dixie Lee Anderson

Names: Anderson, Dixie Lee
Title: The Last Magnolia/Dixie Lee Anderson
Identifiers: ISBN 9781703434026

Photograph of Author by Moa Boyles
Photograph on Cover by Sarah J. Anderson

DEDICATION

For the perfect daughter, Sarah Jo Anderson
Who encouraged and worked with me to return to the story

and

For my beloved son, Kenneth Curtis Anderson,

And With
Such Wonderful Memories Of
My Husband
Kenneth W. Anderson
Best Friend
Mentor
Lover
I wish you were somehow here again.

Acknowledgements

This story and the stories within it were read, liked and recommended enough for me to continue to the conclusion. Good friends, interested individuals, fellow writers, readers and family helped to put it together. Even the people who watched me swim laps at the local swimming pool. They all complained that they couldn't read my lips as my head came out of the water with each stroke, but they knew that I was writing some dialog.

Thanks to Betty Jo Webb, the editor with a smart pen. She has been so much help to me.

Dina Santorelli, my many talented friend, and excellent author, for encouragement and praise ("Dixie I can hear your voice as I read this" or "Dixie, when I grow up I want to be like you!").

My dear husband Kenneth gone for so many years now, who tolerated my writing time and educated me as to aircraft, bombing missions and secret missions during the first war of several he served in.

My family Ken, Sarah, Curtis and Lisa who saw to it that I remained their mother who cooked, gardened, wrote, loved and praised them. Norma and David, their children who grew up and presented us with Great-Grand's who with busy padding feet and skill on the surf are still keeping us informed and busy, full of laughter, and that means happy.

To my readers who added suggestions, criticized and asked for corrections, and praised to send me back to the keyboard. Judy Allen, Mary G. Anderson, Gayle Friedman, Beth Huff, Patricia Minnick, Vivian Greenberg, Norma and David Carlson, Charlie and Sue Damitz, Annmarie Carbin so many so helpful. THANK YOU!

Chapter 1

JOHNNY

August 1931

Crispin, Nebraska

"That's it boy, the third house in the row. You'll find your mother upstairs. Go! Get her. Bring her back to me. Bring her back to the car." Short, terse and tense, the commands were punctuated by the man's arm as it was flung forward to point down the street.

"What shall I say, Dad?"

The boy, blond, tall, probably ten years old, maybe more if height were to determine his age, climbed on to the running board, and holding the open door for support he hesitated. He was dressed immaculately in starched denims. A white shirt, open at the collar, was only beginning to go limp in the summer's heat, and his crisp, sun-bleached hair had been carefully combed with water that still glistened in the comb's tracks.

There was emotion, turmoil, perhaps even an underlying shade of grief in the boy's voice but his straight, obedient, eager-to-please demeanor masked it childishly.

The black Ford touring car, large and cumbersome on its thin wheels, had come into this town of Crispin, Nebraska the back way. It had climbed up and over the steep grade of the railroad tracks, bumped across them, and pulled to the side, just opposite

1

the grade. It was from this vantage that the older man instructed his son. "Your grandmother had a call from a woman here in town. Said she saw your mother at the store and found out where she was staying." The man asserted his authority over the young boy with a direct, dominant expression. His own emotions were held in check by this forceful assertion. His pride had been stung by the act of desertion. His young wife had left him for another man. "You can't hide much in a town this size, Johnny." The man slumped slightly and let out a heavy sigh of breath, but just as quickly the starch of a command asserted itself. "Go now. He's at work, so she's alone. Tell her you want her home."

"Who's 'he', Dad? Is it Fred?" Johnny needed more answers than he understood, still he was afraid to anger his father with too much curiosity. "Is Fred sick? Why would mom be with him? Is she taking care of him?" The boy's innocence triggered an anticipated response of anger. His father's voice snarled, "Get over there! There's enough scandal over this without us sitting here in Crispin to be stared at." The man quieted some and added, "See there, it's the third house on the left, the house with the big elm tree in front. Just go and tell her you want her to come home." The boy made a false start. He wasn't sure he wanted anything to do with this.

There was something wrong, something he didn't understand and he didn't know how to get out of it. "You come too, Dad," he turned to look at his father closely, "you can tell her better than I can." John senior pushed his son's shoulder, "Go Johnny, she's always favored you. She'll listen to you."

Johnny started down the street slowly, feet dragging in the gravel. He didn't turn back to his father again, nor did he look up in the direction he was taking. Head down, he tried to answer the many questions he had for himself. He knew he had been given a difficult task, difficult in that he simply didn't understand. As he scuffed along, he thought, thought about words. What could he say to his mother, the woman who was the brightest light in his world? She shared with him, depended on him and loved him. He knew that and loved her with the only emotion he really knew at this tender age. What could he say to her? She had left them all without any explanation and had stayed away for nearly a week. Her absence had created a distance much further than the house where he had been sent to fetch her.

Only a few hours ago, at noon, his grandmother had come to the farm and her talk with his dad had been secreted behind the parlor doors. When the two of them came out, they saw to it that he was cleaned up and put in the car with his father. Now here he was, questioning, nervous, occupied with words he was trying to put together. A frown of concentrated sadness created a creased brow on Johnny's young face.

He passed the first house, stopped, only a slight hesitation, and then took the next step to move with determination past the second house. Still walking in the center of the street, he paused at the front of the third dwelling. He crossed to stand under a large tree for the coolness of shade, and then turned towards the front window and stopped. His eyes moved up to the white curtains hanging limply on the open windows of the second story.

Over to the side of the house he saw wooden steps leading to a landing and a door that probably opened into the rooms at the top. His gaze returned to the windows. He felt terrible. Embarrassed. What did they expect of him? There wasn't any movement upstairs that he could see, and his head went down again as his freshly shined boots dug their toes into the gravel, trying to stir up summer's dust, trying to kill time. The shadows of the late afternoon were long, yet the temperature and humidity were even more oppressive than they had been at noon. A trickle of sweat came from his hairline to his eyebrows and stayed there. He wiped it away with his right hand as he started back to his father who was still sitting in the parked car. His father gestured broadly with stressed authority, motioning towards the steps, urging him on.

Why me? Why does he want me to do this the boy asked himself? He looked up again at the motionless windows and cried softly, "Mom, it's me, Johnny. Mom, please come out." A curtain stirred on the first floor front of the house, but no one could be seen. He knew though, there was someone behind that curtain, watching him. Ignoring the hidden person, he continued to speak softly, but with an overlying strength, "Mom, please come down here and talk to me."

There she was! She was just as beautiful as he remembered her. His heart skipped a beat.

She leaned forward slightly from an upstairs window. Thick blonde hair capped her head and framed a beautiful face accented with brown-yellow doe-like eyes. Otherwise the face was vacant. Resignation, perhaps pain, seemed to be the depth of her expression, it was dull and accepting, but there was also concern for the young boy standing below and looking up at her. She had known something like this would happen. Fred had assured her that they would be all right, but she knew, knew John would find her. Her heart turned with heaviness. Fred. Where was he now? He had really made her believe that eventually, when they got their feet on the ground, they would send for her children. She should have known she couldn't walk out of her unhappy life with John into the joys she had pictured with Fred.

What was joy? She sighed inwardly. She would never know it, she guessed. A vision of the well-kept farm she had deserted passed through her mind. She felt guilt, but only over the children. There was no remorse over her husband John. Life couldn't work for them anymore. It really never had. The children though, Johnny, standing down there now, was her first born, Donna, the daughter she had wanted so badly, and the baby, just a little over a year were the ones she loved and couldn't leave behind. She and Fred really meant to go back for them, but it would take time. The realization that time wasn't to be hers made her shudder when icy knives pushed between her shoulder blades. Looking down again at Johnny, her big boy, she wondered, how could he understand? He was so young. Heavily in a stage whisper, she said, "Johnny, go home. Don't yell in the street like that. Go home, Johnny."

The conflict of authority between the parents confused the boy. Who should he listen to? There was his father, back there insisting that he talk to his mother, bring her home. Here, up in the window was his mother, hushing him, trying to send him back alone. He thought for a minute and made a decision. His was an important task. He had to bring his mother home. That would be the best for everyone. His voice gained in strength, "Mom, please come down. I need to talk to you," he swallowed, this next part was something he had never said out loud before, this was the hard part, "Mom, I love you." Rushing on quickly, as if to cover those last words, as if he shouldn't have said them, "We all need you. Donna and the baby are waiting for you at home. Dad and I promised we'd bring you back to them...back home," now the words tumbled out of the boy's mouth, "Grandma just found out where you were and we came to give you a ride home, Mom." He paused, then added, to assure himself that he was talking her language, "The baby is crying all the time for you." At this point Johnny's voice broke, and the tears coursed down his face. Tears poured steadily, his hand couldn't keep them wiped away, and his voice became a little boy's voice now, nagging, wailing, like that of a small child begging for a treat. He wasn't in control of himself anymore.

"We have Grandma's car here, please come back with us. We need you so bad." Sobs wracked his body and the handsome face twisted with a combination of grief and shame because he was crying, and tears continued to run down his cheeks. She moved from the window and crossed to the door leading to the steps. Of course they had Grandma's car. She had known when she bumped into Mary Gillam's mother at the store that she was found out, knew they would come to get her. Somehow she had pushed the fact back to be covered with her happiness with Fred, and her hope for the promised future. Now reality had arrived with her young son crying in the street.

She shook her head. What did John think he was doing, sending this child out in the street to beg for her? Anger and pride pushed her through the screen door and she started down the steps towards her son as fast as she could move.

Johnny, still crying, turned once more to look at his father, to seek the assurance of more directives, but out of the corner of his eye, he spotted his mother coming down the steps. He ran to her and threw his arms around her waist.

She looked around at the curtains that obviously hid someone behind them, watching this scene, this humiliating scene between errant mother and sobbing son.

"Come upstairs with me, out of the sun," she rubbed the boy's blond hair, so like her own, back and forth as she held him close to walk up the steps.

Unable to stop the wet tears, Johnny was still sobbing with heaving gasps for breath. He tried to fit as close to her as possible. This was the woman who had been his playmate, his friend, his protector. A great swelling surge of love gave him the closeness to his mother he needed, and any confusion about his mission or the reasons for it was erased. He was with his mother now, the most important woman in the world, and he was going to take her home.

Once in the upstairs room, she sat him down on a kitchen chair and went to a stained, raw open sink where she ran water on a small patch of cloth. Threads clung to her roughly callused hands as she wiped his face.

"Don't cry anymore Johnny," she kept dabbing his face with the cool rag as she looked at her son with sad, open love and regret over the pain she had caused the boy. With cool comfort satiating and relieving his tension, Johnny looked around the room where his mother had been living. He had no knowledge of beauty or of style or abundance, innocent as he was about those things, he realized the oppression of his mother's present surroundings. A sharp flash of momentary maturity enabled the boy to understand the depths to which his mother had dropped when she left home. He felt, with his love, a great pity for her.

The room was awful. As he looked around he saw a bed with a visible sag in the middle. It was covered with a chenille spread that had lost most of its tufting. Beside the bed was a small table and over by the front window a straight wood chair was positioned to face the window. On the opposite side of the room, a chest of drawers with knobs missing, and scars of use etching its finish, stood against the wall. There was a nicked porcelain sink. It had been white once but was now brown-yellow and stained. He pictured the beautiful white sink at home, saw the warm farm kitchen, its cupboards filled with her treasured nice things.

How could she live here? Why would she leave the good things they had to come to this? The boy couldn't find any answers and he was embarrassed for his mother. He hated to look at her for fear she would read his thoughts and feel bad. When he finally did turn to her he nearly cried again. Large tears balancing on the lower rims of her eyes were ready to spill over. He sensed her shame, knew he needed to help her.

In an effort toward making her more at ease, toward wiping away her tears, he said, "Mom, Dad says you can come back."

She recoiled visibly, but Johnny missed the reaction as he went on, "See Mom, he sent me to talk to you, and bring you home." Another sob caught in his throat and he went on, "I really need you. I can't take care of the kids. We need you." He took a deep breath, plunged on, "The baby cries all the time." She watched her tortured son closely as he continued. "Come on home Mom, come back."

She turned away from him to look out the window. Expressions played over her face. There was resolve, loss, resignation, most of all, anger. Everything is such a mess she thought. Walking back to Johnny, she patted him on the shoulder, "Yes son, I'll come with you."

She pulled the curtain covering the small closet back, and retrieved a wicker suitcase. "I'll pack."

Johnny leaned back in his chair and the air came out of him

in one deep, shuddering breath. She was coming home! He felt relaxed, happy and eager to leave this shabby room.

She moved from the closet to the suitcase, to put clothes that were familiar to him inside. In only minutes she fastened the suitcase shut. "That's all, I guess." Pulling the case from the bed, she handed it to her son, "carry this for me, John."

There weren't any more tears for her. Resignation wasn't even evidenced with a sigh as she led the way to the screen door and held it open for the boy.

He stepped out, and she turned to give the room a final look. This was where she had experienced the first kindness in her life, the first real love. Her eyes lit on a box of red velvet raspberries sitting in the stained sink. She had bought them only today, hours before, for Fred's dinner. There had been such happiness in those plans. And as she remembered, heavy fringed eyelashes lowered over her eyes to squeeze back moisture. Turning, she let the screen door slam behind her as she started down the steps.

The black car had moved up the street and was parked across from the house. "Put the bag in the back, Johnny." His father didn't look at his wife or acknowledge her presence.

The boy opened the back door of the sedan, happy in his accomplishment, but disappointed that his dad gave his deed no recognition. He pushed in the bag and climbed in behind it. His mother walked around the back of the car, put her right foot on the running board and swung her body up and onto the seat. Before she had pulled the door completely shut, the car was put into gear. It plunged forward with a jerk, snapping her body forward and then back against the seat. The man didn't say a word.

She looked over at him, and sat up straight, as courage or

perhaps one last attempt at hanging on to the strength of her few days of independence took hold. Gazing straight forward she said, "This was wrong John, you shouldn't have sent our son to do this. He's just a little boy."

John Knowlton Senior never took his eyes from the road, and his retort was strong, bitter and forceful. Forceful and quick enough to take the square from her shoulders and slap her verbally back against the seat of the car, erasing any new-found courage in dealing with him. "The wrong is yours, Mildred, you're an adulteress, just that. Don't forget it. I won't." He spit his words out in fury, "From now on, you stay home and take care of your family. How I'll live this down is beyond me. I'll live in shame for the rest of my days, and you're the cause of it. From here on out girl, you just stay home and tend to your chores. I'll have no other need for you." He was chewing tobacco and he punctuated the last words by turning his head and spitting a dark streak of tobacco juice through the open window.

Johnny, sitting in the back seat, his face grimy from tears, dust, sweat and humidity thought, I did it! I did the right thing. His mind wandered. He had tried to please his father by doing what he'd asked, and that, he decided, must surely please his mother too. He knew that having her home with them was what he wanted, and with the ignorance of childhood, he assumed that since she had agreed to come with him, it was what she wanted too. To young to realize the heartache he had been a part of on this day, he pushed Crispin, the awful house and Fred out of his mind. Now he was sure. Things could be back the way they had been before. His mind wasn't yet ready to form opinions or to make judgments. He was still a boy who had done what he had been told to do. Reality left him along with the responsibilities of the afternoon, and daydreams began. Someday he'd have a car like this, he dreamed. There would be a difference though. He'd be in front, driving. He lifted his hands as if to hold the edges of a steering wheel and drifted further into his dream of the future. A smile crept across his face. There was an uneasy, peaceful feeling in him. His mother was coming home. They were together again.

Chapter 2

MILDRED

August 1931

Harper, Nebraska

The day's drudgery had begun. She was home again.

As she scoured the milk cans, a look of tedium crossed her face. That's it. Milk cans to do... baby...she glanced over her shoulder to be sure he was all right. Children. Canning. Chickens. Dinner. Oh Lord. Why?

Tears rimmed her lower lashes. The life of a farm wife in the thirties was desolate. Especially desolate if, like Mildred Knowlton, you hated your husband.

A soft smile crossed her face as she placed herself in the world of her yesterday. She hunched her shoulders as a ripple of chilling pleasure passed down her spine. Fred. Where was he now? What had he thought when he came back to their room in Crispin and found her gone? Would he understand?

The shrill wail of the baby broke her reverie. Then the voice of her other boy, "Hi Mom."

She turned towards Johnny, standing in the doorway. He seemed so relaxed, so sure of their surroundings. How could he know how miserable she was?

"Bring in the wood for the stove son," she said tenderly, fatigue already showing in her face. "Then bring in the tomatoes, I'll get them put up before dinner."

Johnny flashed his ready smile and, moving quickly, the strain of yesterday gone, went about his chores. She knew he was happy to have her home, she realized his need of her.

"Donna," she spoke briskly to her little girl, "you can slip the skins from the tomatoes and put them in the jars for me."

Assuming her drudging efficiency, her day's work was under way, and she delegated the authority necessary to get everything done while she tried to slip mentally back to a happier time.

Mildred Meiner Knowlton had been raised by a strong-willed mother, who when widowed early had taken on the business of running the vast sections of Midwestern farmland left to her.

Mildred's mother had learned to manage frugally, carefully, and with a ruthlessness usually credited to a strong man. Her land was pushed to yield far above its expectations and she had built a small fortune, even as neighbors and friends were wiped out by nature and the depression. The ruthlessness had enabled Frances Meiner to keep her head above water and she sowed with cruelty and reaped with ferocity and total disregard of any man, woman or child. Mildred had never been allowed to attend school. Her mother felt that lessons in life, if taught hard enough, were all her children would need to maintain and succeed with the land, their heritage. At sixteen Mildred showed some of her mother's spunk when she insisted she be allowed to attend school. Her mother refused permission and told Mildred she could help with the farm or get out. This was the challenge Mildred needed, and she began to search for the quickest way to leave the misery of her mother's domination. She didn't have to look far to find the escape she sought. In escaping, she moved from one hell to another.

John Knowlton, a man eighteen years her senior, and a bachelor, neighbored on a farm nearby. Mildred gave all of her attention to encouraging him in a fast courtship. Before the year was over, they were married and her new husband became a tenant farmer on one of her mother's many properties. This was only a case of exchange for Mildred. Her farm labors simply moved from one farmhouse, one barnyard, to another, and her mother's dominance coupled with the dullness of her new husband made the new life barely endurable.

Mildred watched Donna pack the jars with the peeled tomatoes as she worked to get dinner on the table. A haze of memory crossed her face and covered her eyes. Was it only yesterday? She pictured herself as she must have looked as she walked on the main street of Crispin with her new-found joyful freedom.

She had never experienced this kind of liberty before, and she shopped with joy for supper she would prepare in her life with her lover. Some outside force, luck if you could call it that, had drawn her to the town library. She walked up the steps of the library and spotted the stern librarian.

The librarian looked up and thought, I've seen this girl before. Yes, it was yesterday. The librarian's head was in the constant movement of a palsied condition and it was never certain whether she was cautioning you with a negative nod, or if her condition only made it seem that way.

Mildred approached the old carved oak desk. "Pardon me, I was here yesterday, and I just wondered ...I thought..."
Courage left her.

The librarian's head bobbed back and forth, her eyes never

left Mildred's face. "Yes?" Mildred went on, "I wondered if you might need cleaning help, or filing or," she ended weakly, "something I could do?"

The older woman's immediate reaction was negative. "No, there's not that much to do. As you can see," her hands swept the empty room, "we don't have many customers."

Gaining confidence, Mildred headed for one of the reading tables. "Perhaps I could help you put things away," She picked up a small stack of magazines to put them in a rack behind the table.

"No, no. I do that in the evenings, just before I lock up." Mildred walked back to the desk. "I can dust your shelves. Oh, please." Her tone was soft, a plea, "I need work so badly."

The nodding head watched the young woman. She sensed sadness beneath the desperation. "Where do you come from dear?"

"From one of the farm towns west of here," Mildred answered.

The librarian thought for a moment, this young woman needs help.

"Well, I couldn't use you every day. Perhaps you could come in on Fridays. I'm closed on Saturdays and Sundays, but you could help clean up at the end of the week."

Mildred hugged the magazines she was still holding to her. There were tears in her eyes.

"I couldn't pay much only a dollar for the work." The librarian watched the pathetic happiness kindle the beginning of a smile in Mildred's beautiful eyes.

"Oh, that's fine," the face became radiant with happiness as she thought about the dollar. She smiled broadly and in doing so, her beauty came into being. "Oh yes, that would be fine,"

15

The Last Magnolia

Mildred tipped her head to one side, "and, would you mind," she paused, not wanting to ask for too much, "would you mind if I came in on other days? I mean, I wouldn't charge you. It's just so lonely here in town. I don't know anyone and I'm not used to being alone." She stopped. She couldn't give out too much information about herself and Fred.

"Come in all you want dear. You could be company for me."

"Oh, I'll help. It'll only cost you a dollar." Mildred extended her hand, "My name is Mildred Know….ah….Hanson." She had used Fred's name for the first time. She might as well get used to it. After all, she was going to be Mrs. Fred Hanson soon. The librarian shook the extended hand, "I'm Mrs. Hardesty," she said kindly, "and I'll call you Mildred. We're going to get along just fine Mildred. You come along any time you want. Just remember," there was a twinkle in the woman's eye, "only one dollar."

Mildred nodded happily. Turning to leave there was a lilt in her voice, more like the young woman she was, "I'll be back tomorrow Mrs. Hardesty. Oh...thank you!"

Mrs. Hardesty heard a slight break in the young voice, almost as if the girl was crying. With joy, I hope the woman thought, happy that she was able to do some little thing for someone as grateful as Mildred.

The sharp cry of her baby interrupted Mildred's reverie and she found herself in the hands of reality, back in her farm kitchen. She moved quickly, sweat showing in beads on her forehead, to take him from the highchair. Kissing him on the cheek, she sat him on the floor.

Oh my! Was I in that library only yesterday? Memories flooded back. Yes. I went to the grocery store and bought the things for our supper and Mrs. Gillam was there. I should have known when I saw her that she would get word to John and my mother. Memories spread before her and she slumped against the kitchen sink. Yesterdays were gone. The tenderness she had taken from Fred was out of reach and only a memory. Her tomorrows were bleak.

The wail of a bored baby kept her in today's world and she began to gather dishes to set the midday dinner table. The activity of the noon meal brought Mildred's husband and the youngsters to the table, they ate silently, and she began to clear the dishes and watched to be sure her husband was out of hearing range. She turned to her son, "You've done enough for now Johnny." She wanted to make it right with him, to show him that she loved him but how could she, in good conscience, thank him for bringing her back to this hell? Oh well, he had no way of knowing...he deserved more than she could give. "Take your gun and go down to the creek for awhile. Just be sure to get back in time to get the cows in," she cautioned.

The look Johnny flashed at his mother was bright with anticipation. "Thanks Mom, don't worry, I'll be back in plenty of time."

Chapter 3

JOHNNY

August 1931

Harper Nebraska

This was the first time Johnny had gotten away since his mother left. The exhilaration of the freedom plus the joy of having his mother back created a happiness for him that he didn't realize most of the time.

His horse's name was Wind. She was one of his most important possessions. The other item of ownership and importance to the boy was his rifle. Being equal in Johnny's estimation, neither of these possessions took precedence over the other.

The gun was an inanimate object, important for its function.

Wind was a living, breathing creature. She was old and slow, but his. He kept her curried, fed, clean and exercised if only for a few minutes each day.

Holding the reins with one hand, the gun with the other, he moved with Wind, urging her to a faster clip with the gentle pressure of his heels in her side. She responded by breaking into a relaxed sure-footed trot. The breeze of riding pushed against his face, and his hair blew free to heighten the joy that was his.

As they reached the rim of the gully, Wind came to a rapid stop in response to the light pull Johnny applied against his reins. The boy dismounted, wrapped the reins around a thin tree in a grassy spot and left his horse. He slid down the still damp grass into the gully. Rocks and mud tumbled with him and then he hit the bottom. A small stream only about five feet wide gurgled and rippled over high and low spots and stones along the way. The water was clear and Johnny soon had his boots and socks off and thrown aside and was wading slowly along the pebbled bottom.

There were no thoughts, no speculations, on the way things had been yesterday and the way they were now. There was only the feeling of the water as it chilled his feet and felt wonderful between his toes. A canopy of green covered this secret place and the cool relief from the summer's heat added more to his feeling of freedom as the crisp leaves overhead murmured softly when they touched one another in a gentle breeze.

He walked downstream, around a slight bend and bent to inspect a trap. Empty. Somehow it didn't seem to matter today.

He walked a little further, the stream took another turn and there, just at the bend, was his fishing hole. He'd caught nice fish there, but there wouldn't be any fishing today. Today he wanted to set up targets and use the rifle. When the targets were set, he scrambled back down to the stream, crossed and picked up his gun. He pulled six 22 caliber shells from his pocket, loaded the gun, took careful aim and pulled the trigger. A gratifying ping told him he had hit the first can. With five more shots to go, and time his own, he leaned back, rubbing his gun with the affection of a practiced rifleman.

Someday I'll have more than this gun. I'll add more guns and I'll have a collection. I'll be one of the best shots in America.

Dreams took over as he leaned back on the slope of the gully's rise and fell asleep. This was his special place to dream. Johnny needed dreams.

Wind's soft whinny woke him with a start. He knew immediately that he was late.The sun was low. Why did this have to happen? His father was a hard disciplinarian and Johnny knew he would be punished for being late. Picking up his boots, he pulled them on, grabbed his gun and climbed the slope.

He rode fast now, pushing Wind hard. The roar of air in his ears deafened him as he urged the old horse impatiently. As he rode, he tried to work out his feeling about his mother.

He still didn't understand, or didn't want to understand why he had to be the one who went to Crispin to bring her home. He knew how badly he needed her, and he finished his analysis with the assurance of youth that told him all was well now, and his mother was in her proper place. He rode into the farm yard to hear the bellow of the cows. Now he was in for it.

His father had brought them in and was standing to watch, as John swung down from the horse's back. "You missed the time again, boy," his father was angry, "Who told you could go to the creek today?"

Johnny rushed, gathering the necessary equipment to start the milking, "Mom told me to go Dad, she said it would be all right."

The old man gave a grunt and sat down to start milking. The steady ping into the metal bucket indicated there would be no more conversation.

Johnny picked up a half-filled bucket. Three cows to go, the separator to be worked. He'd get it done.

"If I have to work this place alone," his father broke the silence, "God knows I can't take the chance of bringing another man here so then you're going to have to start acting like a man, boy. You have to be the help and that means there won't be any more creek time until I say so. Do you get that?"

Johnny dared to wonder silently if the old man would pay him the hired man's wages.

"I said, do you get that?"

"OK. Dad, I'll do better. I promise I will."Why did he have to feel guilty, the boy wondered? He moved to the next cow while his father milked the last one.

"Finish up in here and then get in to supper."

The boy hung his head. He wasn't sure whether his punishment was just or not, but he knew he would have to stay away from the creek as his father ordered until the old man forgot today. Johnny worked fast and ended the chores, closing the door to the barn behind him. As he drew closer to the back of the house, he noticed his grandmother's touring car parked in the yard. He could hear her loud, commanding voice coming from the kitchen.

He pumped water from the yard well to wash his face and hands, then slicked back his crisp hair with the dampness on his hands. Hesitantly, he walked to the porch. He didn't think the one-sided conversation coming from the kitchen was meant for his ears, or maybe it was that he didn't want to hear what his grandmother was saying to his mother, but as he sat on the steps to take off his boots, he couldn't help hearing the older woman's voice drone on.

The smell of leftover chicken scorching on the stove wasn't pleasant and added to the oppression of the evening.

"You disgraced me. You shamed your husband. Only the Lord knows what marks you have put on your children. There have been years and years of friendship between your family and your husband's people. Both families have built a fine reputation. Now you've put us all face down in the mud with your little vacation. Your little trip away from home."

Johnny could see his grandmother through the screen door as she leaned on a cane. Her right leg was deformed with a form of elephantiasis, and the cane was a necessity for standing and walking.

Unaware that she was observed by her grandson, the old woman continued her tirade against her daughter, who stood, holding onto the kitchen sink in total defeat, her head was down, her back was to her mother..

"You're lucky John and your son had the gumption to come to get you. You just forget that no good tramp. He's forgotten you by now. No sir, I'll bet he won't come looking for you. To think we trusted him on our farm and he had the stupidity to make eyes at you."

The old woman shifted her position on the cane, and Johnny was fascinated, watching and listening. The tirade continued.

"And you...what did you do to egg him on? Plenty I bet. Then you had the stupidity to follow after him like some kind of a...a...whore! A chippy! That's the way my daughter acts after all the good breeding and training I've given her! Agh! How can anyone even stand to look at you anymore?"

Johnny started for the door. He didn't want to hear things like this about his mother. He didn't want to know these things...didn't want his mother to hear them. He had to stop the old lady.

The old woman rocked back and forth on her cane, and her over-loud voice went on. "John's afraid to bring anyone here to work again because he can't trust you anymore. Do you know that?" There was no reply.

"Let me tell you this, Mrs. Runaway. Don't ever try to do it again. I'll disown you and all of your children if you do. You had better give them a little thought. Do you hear me? Not one red cent will they get from me if you leave again!"

Frances Meiner shook her fist at her daughter and turned to hobble to the screen door. As she pushed it open, Johnny was pulling it and she nearly knocked him down.

"What are you doing young man? Spying?"

"No ma'am, I was just..."

"Don't talk back to me young man!"

His grandmother walked through the yard like a conquering Trojan, using her cane for support, and crossed the dusty driveway to her car.

Johnny ran ahead and opened the car door for her while she climbed behind the wheel laboriously. Not another word was spoken and the boy stood back as she drove from the yard, out to the county road that would take her back to the main house, her home.

Johnny heaved a heavy sigh. I never know how to take her, he thought as he walked slowly back to the house. She isn't ever nice to anyone. He hadn't liked the things she'd said to his mother, but no one could stop her. He was frightened enough of her to know that.

He opened the fly-covered porch door and the acrid smell of the now badly burned chicken permeated the air. The family was at the table for supper, his father at the head in his usual place. Donna was playing a finger game with the baby in the high chair, and his mother, face glistening with sweat from the heat of the stove, was carrying the food to them. Her face had no expression. She said nothing.

His father was reading the carefully folded weekly paper. Johnny slid into his chair across from Donna and the baby and waited for his father to fill their plates then Johnny would be permitted to fill his own.

It was standard farm fare, the supper. There was the reheated, now burned chicken, left over from the dinner at noon. A thick white country gravy, fried potatoes and applesauce along with sliced tomatoes from the garden. Bread was stacked on a small plate, and Johnny helped himself to a slice. He poured the thick gravy over the bread. The chicken couldn't be eaten, so he'd fill himself up with one of his favorites, bread and gravy.

The table they ate from was always covered with a piece of cracked oilcloth, and on the cloth were the condiments for every meal. Homemade jam in its preserving jar with a spoon standing in its middle, salt, pepper, a small jar of bread and butter pickles and a mound of freshly churned butter were there. When the meal was finished these things were left in the center of the table and covered with a piece of cheesecloth.

There was no conversation at the table. The scene was set for the destitution of love and emotion in a family oppressed by a lack of feeling.

The baby cried fretfully now and then, and Donna seemed unmindful of any strain. She looked at Johnny across from her, and in her nagging little voice said, "You got caught coming in late again, didn't you?"

Johnny ignored her.

"You can't go back! Ha Ha. I heard Daddy. Serves you right! Maybe someday you'll learn where you belong at the right time!"

"Shut up, Donna!" She's already beginning to sound like my grandmother, Johnny thought.

"That's enough!" John senior put down his fork, "Eat your supper, all of you."

The Last Magnolia

Silence hovered above and around the table again.

The baby fretted for another piece of bread and jam and Mildred spread a small finger of the coarse homemade bread to put it into his fat fist.

Her husband rose and went to the cupboard above the scarred work table to get a toothpick. He walked to the back door, allowing it to slam softly behind him.

Donna stacked the plates, piling the dirty silverware on top of them to carry them to the waiting pan of hot water that Mildred had filled from the large tea kettle at the back of the stove.

Johnny stood up from the table, walked over to Donna and hit her sharply on the arm. "Ow! Mom! Johnny hit me!"

"That's enough! Donna you take the baby, wash his hands and take him out in the yard for awhile."

"Here Mom, I'll wipe." Johnny picked up a dish towel and his mother rinsed the dishes for him, wiped the table clean and poured the dirty dishwater down the sink.

"Thanks son." She took off her apron, pushed a damp curl from her forehead and walked towards the back porch. Passing her husband, she went to the front of the house where Donna and the baby were playing on the grass beneath a large elm tree. Here, finally the day's work nearly done, she could be cool with only an occasional fly to swat. The baby toddled among the grass, stopping to sit suddenly, and then laboriously lifting himself again to stand and toddle a few more short paces.

Mildred was tired. She leaned against the tree. I can't take it anymore, she thought. I can't listen to my mother. I won't take the silent treatment from John. She laid her head back to rest on the tree trunk. I think I will lose my mind. Moving again, she rested her chin on doubled knees. She was so alone.

The Last Magnolia

A sharp cry pierced the air, "Johnny, that's no fair. That wasn't fair! You hurt me! Da-a-d!"

Johnny jumped back as his father came from the back of the house.

"Johnny! How often have I told you that you're too big to scuffle with Donna?"

Mildred watched her children and her husband as if she weren't a part of the picture, as if she were suspended, looking down at them.

She was brought back to reality as the baby threw himself against her, crying the nagging little whine of a sleepy child. She held him to her, using him for solace, nestling her head into his fat little shoulder, she rocked him back and forth

Oh dear God, I just can't do it.

The skies darkened and the last lightening bugs of the season appeared to begin their dance of seduction. The silent family watched the twinkling lights and thunder rumbled in the distance. Mildred headed for the house, carrying the baby.

"I'll help put the baby to bed Mom." Johnny jumped up from where he was lying on the grass and walked alongside her. He knew she was tired and he would do anything to keep her here.

"It's late dear, go to bed. I'll do it."

She looked at her son with great concentration as if to imprint him on her mind for the rest of time. The boy, in his blind comfort at having his mother at home again, sure that his help would keep her with them, was not aware of her look or of her misery.

"God bless you son, good night."

"Night mom, see you in the morning."

The Last Magnolia

There was no answer.

Chapter 4

KATE

August 1931

Harper, Nebraska

Her footsteps sounded with authority and purpose as she clipped down the back stairs to the kitchen. A small plump woman, her rapid but precise movements left no doubt as to the extent of her efficiencies. Her age could not be determined. Red rosy cheeks, dark piercing eyes and snowy white hair cut short to frame her face put her at probably, fifty. Her facial features were coarse, nearly man-like but her comfortable figure pleasantly announced that she was indeed, a woman. She was so much of a woman that one knew at a glance that she could be sought after for any kind of help. In return they would be treated with soft kindness and understanding if they needed it.

Without the slightest hesitation she crossed to the large black cook-stove and the ritual of starting a fire in the morning began. When the flames had licked paper, kindling was added, then splits of wood and, still in motion, nearly like a dancer, the woman leaned toward and picked up the tea kettle, filled it and put it on the stove.

Arms akimbo, she surveyed the neat kitchen and tried to decide what she could put on the table for breakfast.

This was Aunt Katie. Katherine Irene Knowlton, spinster sister to John Knowlton senior, the daughter of early German settlers and a friend and helper to all who knew or needed her in the community.

Kate had birthed and mourned, served and smiled for vast numbers of people, and her life was enriched by all she touched because it was the way she wanted to be. "Call Kate," was the byword in the area, and anyone she worked with would tell you with affection and love that she was one of the finest women you would ever meet.

She was a perfect lady with a sharp wit that brought a special light to any situation, but a strong will that insisted on doing things the right way. She tempered this assertiveness with wisdom and character.

The mainstay of her own family, Kate had accepted each mission of need with a calm loving attitude. Her spark of humor always made it bearable. She had taken care of her parents in their declining years, and then remained in the small town of Harper to live in their house. Her lifestyle was supported and filled by the help she gave to others.

There hadn't been any time for her to marry and now, when she might enjoy life with a man her age, she had become too independent. When she was teased with the possibility of a spouse, she would laugh and put aside any suggestion of a possible alliance.

Now, as she stood in this kitchen that belonged to another woman, she was troubled.

She was shocked and disappointed by what had happened to her brother John and his family and knew she was going to have to fill many roles before this day was over. She faced a heavy burden of decisions that she'd be called on to make, but her strength would help her face each one. One at a time. Still she needed some more answers to what had happened here last night.

At close to midnight Frances Meiner, Mildred's mother, had driven into Kate's yard in town. She'd gone to the front porch where Kate met her, pushing the light switch to show the way as the cumbersome old woman pushed her way up the steps.

"My daughter has left again Kate, and John has gone after her. Why he would bother to chase the little chippy, I don't know, but he did, Johnny told me he did."

Mrs. Meiner, dressed only in a nightgown and a wrapper, continued, "The boy rode over on his horse to tell me they were gone. I sent him back to take care of the younger ones. You come with me Kate. It's your responsibility to stay with your brother's children."

Kate held open the door. "Come in Frances, sit down and tell me about it. I didn't know Mildred was back. When did she come home?"

The steely old woman evidenced her mortification and shame as she told Kate the past day's events.

"Then late tonight after they'd all gone to bed, Johnny told me his dad heard noises and went to check on her. She was gone."

The old woman stifled a sob, and Kate thought how unlike her it was. "Gone heavens only knows where. She left her children again and Johnny says his dad was so mad. He went after her!"

Kate patted her on the shoulder. "Just sit right there. I'll pack a bag."

As she hurried up stairs, Kate tried to put all the pieces together. Packing was fast and she was ready to go.

Pulling the door shut behind her, Kate followed Mrs. Meiner

across her yard and climbed into the car for the trip to John's farm. Both women were silent with their own thoughts as they traveled along the county road.

In the farm yard, Kate lifted her bag out of the car and the old woman, returning to her usual abrupt manner, turned the car and drove out of the yard without another word.

Kate walked to the back porch and into the kitchen where a light had been left burning. She checked the children in their rooms and went to the guest room to sleep. As she lay, pondering the tasks ahead, she thought she heard muffled sobs coming from Johnny's room, but she felt it was too late to talk to him now....tomorrow morning would be better. But that was all last night she thought, and shrugging off these recollections, she continued the morning chores familiar to any farmhouse. Kate pulled herself up short as she realized in her practical manner that she was probably faced with the prospect of running this farm, tending to the needs of the younger children and generally becoming a substitute mother to them. She smiled to herself. It meant she'd have Johnny. He was her oldest nephew and her favorite. She looked on him as the son she'd never had. A special bond existed between them. She would have to fill the slot intended for both of his parents until his father came back. Could she do this, she wondered?

She poured herself a hot cup of coffee and stood for a moment, reflecting, leaning against the hard rim of the kitchen table in the center of the room.

The door to the back stairs opened and Johnny came into the kitchen carrying his rumpled sleep-flushed baby brother. Johnny's eyes were swollen, so she knew she had indeed heard crying coming from his room. What could have happened?

The boy didn't look up; actually it seemed as if he were avoiding direct eye contact. What a pity, Kate thought, to have parents who had created this deep sense of shame, or was it something else in the boy? This wasn't the same Johnny that she cherished.

"The baby was crying so I changed him and brought him down. I guess he's ready for his breakfast." Johnny spoke with little or no expression and his entire manner was of deep grief. As he turned towards her she caught his eyes, and his expression immediately turned to one of fear. The fear of revealing something he shouldn't. He recovered quickly and Kate watched as he regained an almost normal countenance.

"Morning Aunt Katie, thanks for coming," tears came to his eyes, "I needed you, and as always you are right here for me, aren't you?"

Kate walked to him and put her arm around both him and the baby he was carrying. She pulled them close to her ample, soft bosom.

"They're both gone now," the statement was flat, as if its meaning had no significance.

"Oh Johnny, things will change....your father will be back...

"No! He's gone....the statement flattened....not coming back here." The eyes dropped again, Johnny wouldn't look at her. What was wrong here? She watched him closely; this just wasn't her Johnny at all.

"Yes honey, things have changed, but we'll try to put it all back together for us." She decided to bide her time, to let him tell her in his own good time what was bothering him.

"Aw Kate, I tried so hard. I knew it was bad for her and dad. He was so mean. He wouldn't even talk to her. He hated me."

Johnny gasped, "Aw, I tried....I tried so hard...." tears coursed down his cheeks.

Patting him and petting him, she wondered what she could possibly do to make it better.

Johnny pulled away and with a deep cleansing breath wiped away his tears. They would be the last tears Kate would ever see him shed.

"I'd better get to the barn and start on the chores." He moved towards the door, "I shouldn't have done it...I could've helped her more....she could've stayed....she said she would..."

Kate watched him with a sixth sense....there was something else., something Johnny wanted to tell her, and then the moment was gone and the boy bolted out the back door as though he had reached a decision. It was a decision that would affect the young man for the rest of his life. Kate wasn't going to be included nor was anyone else.

He ran to the barn. He couldn't have stayed in that kitchen for another minute. The pressures of everything that had happened would have come out....he couldn't have that. This farm was what would count now, the farm, his sister Donna and the baby. He tried to take a breath, but to force the air that was taken in from his tightly constricted chest seemed impossible. He felt lost. His mother was gone. Everything he had done for her had been for her good, and she'd left anyway.

Walking into the barn he considered the myriad thoughts that were creating a turbine of inadequacy within him. Sorting it all out, his helplessness turned to self pity, and the small beginnings of hate began to creep into his being. The detestation encompassed all who in his mind, didn't love him enough. His father, who used him as a hired hand. His grandmother, who hated him as she hated the world. His mother, who hadn't wanted to leave just his father, but him as well.

He decided he could take lessons in hate from his grandmother. She was a master in taking all, giving nothing. If he learned to be like her, he couldn't be hurt or ever afraid again.

Pulling Wind from her stall, he clutched the reins, mounted her and rode out. He needed to be alone, to push all of the past day and night out of his mind, out of his life.

Pushing the old horse as fast as she could run, he ended the ride with a sudden hoof-sliding stop when they reached the gully. Jerking back on the reins, too heavily for the gentle old horse, he jumped off and dropped them to throw himself on the grassy bank at the top of the gully's fall.

There couldn't be any more tears. He couldn't be afraid. He had to be the man now.

He lay on the grass, spent, with only a hard large core of emotion, like a tumor, growing into the pit of his body.

He felt the pain of this new tumor created by last night's happenings. He welcomed it and learned too soon that this was to be maturity. He had reached the end of the life he had known. The childlike trust and complacency that had been his rights as a ten year old boy were gone.

He lay very still, allowing the emotion to drain and the memories to disappear.

The grass was soft, the countryside quiet, as the removal, the 'Ectomy" without the aid of a scalpel, was completed mentally and the too-young boy steeled himself for manhood. The tumor was gone. It took away the child of yesterday and hid a fearful secret that he would not, could not ever divulge.

In a relatively small space of time, the boy-man lifted his

body from the ground. Mosquitoes were biting him and he slapped at the fast-flying humming bugs on his neck and arms. As he stood it seemed he was taller in this new forced maturity, taller than he had been earlier this morning. He climbed back on Wind to ride her home.

Kate, with a searching look of tenderness, met him at the kitchen door. With her natural insight and her ability to understand, she sensed this young boy had taken a turn in his life. She wanted to be able to judge and to understand how to deal with this change.

"Let me fix a sandwich for you son. You missed your breakfast, and it's already time to think about dinner."

Johnny walked to his aunt and kissed her.

"I'd better get to the cows and the chickens. I'm sorry to be late Katie, I'll get it done now."

"I have the milking done and Donna took the cows to pasture. The eggs are in and the chickens are fed."

She was back at the kitchen table now, spreading butter and jam on a large piece of bread.

"I have to talk to you Johnny. We have to decide what we're going to do until your father comes back."

Johnny's eyes didn't meet hers, and she thought there was a quick gulp of air on his part.

"I don't know Katie, could we stay here? Could you and I do the farm alone?"

Kate sensed his need for one last tangible connection to his past. "If you want to stay here, we'll try it. I'm sure your grandmother would send over some help for us, and the two of us could work together." She wanted to help this boy who had been robbed of so much in such a short time.

Johnny munched on the bread and jam. He took the glass of milk she offered him, "I think we can do it Aunt Kate if you help. I'll go over to see Grandma."

Actually he dreaded this confrontation. He never knew what would happen with his grandmother, but if it was up to him to keep this family together, then he'd approach her to see if she would help him. He finished his lunch, and as he walked to the porch, the sound of tires on the gravel in the yard stopped him.

His grandmother drove in, stopped the car and got out to walk with her cane supporting her, to the house.

Sitting in the kitchen, she leaned forward and the cane, held by both of her hands, one on top of the other, became a chin rest. The old lady watched Kate and Johnny closely as she delivered her edict. Her words were cold, heavy covered with a speculative shrewdness that showed in her eyes.

"There's no way I could trust one of my valuable farms to a ten year old boy and a spinster!"

Johnny and Kate recoiled as if they had been hit. Kate started to speak, stepping closer to the fat old lady.

"No! Let me finish," the grandmother said, "I want you out. Kate, you have that house in town. You take these children. They are your brother's family and you are responsible for them."

Johnny, strengthened by his new maturity, interrupted, "Grandma, we're just as much your family as...."

"Don't talk back to me young man! I told your mother only yesterday, if she pulled another one of these stunts, I'd have nothing to do with her or her children." Assuming an aggrieved look that didn't match her hardened face, she continued, "Lord only knows where this bad seed came from, certainly not from my side of the family." She shook her head as if trying to sort out

The Last Magnolia

why such tribulations had been put down at her doorstep.

Kate watched closely....it was part of the old lady's act....another way for the old bat to shift responsibility. She started to speak up, to contract. Instead, she put her arm around Johnny's shoulder. They each took comfort from each other and seemed to relax, waiting for the next command from this heartless woman.

"I have another tenant and his family coming here today. Kate, I want you to have these three children packed up and ready to go by supper, Frances smiled condescendingly, pursing her lips as if she were sainted in her next offer, "then I'll drive you in to town."

Kate gasped and Johnny sat down. Hard.

"You be sure the place is clean and neat. I have enough scandal hanging over my head with the disgrace these children's mother has sent to my door. I won't have people saying she left a dirty place."

The old woman stood up laboriously, no one went to her aid.

The baby started to cry as if he knew what evil had just taken place in the room.

"I'm going to town, and when I get back I want the place in order and the bags packed. Don't try to take anything that isn't yours."

Donna came down the back stairs just as her grandmother completed her last sentence.

"Grandma, I don't want to go with Aunt Katie," she whined. "You'd better learn to stop whining and take what's coming to you, young lady!"

The unyielding old lady dismissed the little girl and turned to Kate. "Get these children into your little house in town Kate. You can take care of them there and they can go to school. When your brother gets back, he can pay you what he owes you. I can't and won't be of any more help because this is your responsibility until John returns." She limped to the door, "Be ready now. I'll be back at five!"

Johnny ran to the door and started to pull it open. He was livid.

"No John, don't do that. She doesn't know what she's doing," Kate looked at Francis with contempt, "or maybe she does," she held John back, "town for all of us will be the right thing. Come on, let's get going!" Kate knew that activity and determination coupled with their combined anger would salve the loss that this little family had incurred in the past hours. Moving swiftly for the back stairs, she spoke over her shoulder. "Bring some of those boxes from the porch. Let's take what's yours and get out of here. We'll all be fine in Harper. We'll make it fine!"

Johnny seemed to welcome the activity and he moved quickly. Kate was right. This was the new life they'd learn to live and it would be good to leave this farm....the barn....the chores. He began to account mentally for the things that needed taking. He wanted to be sure to take the gun and the ammunition. And what about Wind? His mind raced to the chores and the sure sacrifices ahead.

Chapter 5

KATE AND JOHNNY

October 1938

Harper, Nebraska

Seven years. The lack of funds, the doing without, all of it has been worth it, she thought as she watched the young man working alongside the house. He was the son I would never have had and what a wonderful son he has been!

"That's the last basket for the fire Kate," Johnny yelled as he poured another container of leaves on the smoldering fire, "now if you'll show me where you want to put the mulch bin, I'll empty the end of the rakings and we'll be done."

Kate leaned on her rake and watched the fire die, smolder, then flare up again. It had been seven years since Johnny had come to live with her in town. Those years had all been golden ones. That boy, she grinned, has kept me young!

Johnny's world of activities involving young friends had given her the opportunity to know a new generation, and to grow all over again with the fun of the young people's ideas and activities. Kate sobered as she recalled that terrible day when Johnny had appointed himself the man in his family. He was only ten and she in her careful, understanding way, had allowed him an equal position of authority and leadership in her household. That way, she had ascertained, he might be able to bridge the terrible loss brought about by the desertion of both his mother and father.

Three children had been left in her care back then, and Johnny was the oldest. She knew that even after years of happiness with her he would carry scars that only he knew the depth of for the rest of his life.

She had brought the three children to Harper on that hot August day, brought them into her house to make as normal a home as possible for them. Her heart had been in her mouth. She didn't know how she could support all of them.

The baby hadn't been two years old and Donna, eight, was a willful child, hard to deal with. She pouted a lot and loved no one. She didn't seem to miss her parents. Her main mission in life, it seemed was to make Johnny miserable.

Johnny took all of the grief Donna had to give and, in an admirable way, applied himself to taking care of her. Considering he was only a few years older, he had done well.

Kate shook her head, remembering, then she applied herself to today.

"Over there, back behind the strawberry bed John, that's where we'll put the rest of those leaves." Picking up her rake, she walked briskly back to the rear of the lot.

"There's a tarpaulin in the shed, we'll anchor it over the leaves with these rocks."

While Johnny dumped the leaves, her mind moved back to the past, to the years of being a mother to Johnny. He was as a son would have been and her life had been richened and ripened with the experiences of motherhood. She hoped fervently that she had done everything right. His strength and character could carry him through life with assurance and happiness, and Lord knew, he deserved that much. She had done her best, and so had Johnny.

"O.K. Kate, let's get a cup of coffee and call it a job well done," he walked over to her and pulled her towards him for an affectionate hug.

The fall air was nippy and the leaves were nearly off the trees now. Kate had waited for a Sunday when Johnny wasn't busy and could help her get the yard and garden ready for the winter. It was nice to know the job was finished. They worked together well, always good naturedly.

The financial burden had been alleviated somewhat when Mildred, Johnny's mother returned to Harper two years after her disappearance. She said she had divorced Johnny's father and married Fred, the man she'd left her family for. She seemed happy and said they had room for two of Mildred's children in their new life in California.

Kate had watched her Johnny die a little more inside of himself when his mother said she was taking the younger children with her. His eyes filled with un-spilled tears, and as his head went down, his toes scuffed at the hard dirt in the side yard where they stood. "But Mom....what about...." and his sentence died in mid-air as his mother said, "You stay here and help Kate, Johnny. She needs you,"

Johnny, head down, had walked to the back of the house. He didn't come out to say goodbye to any of them. When they drove away, he came back to Kate. It was like that hot day on the farm when he lost both parents to desertion. He walked away from the hurt only to return to her as an older and wiser boy. He never mentioned his mother again.

Kate rejoiced at being able to keep the boy, but that joy had to be kept inside because she felt the depth of hurt that this young boy was hiding. His scars from rejection were so deep Kate knew they could never be erased....not by her love, not by anything.

Nor had there been any word of Johnny's father.   In this small mid-western area of closely integrated communities, no one had ever seen him. Kate assumed that he had gone west and stayed. She was sure his pride had suffered so much he would never show his face again. How silly! And look what he's missed with this wonderful boy, she thought.

High school had opened new avenues for Johnny and he had become intensely involved in any activity, no matter whether it was extra-curricular, or involved with the curriculum of the school.   His grades were at the top of his class, and he played baseball with the spring team, and basketball in the winter. A popular athlete, the citizens of Harper and the surrounding communities supported all of the teams and their teams by attending the games and cheering them on to occasional victories. Kate had been right along with them, proud that her "son" was one of the team.

The word "son" brought her up short. He was like a son to her, and she hoped she had given him the best possible mothering.   Still, there was something missing, something that seemed to be hidden in Johnny. Hidden since that first morning after his parents left him. He had never talked about it again, but Kate was bothered, because Johnny had buried something very deeply inside of himself, and he had never confided in her.

She felt that Johnny was probably happier than he had been as a child, living with the tension and lack of love that must have been found on the farm with his parents. She hoped that he would carry with him memories of a good life with her for all of his life.

When they reached ninth grade, all of the youngsters from

Harper were sent by bus to school in Bratton Falls, the county seat. There, during his freshman year, Johnny met and played basketball with Erwin Wallace. The boys became fast friends.

George Wallace, Erwin's father, owned and operated the small airport that served the county. It was outside of Bratton Falls, only ten miles from Harper.

In the beginning weeks, as friendship grew with common interest in guns and hunting, Erwin introduced Johnny to the airfield and the adjacent home of his parents.

The large, rowdy, happy Wallace family welcomed Johnny as they did any new acquaintance, and he quickly fit into their family activities. There was always lots of laughter, boisterousness, teasing and fun, but the operation of the airport fascinated Johnny. It was here that his love of airplanes began.

His enthusiasm and interest in everything that went on at the field had no boundaries. Under the Wallace's tutelage, and reading all he could find on the subject of aircraft, he soon became more knowledgeable than his instructors expected. His greatest wish was to fly, and he knew that one day he would have the money he would need to take lessons.

Working at the airfield with machinery and engines was not completely new to Johnny because he had shown a keen interest in and a natural talent for mechanical works since his early teens. Friends had come to him with broken things to be repaired. He worked at Harper's only gas station during the summer months, pumping gas and learning how to fix things by watching. By the time he was thirteen or fourteen, he had earned a good reputation in the community because he seemed to know more about the repair of engines than the man who owned the service station.

Now and then Johnny would be sent for by one of the local

farmers who needed some farm equipment fixed. The pay was always fair for these jobs, and it helped Kate manage their living expenses. A little bit of that money was always tucked away for the future flying lessons.

Several times his grandmother, Frances Meiner sent for him to repair machinery on one of her farms. When called, Johnny had always been in Bratton Falls, working at the airport, so hadn't been available to do her work. It was a source of irritation to the old lady, who felt that if Johnny did her work, he couldn't charge her because he was her grandson.

Kate smiled when she remembered this. She had made sure Johnny never got the messages from his grandmother, and that he wasn't available to help her. He owed that old harridan nothing in Kate's opinion.

The first plane Johnny had become familiar with was a silver Stinson. When it stood on the ground it seemed high in the air. "My gosh Kate, when I looked up at it, it might as well have been flying!" John told her, his eyes shining.

"That did it Kate. I knew I had to fly!" Kate knew the boy's determination would make him a pilot.

Elated, John touched and learned as his hands, nearly in synchronization, jumped from one dial to another on the instrument panel. He likened it to the dashboard of his grandmother's car yet there were many more dials to be read.

As Johnny's need to know more about flying had intensified, Kate remembered, Mr. Wallace agreed to let his son and John trade chores at the field for flying lessons.

From that time on, Kate didn't see much of John in his spare time, because in days, months and years that followed, the boys, under the guidance of a hard master, learned how to perform minor repairs on aircraft at the field. They worked so hard, Kate thought, but there was always that goal shining at the end of the chores as they earned their lessons. She smiled. The lessons they learned the best of all were the flying lessons and in a short time they were ready to solo.

She felt as if she knew as much as they did because the planes were all that Johnny talked about.

The solo flight was in a Waco, a three-place bi-plane. Kate was at the field for the first flight with her heart in her mouth as she tried to be as supportive as possible. The open cockpit frightened her, but the look on the boy's faces told her about the exhilaration they felt and she knew, watching them, they would make flying one of the important parts of their lives.

That Waco was only the beginning and in their spare time the boys learned to fly the other planes on the field.

And I learned too, Kate smiled, whether I wanted to or not.

From the Waco, the boys moved to the workings of a Curtis-Robin, then to a four-passenger Stinson that was used as an air taxi.

Johnny and Er shared their dreams with Kate and the Wallace's and they learned about their plane's workings as they waited eagerly for the day they could be licensed pilots and fly the air taxi service.

I wonder if they realize, or can foresee coming years, Kate mused? But of course they can! She knew from watching their enthusiasm, and the constant quest for more knowledge about the planes they loved so much, that they would both work themselves into the aircraft industry in some way. It was a new field, and these boys, through their enthusiasm could apply themselves to bigger and better planes for the rest of their days.

I hope I'm here to see it, Kate thought. She had always believed and tried to teach Johnny that any effort you put into reaching for a dream helped you achieve it. She tried to teach him never to worry about dreams of achievements but rather to work towards a goal. Johnny had surely done this with the airplanes, and it showed her that he would succeed. She was proud of him and his achievements. There were many more to come, and she wanted to support him and cheer him on as he reached the pinnacle of every goal he set for himself.

Wallace had promised that if the boys learned "everything" about the planes on the field, they could fly his Davis Monoplane. This was to be their high school graduation gift.

The Davis, often referred to as the Davis racer, was the fastest plane Wallace had. It was the boy's favorite. The greatest flying thrill they could imagine would be taking control of the stick in the Davis.

Each fall and spring, a traveling air show stopped at the field and this was a busy time for Johnny and Er. Kate saw little of her ward.

The boys ran errands, helped with the maintenance and upkeep of the performing planes and were on hand for dozens of small assignments. They worked hard and fast because it was a treat to spend time with the performers, listen to the flying jargon and be included in some of the conversations. Watching the stunt flying, the swing walking and all the other daredevil activities featured in the show led both boys to bigger and better flying ambitions. This fringe acceptance was a part of their education and they listened, watched and absorbed what was as valuable as a college education.

When John was away from school and his jobs at the airfield, he worked with Kate. He had very little social life, other than activities at the Congregational church where Kate was a regular member of the flock. It was through this affiliation that John had gotten to know the minister's daughter. She was Janice Adams, three years his senior, a nice girl and a good friend Kate thought. Janice's mother had been killed in an automobile crash the year she graduated from high school, so she had stayed in Harper, acting as her father's secretary, hostess and housekeeper.

Janice and John didn't date. He didn't have enough money to take anyone anywhere. The two did pair off at church socials and did lots of talking.

Telling her about his dreams and ambitions, I suppose, Kate thought. She knew what those plans were and she couldn't find a way to support them. John wanted a degree in engineering from the state college. He didn't know how to achieve his dream. Both he and Kate knew it would take money they didn't have. There had been talk at the high school about a scholarship and John had applied, but so far, nothing had come through and in the spring he would graduate.

"I would do anything, anything at all to help," Kate thought," but there aren't any jobs for me that will bring in enough money for college."

Kate hung her heavy sweater on a peg in the tiny cloak closet under the stairs. She tried to hide the worry of her thoughts from John. There just had to be a way.

She walked into the kitchen and took the coffee pot from the back of the stove. John was sitting at his usual place at the kitchen table; he was so deep in thought that when she walked in he didn't even look up.

"Kate, if I can get the scholarships and earn some more

money during the summer, I'll be in college when you need this work done next fall."

Don't give it a thought," she poured herself a cup of coffee, "I've been thinking about how to earn a little more money, I'm going to start looking."

"It can happen, Kate."

"I know it can, and we'll work something out. I always think of my mother, she used to say, "When everything is all said and done, you'll be in your place," and Johnny, college is going to be your place. We are going to keep on working for it and you will go in September."

"Well, in the meantime Miss Katie, Er has his dad's car for the evening, and he and I are going to take Janice to the Fall Fair in Crispin. Er's girl couldn't come, so there's room in the back seat for you. We wondered if you and Mr. Adams would like to tag along?"

Kate laughed. This was just like her Johnny.

"Mr. Adams? Are you trying to match-make young man?" She looked over the rim of her coffee cup, "He's too old for me!"

She was excited about a chance to see the fair and its elaborate harvest booths, but teasing Johnny to see his slow grin was a part of the fun of their relationship and, in the case of right now, stopped their deep concern about his future.

The grin didn't come. Instead, a slight frown creased his brow, "Ah Katie, of course he's too old for you! I'm not pairing you up. I just thought if you wanted to go.." then the grin started as he realized he had bitten her bait..."but now that I know you don't want to go, we'll just take Mr. Adams."

She'd been had! "Johnny Knowlton of course I want to go!" She was flustered, sure of the twinkle in his eye, but thwarted in

48

her own effort to tease. "What time? Do I have time to get cleaned up?"

Johnny's laugh was rich, "You have exactly one hour ma'am and I'd like a chance in the bathroom too." His laughter followed her as she moved quickly up the stairs.

When she was gone, he sobered. She's been such a good mother to me. I wish I could do more for her. His dreams drifted in, I will do more. When I have that degree and a job, Kate can come to live with me and I'll be the caretaker.

He had to go to college! Janice's father had explained that if John attended summer school, he would be able to finish in three years. John knew he could find work on campus and if he didn't live in a dormitory, he would have money for a few extras. He had to get a scholarship!

I'll work on it..it's got to happen, he thought. A new idea began to form in his mind, yessir, there was somewhere else to go for help, and he'd try! His step was light as he headed up the stairs.

Chapter 6

FRANCES

October 1938

Harper, Nebraska

Frances Meiner stood up from her desk and walked to the large window facing the front road. Walking was difficult and her progress was slow.

Early October was bringing on heavy weather. She wondered if this was a sign of an early winter. The day had begun sparkling and clear as a fall day should be, then as afternoon wore on, the air became brisk and the wind blew dust and leaves into cruel little eddies and swirls as the sky began to spit snow.

As cold and miserable as the weather, she changed directions and walked with her cane supporting her, into her office.
Something on the road caught her eye. A tall man, bent into the wind, without a coat was coming up the gravel driveway. The wind was whipping the shirt against his body as if it was hanging on a clothesline to dry.

What could anyone want at this time of day, she wondered? It was nearly dark. Why would any fool be out in this kind of weather in just a shirt? As the figure came closer, she recognized her oldest grandson, John.

Isn't that just like those Knowltons, she thought, never did have sense enough to come in out of the cold.

The Last Magnolia

In the years since her daughter ran away with the hired man, causing heartbreak and scandal the old woman had convinced herself that the Knowltons were responsible for the disgrace that had followed her daughter's acts. This self-indulgent defense mechanism enabled her to watch her grandson now with contempt as he approached the front of her house. The strong wind flapped against what she now realized was a jacket, and the boy reached the door with his head down to shield his face from its ferocity.

"John! Go around to the kitchen door," she yelled through a crack in the door before she slammed it shut, "you know we don't use this door except for company."

The young man, surprised by his grandmother's voice, lifted his head with a start. The wind was cold and he hesitated just a second before turning to run around the corner of the house. The old woman walked laboriously to the kitchen where she could hear him knocking on the latched door. She lifted the hook, opened the door and let him in.

"My heavens, you look blue with cold, John. How did you get here?"

The boy was rubbing his hands together to warm them, "I walked out from town, Grandma. I tried to hitchhike, but there wasn't anyone on the road."

He noted the disapproval on her face and continued, "It was really nice when I started, I didn't even think about bringing an extra sweater. Boy, the weather really changed fast, didn't it?"

"You have to expect changes like this at this time of the year. Surely at your age you should know that." She stopped, as if to show him that her word was the last word, then went on, "This could be a warning for a bad winter. The farmers are ready though. The crews finished up the harvest and the plowing last week."

She walked away from him and then swung around heavily, "We had a good year John."

What was the closest she would ever come to a smile crossed her face, but it reminded you of a sly cat who has just taken something away from someone, "It's hard to believe that every year the price of corn goes up."

The chill of the outdoors was beginning to leave John, "It's good you did so well, Grandma. Kate and I really hoped you would let me work for wages last summer. I would have done good work for you. I have my full growth now, and the money would have helped us."

There was no understanding or regret in the old lady's voice, "You know I have my regular workers John. To pay family....to pay you....well, that just isn't necessary." She was warming to her favorite subject now.

"Anyway, the times I did need you, the times you could have fixed some of the equipment, you were never around. Right? How do you explain that?"

Johnny looked down at his brown, dusty and scarred shoes and thought, she probably wouldn't have paid me for that either.

Her tuneless voice found yet another barb to throw at her grandson to make him as uncomfortable as possible. Her lip curled in contempt and with a sneer she asked, "What do you hear from your mother? Do you see your dad? What's your sister doing now?"

Damn her! John faced the tyrant and held his temper, "You know I don't hear from Mom or her family, and you know I don't know where my father is." He spoke carefully and she realized she had gone too far with her less than subtle taunts. My gracious, he certainly was growing up, she thought.

"Humph. Some family you come from young man."

John bit down on the sides of his cheeks. He wasn't going to argue with this old bat. He wanted something from her and if he had to eat her words, he was going to try to get it.

The fat woman had squeezed her corpulence into a large slatted oak rocker in the kitchen and she rocked back and forth as she talked to the boy.

Rubbing her tongue between her protruding false teeth and her upper lip, she looked her grandson over.

He was tall, well built, perhaps a little thin. A nice looking boy, she thought. Good, even features and he's clean. Well, he was clean except for the wind-blown condition his walk from town had created.

Assuming an attitude that was more agreeable she asked, "What brought you here today, John? Did you skip school to come out here?"

"No Grandma, I didn't. School's closed today. I came out here to discuss some business."

"What on the Lord's earth could you know about business boy?"

The tongue rubbing between teeth and lip changed her facial expression, and she looked like a baboon.

"You just seem to know anything about cars, trucks and tractors. Oh yes," she nodded knowingly, "I hear about all the work you do for the farmers around here. You only do greasy dirty work, what on earth could you possibly know about business?"

Unabashed by her cruelty, John remained calm. He had

thought this all out, had planned each word of the proposition he brought to her today and, no matter how distasteful the whole thing was to him, he wouldn't let himself be foiled by losing his temper.

"Grandma, you know that in the spring I'll be finishing high school over in Bratton Falls."

"Finish?" She pressed forward to lean on her cane, "Does that mean you're through with the eighth grade? I never gave much thought to school you know, none of my children were allowed to go." She tapped the cane on the kitchen floor to make her point, "Good hard work, that's the only school they needed, and as far as that goes, that's all you need too!"

He dismissed the sound of her voice and the things she was saying. "No Ma'am, I've finished twelve grades now. I'm a senior in high school this year."

"Well, there's just another good example of the waste your Aunt Kate has allowed you, isn't it?" She took a deep breath, "That Knowlton outfit were always impractical, probably why they never did much with their land. I'm sure that's why they lost it in the Depression." She seemed to have forgotten the boy was there, and he stood, letting her ramble on.

"Twelve years of, just school when you could have been out working?" You could have been out picking corn, helping to support that poor household you live in. Why didn't you come out here to live and work, boy?"

He had taken enough. His anger couldn't stay frozen in his throat in one giant lump any longer. He disgorged the lump, spewing words forward, uncaring as to his mission, intent only on contradicting this miserable, mean woman.

"You didn't want us, Grandma!"

"Don't get sassy with me young man! Now," she waved a limp hand at him, "state your 'business' as you call it, humph, as if you knew anything about business."

The whole scene was ridiculous, he shouldn't even go on, but he paused, put his thoughts back together slowly and carefully. When he was sure of his words, he began, "Grandma, Mr. Slade, the principal at the high school has talked to me about going on to college. You know, I'm going to be the Valedictorian of my class." There was a note of pride in this statement, but he covered it in a rush, "that means I'm the student with the best marks in the class for the whole four years of school." He didn't want to boast, but he wanted her to realize the reasons for educational pride.

"Anyway, Mr. Slade feels I should go to the state college next year. If I work part-time and go to summer sessions, I can get a degree in engineering in just three years."

"College! What on earth are you talking about, John?" The old lady was sitting stiff and upright in her rocker. The rocking had stopped.

"Engineering! We've all been farmers in your family and mine since time began. We've had no need for a college education. Engineering? What does that mean? That you can get all greasy and dirty under some truck or tractor and you'll have some kind of paper saying you went to school to learn how to do it?" The chair now rocked back and forth, carrying its heavy load with great agitation.

"No need for you to go to school to get your hands dirty, you already know how to do that, I guess. Who does this Slade think he is, putting all these fancy ideas in your head?"

John's stomach curled inside of him like giant worms but he

stood his ground. I shouldn't have come. It isn't going to work, but I have to finish, he thought.

"Grandma, I went to Mr. Slade hoping he'd be able to help me get some scholarship money for college. He's helping, but so far, nothing has come through in the way of money. I have to get my registration taken care of now, and I need money to do that." The discipline with which he had prepared his appeal left him and his words came too fast, "Kate would be so proud, she really wants me to go."

"Kate! No practicality as usual. She takes a lot for granted, you know. Seems to think that because I've allowed you to live with her, she can have something to say about what and will not do. Well let me tell you, and her too," the grandmother shook her hand at him, pointing with a half-curled index finger, "I'm your grandmother, a blood relative, closer than some Aunt Kate, and I won't hear another word about college for any member of my family!"

"Grandma, I'm not asking you to approve of my going to college, I'm here to make a deal with you." John's voice was low, under control again, and he spoke slowly, knowing all the time that his appeal was useless with this stupid old woman.

"Grandma...."

"Stand up straight!" The old lady watched him with shrewd eyes.

"Would you lend me the money to start college with? I'm sure I'm going to get the scholarships, and Mr. Slade will help me find part-time work on campus." He stopped, looked to see if he was having any effect on the woman, the rushed on with his request before she could over-ride his words with her cruelty again. "Then Grandma, I could come here to the farm just as soon as I graduate from High School and work for you all summer to pay back the loan. You wouldn't be out one red cent."

She didn't stop rocking and her voice didn't waver as her steely eyes met his, "John, you're living in a dream world. There'll be no money from me. When your mother left her life with you and your father, I warned her that if she disgraced me, I'd cut every one of her children out of my life and my will. I've done just that and I won't even consider helping you with the foolishness of college. I've said it before and I'll way it again, this is a farming family. This is a farming life and there's no room for the likes of you at some big college." She stopped her recitation to look out the window.

"Now, you'd better get yourself back to town. That storm out there is getting bad, and you didn't even have sense enough to wear a coat!"

John looked at her distastefully,

"Grandma, I don't have a coat. Kate asked for money for a coat for me two years ago, and you didn't have time to listen to her."

The rocking became agitated with rockers squealing slightly with strain as the chair's occupant pushed out more biting words, "If you want a little advice from me young man...."

"You have advice to give? Yes. You always have something to say, don't you? I wish you could have stopped talking, stopped advising long enough to find some room for me. I wish someone here had time, just a little time so I could have been included, but no. I just have to listen, don't I? I count for nothing!"

The chair stopped again. Somehow the hulk knew she could not bully the boy anymore. She realized he was through with her. It frightened her and she seemed to shrink in stature. Her voice softened.

"You can work for me in the spring son. I won't guarantee wages, but if you want to work here, you can."

"I won't be here in the spring. You don't need me and I will never need you again!"

John walked to the back door and opened it to leave.

"Close that door quickly," she snapped, "don't let the cold in."

Hunching his shoulders, John lowered his head into the wind and began the long walk back to Harper.

The door banged open and shut, open and shut and the cold air fanned into the kitchen to chill the fat old woman who was struggling to get out of her rocker to close it.

Chapter 7

JESSIE

December 7, 1941

State College

She leaned toward him and touched him. He didn't stir. His breathing was steady and deep as he slept the sleep of satisfaction. It was a shame to wake him, this handsome angular young man that she at age forty-five had taken as a lover.

She decided she'd give him just a few more minutes. Poor kid, he'd needed this little diversion badly. She was glad she'd come to see him in his off- campus poor third floor walk- up room where he had lived the entire time he had been in college.

One window, one door and a cot, there wasn't much more to his living quarters. He had a desk that was piled high and cluttered with books and papers and a sturdy wooden chair that matched a scarred dresser. There was a bathroom down the hall that he shared with other tenants... This room and these objects had been his only surroundings for the entire three years. How could he stand it?

While she watched him, he began to waken and to move. She leaned over and down to his soft, warm mouth and kissed it.

Without any waste of motion, he surrounded her suddenly with strong arms, and pulled her down against his chest. "What is it that's so nice to look at, Jess....Me?"

No sirree. You're not it honey....you're a smart kid, because

59

you've learned your lessons well, but you're not that great to look at," she pushed up and away from him, knowing full well that she was lying in her teeth....he was a handsome man!

"What am I best at learning, Jess? What the university had in mind for me, or what you teach so well?" His grin was infectious, and he taunted her with his words.

"Come on, Jesse, teach me some more."

"Johnny, you're just too much! Let go of me now," she slipped from his grasp, "how in the world I ever got involved with you, I'll never know."

She did know though. This boy, Johnny Knowlton had come to work for her in his first year at school. He was a good worker, needed money badly, and what little he picked up for the hours he worked under her supervision in the campus cafeteria, paid for his books and his living expenses, that is, if you could call this room living.

He had scholarships to help with tuition and had stayed at the college the year around to complete his degree in just over three years.

As she slipped into her bra and slip, she realized their relationship was nearly over. She knew that on graduation, he would move on to bigger and better things, and to younger women. She knew she wouldn't be in the picture anymore. Her heart skipped a beat. She really cared for Johnny....

How had it all begun, she mused, now that it was about to end? She had been his first woman. Shortly after he came to work for her, she had asked him home for a good meal. He did not suspect she was going to take him to bed.

Johnny learned well and fast the many ways there were to satisfy her. His tension lessened with the release she offered, the release of satisfying sex.

Johnny continued to come to her, to make love to her, because there were no strings, no requirements. She had been the only companion he made time for. She offered him friendship as well as short escape from the stress of studies, work and college.

He wrapped a hand around her thigh, "Come on Jess, come back to bed," his voice was throaty, deep, sleepy and suggested more than just bed.

"John my boy, you have work to do. You promised to go back too it if we just dallied a little bit. I promised to go back to the cafeteria. Well honey, we did and now it's time to go." She pulled away from him again. His animal magnetism was strong and she was putty in his hands. He'd learned the lessons she taught him well, and now he was the aggressor, a practiced, passionate, wonderful, soft and caressing lover who knew what he wanted. He made her feel like a musical instrument as his hands, his caresses and his magnetism made her want to sing as he lead her into his own special kind of ecstasy.

Pulling up her slip straps she hunted for her panties on the floor. They weren't in sight, so she got on her hands and knees to scout under the bed.

The sting of a resounding slap on her rear bought her up quickly and there he was, laughing out loud at the sight of her as she rose, highly indignant, the panties in hand.

"Ah Jess, you're a life saver! What would I do without you?" Rolling over on his stomach, he leaned on his elbows, and held his head in his hand, watching her, "I have a mean exam tomorrow and I haven't put enough time on it, so there sure wasn't time for us, but here we are....and there we go," he drew in a short, passionate, remembering breath, "you seem to know just when I need you."

"Honey," she laughed, "I can read you like a book," her voice became throaty, deep and ready to participate in any more activity he had time for. His sharp intake of breath alone had begun her trip towards more ecstasy in his expert hands, "and you know kid, you do pretty good work on that narrow little cot of yours!"

She looked down at him tenderly, "Did you ever stop to think honey that maybe this little interlude was for my time of need?"

Once more he reached up to pull her down beside him. The gesture was tender as he cupped one breast and with his other hand began to massage the inner thigh of her right leg. She allowed her legs to open lightly and relaxed as she turned toward him with her body, ready to go on, but suddenly she remembered his work and pulled loose to jump back.

"Enough kiddo, now's the time for the desk and the books and for old Jessie to head out."

Johnny laughed and lunged and she deftly sidestepped him, stepped into her underwear and headed for the back of the chair where she had tossed her sweater, skirt and jacket.

"You make good stuff for an old boss-lady, and you know you can get me started any time, but no more today."

She walked to the door, "I want to see you get that degree." Turning the doorknob, she shrugged into her coat, "Bye lover, good luck, I'll see you on the salad line at four o'clock tomorrow!"

John got up, shaking his head in amusement. She was a good friend, his best here at the college, exactly what he had needed through these years. She asked for nothing more than a good time in bed, here or at her house. She was an attentive listener, a plain talker and gave him good advice. He didn't have to love her, but he did. He treasured her intimacies, patience and understanding.

Pulling on shorts, he stood and looked at himself in the cracked mirror over the dresser. "By God Knowlton, you've done it!" His smile was cocksure. All his doubts and fears were gone. Kate was right. "When it's all said and done, and you've worked hard enough, you'll be in your place...." Here I am! Ready to go!

He had worked harder than most anyone else had to, but he would have his degree in engineering in only a month. He pulled out the books and began the studying that would put him over the hump as far as the degree was concerned.

A voice in the hall and a sharp knock at his door interrupted and he rose from his self-imposed concentration to answer. He thought Jessie had decided to return, and then realized she had been gone for more than an hour. By the time he got the door open, there was no one in the hall, but he could hear excited voices.

Stepping back into his room, he pulled on trousers and a sweater.

"Dirty Japs, and all the while Roosevelt was talking to a bunch of 'em in the White House gardens. Damn those bastards! They bombed us! Parley Harbor I think they said, or something like that. Yeah. Out in them Hawaiian Islands, I guess."

The scraps of conversation reached John's ears, and he wasn't exactly sure what he was hearing. The talk wandered along.

"Maybe they said Pearl Harbor. It's one of them islands out there, I guess. It was an air raid. My God! That means we're at war!"

The Last Magnolia

As he reached the group he recognized another student whom he knew slightly, and there were the two waitresses from one of the local campus night spots. Standing with them was an elderly woman who took in sewing and a crippled, arthritic old man.

"Does someone have a radio we could tune in?" John asked.

One of the waitresses turned and went into her room, leaving the door open. In just a minute there was a crackling of static, and she finally tuned in a local station.

The radio announcer was repeating what they thought they had heard. In the early morning hours, the Japanese had attacked Pearl Harbor, Hawaii, and had accomplished devastating destruction on the Pacific fleet. The President would ask Congress for a declaration of war before noon tomorrow.

"That means war boys," the old man looked at John and the other student, "you're going to be called up. Just like I was in '16. It ain't fun." He wiped his eyes with a dirty handkerchief and shook his fist, "Give 'em hell for me!"

John listened, stunned. He wasn't ready to put it all together. War? Not now. Too much to do. He walked back to his room. The calendar above the desk was marked for tomorrow's exam. His last and final test before graduation and the beginning of the future he had worked so hard for.

The examination would be held at 10:00 a.m. on Monday, December 8, 1941.

Chapter 8

HANK

December 1942

Texas

"She said yes!"

Johnny was shaken from his lonely scrutiny of a beer glass. His roommate in the Bachelor Officer's Quarters and close friend for these past six months of flight training thumped John on the back as he climbed on the adjoining barstool.

"By God, she said yes!"

John smiled as he watched Hank digest his happiness. "She's the kind of gal I've been looking for all these years."

"Hank, how in hell long have you been looking? It seems to me only six months ago you and I were two of the most confirmed bachelors I knew," John observed his friend from over the top of his beer glass.

"Bachelors for life if I remember correctly. It was a pact made over a very important pitcher of beer, right here in this club!" John signaled for the bartender, "Now you tell me you've found the girl of your dreams. Man, you move fast!" His hand on Hank's shoulder offered as a pat on the back as he ordered a beer for his friend.

The bar of the small officer's club was dark and smoke lay in

65

The Last Magnolia

cirrus layers as the exhaled plumes began to fill the room during the early evening happy hour at this small Army Air Force base in Texas.

John continued his scrutiny of Hank, knowing his friend was dead serious, yet completely happy. "I assume you're talking about the woman who's been included in all of our conversations for the past four months. None other than Beautiful Barbara, right?"

"Right good buddy, the only thing is Beautiful Barbara is going to be Mrs. Henry Bailey in about two weeks. John, I'm tagging you here and now," Hank clapped his hand against John's back, "Right now. We want you to be our best man."

Hank's natural exuberance was heightened by the excitement of his announcement, and John felt that same exuberance taking hold. "I wouldn't miss this for the world. Where and when?"

"A week from next Sunday after our graduation on Saturday. Place . . . here on the base, at the chapel. You, me and Barb, her folks and her sister. Not enough time to get my folks down." Hank sobered, swallowed some of his beer and continued, "God John, I thought she loved me." He looked down, picked an imaginary piece of lint from his shirt, "I sure as hell knew I loved her. I know you probably think I'm nuts to get married now with our first assignment coming up."

The expression of apprehension passed momentarily across Hank's face, and John sensed the feeling . . . fear of the unknown, fears of combat and the war they were being trained to fly and fight in.

"Barb and I talked about it. We don't want to lose one another. Too many guys are getting 'Dear John' letters now. As far as that goes, there have been lots of women getting 'Dear

66

Barb' letters too." Hank shook his head sadly, "That's a hell of a way to end a relationship. Barb and I know what we want. We want each other for life."

In only a short span of friendship, John knew every facet of Hank and could sense the deep love he held for his chosen.

"I'm beginning to think I'm as love-happy as you are my friend." John patted his chest, "Even my heart is doing a little pit-a patting. Seriously, you and I have talked about this. You know, so do I, that everything we've hashed over about wartime, marriage, the whole bit, stacks up to just how sure you are about one another. If you and Barb are that sure, and I believe you are, you'd better belong to one another all the way now."

He laughed and punched his friend lightly on the arm, "Barbara is a great gal, and I'm really happy for you. I just wish we knew what was coming up assignment-wise. It would be nice for you to be able to tell your lady where she'll be making a home."

During their close months of living, learning and working together, these two Army Air Corps officers had proposed, thought and dreamed about the missions that would be coming their way when they completed transition training. They'd be graduates of one of the first classes in heavy bombers, and so, they had reasoned, they'd be piloting heavy planes in combat soon after graduation.

Overseas duty had been the dream of both men. If they could fly together, stay together, so much the better. Now, with a marriage coming up for Hank, John was sure his friend was having second thoughts about combat. He knew he should go overseas to fly and fight. Hank would somehow wangle an assignment in the states, an assignment that six weeks ago he would have scorned. John could only wish his friend well.

The two men sat in silent comradeship, hunched forward on their barstools, close to young fellow officers on the left and right. These others were somehow misted into oblivion as Hank and John nurtured their own thoughts.

"We could be headed overseas by the time your wedding day arrives. You know that, don't you?"

"The hell we can! We have leave time coming after graduation. They can't take that away from us." Hank swallowed beer. "I just wish those assignments would come in. I wish we had some word."

John turned toward his friend. "I feel damned bitter about Aunt Kate, and you'll find me pretty cynical about guarantees as to what we have coming as far as leave or any other privilege is concerned." He pulled his head up and anger crossed his face. "The fact that they wouldn't let me go to be with her before she died wasn't right. I obeyed their damned orders, but by God, it wasn't right. Especially not right for Katie. I was all she had and she gave me so much. Then I couldn't be with her at the end." John's grief was evident and heavy for him to carry.

"I love the corps, I love to fly and I love my country, but Kate came first, and now she's gone." He shook his head in wonder, "Hard to believe."

Katherine Knowlton, John's other mother had died following a stroke just at the beginning of his cadet training. Only given time for her funeral, he had returned to the stress of accelerated pilot training with new bitterness.

Hank leaned toward John and with his stocky arm, nudged his friend. He had to raise his voice because the dimly lit bar was noisy now as drink loosened tongues and raised decibels.

"Life's hell, but let's drink to the good times tonight, John."
He wanted John to forget the morbidity, "You know if I've got it
figured right, they really need you and me for lots more than
fighting. We're the only two privately licensed pilots in this class
and we took to the new aircraft like ducks to water. As I see it,
you and I could sure stay right here and help educate a lot of the
new pilots for the good old Army Air Corps!"

"Hank, by golly I hope it happens for you. As for me, I'm
still going to head for some of those Krauts, or better yet, the
Japs. I want to get into it."

Henry Wheeler Bailey had come into John's life the day they
threw their duffel bags on the beds in a shared barracks room in
Texas.

They had much in common and much to learn from one
another. Their destinies would intersect for the rest of their lives.
Both men were licensed pilots. Hank, a graduate engineer, three
years older than John, came from the western states where he had
worked with his father, a building contractor in Spokane,
Washington.

The first mutual contact the two men had was the shared
knowledge that they couldn't admit to their previous flying
experience. Word had reached them that to play inexperienced
was the best way, so they had been quiet about their knowledge of
flying and learned the Air Corps way. When they finished pilot
training and pinned on their wings, they referred to one with their
own coinage as "aircraft experts," because they had learned to fly
twice.

When he graduated from the state college in January of '42,
John immediately signed for the Air Corps. He'd been sent to the
training center in Texas where he'd continued his transition

training, learning about the B-17 bombers he would fly throughout World War II.

As their weeks of training passed, John and Hank became known as the Mutt and Jeff of their class. John stood tall, handsome with light brown hair that waved over his well-shaped long head. By contrast, Hank was just five feet six inches and his body was one of bulk. While not overweight, Hank's round childlike face would always make people think of him as juvenile, short and fat.

Hank was funny, possessing a rare sense of humor and an approach to life that was always enthusiastic, happy and expectant. He fit into any group, and he never met a stranger.

John was reserved. Life with his humorous aunt had given him an appreciation of wit and humor; still he was able to complement Hank's bursts of joviality. With Hank's fresh approach to everything, John found his innate caution easing away and the two men founded an easygoing relationship.

In addition to their many career similarities, they found they enjoyed hunting and fishing. Both had accumulated the beginnings of collected sports weapons.

When Kate died and the property had been sold, John had taken the two guns that had belonged to his father. He added to them the little 22 caliber rifle he'd had since he was a small boy. Hank's guns were more sophisticated. He'd spent time in the western and northern mountains hunting big game, and the stories he told, the hunts he described, whetted John's sporting appetite. The promise of many hunts together gave both men a future to visualize after the war.

Hank's girl was from Texas. John had watched his friend, in his happy-go-lucky way fall in love with Barbara and, while there had been foursomes, they had dwindled as Hank and Barb spent much more time alone.

Barbara, a secretary, was as open and gregarious as Hank, but she had a serious side as well, and her down-to-earth attitude counterbalanced Hank's carefree ways.

John signaled for the bartender and when their beer arrived, raised his glass. "Here's to the best friend I ever had," emotion stopped the words momentarily. "May he live happily ever after." Hank, head slightly lowered, took in the emotion, "Listen old man, what we have, our friendship, can't be taken away because I'm getting married. We've made so many plans. Barb knows what we want to do, and she wants to be a working member of our team."

He swiveled around on the stool toward John. "We've got to consider her as a third partner, you know." He put out his right hand. "Shake on it, John. Our plans aren't going to change. When the war is over, we're all going west to start making money."

John and Hank's plans for starting their own airline or aircraft service and evolved with their friendship.

Neither had any money and their dreams nearly were financially impossible. In spite of those drawbacks, the two young pilots plotted, planned, speculated, and made notes and graphs. They played with figures until they came up with a system of services they knew would be needed at war's end.

Their plans would move them to the Pacific Northwest, where Hank had business contacts as a result of working with this father.

As population and building increased in the far west, the need for new highways, manufacturing and industry exerted itself as remote sites were chosen for industry. Millions of dollars were lost as businesses, builders and contractors met devastating delays in construction or manufacturing breakdowns. Repairs were costly in these operations because the remoteness of sites made it impossible to receive necessary parts of expert repair services quickly.

Hank knew production shut-down occurred at these remote sites while a courier was dispatched by car or truck to the nearest city, sometimes hundreds of miles away, to pick up a part or a specialist. Meanwhile, the plant's and the employee's idleness was costing many dollars.

As Hank explained these problems, he and John formulated a plan to shorten time lost on the job. They would create the possibility of a flow of workers and parts by using aircraft in and out of remote areas. Theirs would be a service supply business that would feature speed and efficiency, and would save their subscribers large amounts of money.

They had labeled their plan, 'Expediting,' and knew with a little capital, they could sell top notch necessary air service. Neither of them had any idea how to finance their plan but, if it was possible, financing would be found.

Their first requirement would be a small airplane. They would maintain it, fly it and deliver the necessary service to customers.

"We aren't going to make enough money in the service to do it John, but we'll find a way."

This was so typical of Hank's outlook that even John, who was much more cautious, got caught up in the enthusiasm.

"Hank, if you say so," John would laugh when his friend was so earnest in his assurance, "but look, neither of us has a nickel to rub together and, as you say, Uncle Sam isn't going to make either one of us rich."

"We'll worry about that when the war's over," was always Hank's reply.

As they finished their beer, Hank reminded John, "Remember, there are three of us in it now, OK John?"

"We three. We'll do it by George. Don't worry. Barb is going to fit into the plans like a cog in a wheel."

Hank slid from the bar stool, shook hands with his partner again, "Come on, Barb and her sister want you to come for a celebration."

John signed his chit and they walked rapidly out of the noisy club to the lot where Hank's 1936 ford was parked. Neither young officer showed any of the insecure curiosity each was feeling about the future as they climbed into the sedan.
****

Hank's wish was fulfilled when their assignments finally reached them. His rationale had been correct when he assumed that their flying know-how would best be put to use by assigning them as flight instructors.

Both he and John had been assigned to South Carolina as instructors for the large B-17 bombers.
John was disappointed. He wanted a direct assignment from
transition into combat, but he was happy for his friends, Barb and Hank. The assignment meant they could be together for their first months of marriage.

They had been in South Carolina for nearly a year now. Hank and Barb were comfortable in a small apartment off the post and Barb was due to give birth to their first child in only a matter of months.

The Last Magnolia

John's life had been filled with his duties and he found great recreation in the salt water fishing at nearby ocean beaches.
He and Hank and Barb spent hour's together, developing plans for the company they still dreamed of founding at war's end.

Chapter 9

MARY ELIZABETH

August 1943

Charleston, South Carolina

Her grooming was perfect. Her skin was fresh and smooth, showing years of kind care, and taking years away from her probable age. Silvered in an exacting tint of blue to create a shine, her hair was perfectly dressed, waved flat to her head, short and elegantly neat.

She was between fifty and sixty, perhaps older, but the excellent care taken of every detail of her body and dress belied any exact age. Her clothing blended in monochromatic harmony in the softest of blues and dove-grays. A perfectly tailored light skirt and silk blouse were accented with a single short strand of pearls and matching earrings. A very large diamond over a band of platinum graced her left hand. The only other jewelry she wore was on the small finger of her right hand, an intricate domed smaller diamond, set again, in platinum.

Sitting at her small kneehole desk, she was straight, regal and proud. While her features seemed relaxed, close observation would reveal that she was waiting for something or someone. She was not ruffled by the waiting, but rather, patient.

The telephone rang and she jerked with as though startled... It was imperceptible to the untrained eye but, to one who knew her, there was a short, quick twinge of muscle. That reaction done, she relaxed, settled back and waited for a third ring before picking up the receiver.

"Mrs. Graydon speaking." The sound of her voice was soft, accented delightfully in the cultured easy vernacular of Charleston, South Carolina. Her diction was perfect and the quality matched the unmistakable caliber of her appearance.

"Yes Colonel Allen, I appreciate hearing from you so soon. Thank you for calling," the understated accent was soft and charming.

She had expected to hear from this man, the commander at the nearby Army Air Base expected and wanted him to call today and he had. Her plans were going well.

Listening as the Colonel spoke, she made several notes on crisp notepaper, shifting the receiver to her left hand as she wrote precisely in tiny, perfected Palmer method. Occasionally she would nod as she listened, as if in approval.

"Why my goodness, Colonel, when I asked for your help with this project, I didn't realize you would be so kind as to lend me one of your own men. I am deeply in your debt sir. You see," she continued, "as I explained to you and your wife last week, it has been so difficult for me this year, as the chairwoman for the White Cotillion, to find enough suitable escorts for our young debutantes. The war has taken so many of our eligible young men, and to find gentlemen who might help us from your station seemed such an impossibility because although I know there are fine young officers in your corps, I simply don't know how to begin to meet any of them."

The response at the other end of the wire was crisp and efficient and, listening cordially, she leaned her head to one side, poised to concentrate on the information she was receiving.

"Yes. This young officer sounds like an excellent choice. I approve of what you have done, Colonel Allen, and I will look forward to hearing from him. I'm sure I will be able to explain to him what the qualities should be in the young men he chooses to fill in as our escorts. Thank you so much." She added the charm of an invitation, "I do hope you will bring Mrs. Allen for tea one of these afternoons. Yes, Thomas and I would enjoy seeing you both." She sat up, if it was possible, even straighter in her chair, "Thank you again, Colonel. Yes, soon." Placing the telephone back in its cradle, she leaned back.

She hadn't been in favor of a Cotillion this year. Her objections were the war and the unavailability of young Charleston men as escorts for the debs. It hadn't seemed feasible or right to hold an annual affair of this size with so many people away but, as her husband Thomas pointed out, the war had deprived everyone of so much, perhaps a dance was what Charleston society needed to cheer it.

At his urging, she finally succumbed but, so that she could be absolutely sure the dinner and the dance would be conducted in the traditional style, had insisted that she, even though a younger matron should have had the responsibility, be the chairwoman for the event.

Rising from her chair, she gathered her note pad and pencil with the small book. Yes, everything was going well, and one of her major problems was solved.

The week before, at a dinner party in the home of friends, she had met the commanding officer of the Army Air Field near Charleston. He suggested that he provide her with the names of young bachelor officers who could be recommended as reliable party escorts. Today his telephone call provided her with the name of a young Captain who was assigned to the base. The colonel assured her she would like him very much. The officer was to drop by this afternoon and together they could work out the details of suitable escorts for the Cotillion.

John parked Hank's old Ford at the curb and looked around. The Colonel told him this woman was from the cream of Charleston society. If the homes along this short block were any testimony to that fact, then indeed this lady must be from the very top of the milk bottle.

He smiled to himself as he walked up the old brick sidewalk. The houses fronted directly onto the walkway and were protected by massive, elegantly decorated gates. A glimpse through the intricate ironwork of these stanchions gave a hint of the beauty to be found beyond.

John's long strides slowed as he looked at the perfection of century old dwellings, and his curiosity peaked as he anticipated the home he would visit today.

Funny how circumstances seem so easily changed. Here I am, a boy straight from a farm in Nebraska, about to be welcomed in one of the grandest homes in Charleston, South Carolina.

When he arrived at the numbered gate the colonel had designated as the Graydon home, he found it fastened. He pulled a bell cord and an elderly manservant arrived to open the way to what would be the loveliest home John had ever visited.

"Good afternoon, I'm Captain Knowlton. Mrs. Graydon is expecting me."

"Good day sir, Mrs. Graydon is waiting for you in the drawing room." The man beckoned for John to follow, "If you will just come with me." He led John up a flight of steps between splendid large white columns to an open, arched doorway.

On entering the house, the first thing John was aware of was a full, sweeping circular staircase. It rose regally to its upper reaches. He stood in awe as he noted the grandeur of the large case clock, the beauty of the oriental carpeting and the splendid woodwork in the large entry hall.

Without realizing it, John had stepped into the very center of this surrounding magnificence. My gosh this is only the entrance, he thought. It's larger than the parlor of my grandmother's old farmhouse, and I thought that was pretentious! He couldn't begin to imagine what the rest of this home must be like. The servant coughed slightly, discreetly, and brought John back to the present. "You'll have to excuse me, I've never been in a home like this before. There are so many lovely things to admire."

"The house is indeed beautiful sir, and Mrs. Graydon will be happy with your appreciation. It has been her home all of her life, and her father's and her grandfather's before that, so you can see, it means a great deal to her."

John was led across the hall into large double doors which were pulled open to reveal a room filled with elegance and beauty that had never been a part of his meager life.

Subdued, yet refreshing, the room was done in cool tones, making it a haven on this warm August day. The large expanse of lovely oriental carpet was made somehow intimate with the use of small conversational groupings of wonderfully rich furniture spaced tastefully throughout the room.

The major seating unit though, was situated directly in front of a rich, cherry paneled fireplace which centered on the back wall. Tall windows reaching from floor to ceiling formed airy walls to let light into each side of the room. The windows were open and covered for summer with soft gauze-like material that moved languidly in a slight but a welcome breeze.

The gay colors of the chintz coverings on large wing chairs added a light note to the elegance. The total effect heightened John's sensitivity and gave him a pleasant sense of order and beauty.

Walking toward him, hands extended was an equally beautiful woman who was obviously born to this elegance.

"Mrs. Graydon?" He shook her hand, "I am John Knowlton." He didn't let the soft white hand go and looked at her steadily. "I am overcome with the beauty and the dignity of your home. I've never had the privilege of seeing a place like this before."

She patted his hand in hers. Why, she thought, he's the same age as our Tommy. The same height and that smile . . . motherly love crept into her thoughts, only for a moment, though, as she noted this young man's propriety.

"Welcome to our home Captain Knowlton. It is so nice to have someone appreciative of it. Come," she pulled him toward a soft sofa facing the fireplace, "sit here with me. I want you to meet my husband. Thomas," she called, "our guest has arrived."

Mary Elizabeth Graydon's family had come to this city in the seventeen hundreds. They had prospered and, along with the wealth of property and businesses they acquired, had maintained a social position ranking with the finest in Charleston. She is a member of the fourth generation of this founding family and has continued to carry on all of its traditions and customs.

As her upbringing required, she had married within her social circle, a tightly bound group of the leading county families. The marriage was arranged and she had born two children to carry on the family lines.

To her great surprise, she fell in love with her husband and him with her. Their life together had been happy. They had shared mutual trust, affection and interest for nearly thirty-five years.

Their daughter Shirley married into Charleston society and had lived nearby in the home of her husband's family until the war had taken him to the Pacific coast where he was stationed with the Navy. Shirley and the children had followed him.

A son Tommy, much younger than his sister, was assigned to the submarine service in the Pacific theater.

Both elder Graydons accepted their duties and sacrifices due to the war, but were lonely and lived quietly, seeing only occasional friends and neighbors while they waited for their children to come home.

"Have you explained what we will require from this young man, Elizabeth?" Thomas Graydon walked from his study with a nearly imperceptible halting stride. An early stroke had partially paralyzed his right side, but determination had created a nearly flawless carriage and he reached his wife's side easily.

"Oh Thomas, I haven't had time. He's just arrived." She turned to John, "Captain Knowlton, I'd like you to meet my husband, Thomas."

John was on his feet and held out his hand for the man, "How do you do sir."

Thomas Graydon looked the officer over carefully and then, turning his attention to the table set for tea, frowned. "Elizabeth, don't you think it's getting a little late for tea and sweet things?" With a twinkle in his eye, he moved toward a small oriental cabinet at one side of the room.

"I should just imagine the Captain might appreciate something with a little more bite to it," he directed his words toward John, "a shot of something on the rocks perhaps?"

John laughed, "As a matter of fact," he looked quickly at Mrs. Graydon to see if there was approval to this change in refreshments. There was. "Scotch would fill the bill. I don't want to degrade the pleasantries of tea, but today has been a busy one, and a scotch might add just the power of relaxation I feel the need for."

"Why, Captain, you can have whatever you like," Mrs. Graydon picked up a small silver bell and gave it a slight shake. From nowhere, the man who opened the gate for John appeared.

"The Captain has decided to join Mr. Graydon and me for a highball Virgil." She turned to her husband. "Yes Thomas, fix one for me too. We have lots to do."

She liked this young man. He seems so like my Tommy, she thought. Or am I just especially lonely today?

"I'm sure your mother must miss you as much as we miss our son. This war with its separations is so difficult for us."

"My mother is gone Mrs. Graydon, and the wonderful woman who brought me up died just a short time ago." There was no emotion; no call for sympathy, the statement was just that, a fact.

How could she guess the hurt and stress created in John's life by his mother? Judging from his reply, it would seem that John himself had put it all aside. Only John could feel the hidden feelings of guilt and terror, and he had buried those feelings so well within himself, it seemed that not even he could pull them forward.

"Oh, I am so sorry. Do you mean you have no family at all?"

The Last Magnolia

"Well ma'am, I have good friends whom I really consider family here in Charleston. It is a fellow officer and his wife. We're awfully close."

For the rest of the late afternoon, pleasantries were shared, details for the Cotillion's requirements were discussed and the Graydons were mutually satisfied that the young man would handle things properly.

John liked this charming couple. He appreciated them and was impressed with their beautiful surroundings. He wanted to please them in whatever they asked of him.

"Mrs. Graydon, I hope the next time I'm here, you will tell me some of the stories I feel must accompany your beautiful treasures."

She beamed. "It would be my pleasure John, I'd love doing that."

"What do you do in your leisure, Captain?" The elderly host was open in his ready acceptance of this new friend.

"Well sir, there isn't much time for leisure. We find we're kept busy, but I read a great deal, and I've learned to fish your ocean waters from the local beaches. That's the best thing about South Carolina I have found, the beach and the surf."

Mr. Graydon listened carefully as John continued, "Actually, I hunt small and large game whenever I'm in a locality where that type hunting is available to me."

"You have your own guns then?"

"Well yes sir, I have a few. I'm trying to be discriminating as to the ones I add to those I have from my family. Right now utility is the keynote of my collection. I use my guns to hunt with or for target practice."

John's host leaned forward, his eyes bright with interest.

83

The Last Magnolia

John's words seemed to be exactly what he was waiting to hear."

"I've been collecting for many years."

"Do you hunt sir?"

"I used to. I traveled to the mountains and fields in season. That was the greatest sport in my life. It ended when I was hit with this stroke. Now I'm afraid my pleasures would be boring to you. I spend most of my time with my guns. I see to it that they are properly cared for and displayed . . ." his voice drifted, perhaps regrettably and he turned to his wife, "My dear, we're off the subject we all joined to discuss," he smiled, "forgive me. Is there anything else we could ask John about?"

Mrs. Graydon pushed her hair back carefully, "Thomas, I feel as if the subject of proper escorts can be put into John's hands with no further concern," she paused. "You don't mind if we call you John, do you? It seems so natural."

"The cotillion is now in my hands Mrs. Graydon, and, yes, please call me John."

"Well that's good!" Mr. Graydon rose, "Young man, would you be kind enough to accompany me to my study. I have a few things I'd like to show you."

They walked side by side towards the door in the paneled wall. As they walked together, John bent down towards the smaller man. "You know sir, targets are quite a challenge. If you like, I could arrange to take you to a range, and perhaps we could give some of your guns the workout you have been preparing them for with all the cleaning and preserving."

Mrs. Graydon interrupted, "Don't take too much time Thomas, dinner will be .... oh! John, will you join us for dinner?"

"That sounds wonderful!"

John followed his host into the den thinking. It seemed as if

84

he'd known these people all his life.

Tidying up the cocktail things, Mrs. Graydon tried to understand why they'd felt so instantly at ease with the young man. He is such a fine young man, and he fits in so nicely. He's so nice to Thomas and they share so many interests. I guess we need to be with young people, she decided. Then again, because we miss our children so much, are we too eager to accept just any young person in our home?

No, that's not it. After all, we have Honey.

Honey Bascomb was the fiancée of Mrs. Graydon's cousin who managed to amuse them with her unannounced drop-in visits. Her lengthy versions of what was happening in Charleston kept them amused and they hoped, informed. Honey was a spirited girl, and Mary Elizabeth wasn't really sure she approved of her. There was no mistaking the fact that Honey did make Thomas laugh. He saw through her very feminine wiles and was always amused at whatever Honey was trying to achieve with her dainty subterfuges.

She tried to place what it was that made John seem special to her. Could she be replacing her maternal instincts for her own son, Tommy? No, it wasn't that really. Yet she felt as if today was only a beginning . . . the beginning of one of the strongest relationships she would ever know.

"Alice, there will be three of us for dinner . . ."

Chapter 10

HONEY

January 1944

Charleston

She tapped her beautifully manicured fingernails on the edge of the table impatiently as she focused on the telephone itself and willed it to produce a voice on the other end of the line. The need for haste was plainly demonstrated as her eyes darted towards the open stair well and then back to the telephone. In sheer exasperation she stamped her foot.

If her mama knew she was calling a soldier on the telephone, there would be the very devil to pay. He'd better come to the phone quickly. She looked around again. Mama could come into the room at any time and then she was caught for sure. Pulling the telephone closer to her ear, she listened as a faint sound came from the other end of the line, then the voice she had been waiting to hear.

"Captain Knowlton speaking."

Finally!

"Well Captain Knowlton, this is a most impatient little friend of yours."

There was a pause. She imagined he was trying to identify her voice, and she smiled secretly to herself. He'd remember. She would make sure of that.

John thought, boy she doesn't give up easily, does she?

This is Honey Bascomb, Johnny." Her voice with its soft southern drawl was sexy and seductive as she pronounced the name that was most important to her, her own.

"Do you still remember me?" A too cute little girl expression crept between the accentuated words.

"Miss Honoria Lee Bascomb. Of course I remember you. How could any man ever forget the first true southern belle, the first magnolia blossom he ever met?" John chuckled.

His reaction was exactly what she wanted. His voice sounded exactly as she wanted it to sound. He was surprised and pleased to hear from her! She knew it would be that way.

"Honey, I'll always think of you as Miss Magnolia, did you know that?" he asked.

Well now...magnolia blossom...she didn't know about that, it might be a little cheap, but then, did she detect a warm caress in his voice? She hoped so, or was she placing more meaning into some of the things he said and the way he said them?

"You just have to forgive me for being so forward, I really didn't want to bother you at the base, but I just didn't know how else to reach you." She didn't wait for his reply, but rushed on in her soft, warm voice, "Mama and Daddy and I would like very much for you to come to dinner one evening this week. Do you think you could make it?"

"Honey, my schedule has been so hectic. I really would like to see you again, but I just can't make any definite plans at this time." He was dodging her and her invitations as artfully as he could. "I hope you can understand."

A small pout became audible in her voice. "Johnny dear, you must know how very much I want to see you again. Things here in Charleston are so dull and now, since I met you ... through the proper channels of course ..." she paused. It was difficult to determine whether that last aside was spoken with sarcasm or propriety. "I think there might be a little bit of fun left here in spite of this stinky war."

As she warmed to her subject, more words tumbled out, "Mama would approve of you as a guest, Johnny ..."

Actually, she hadn't even consulted her mother, but she knew she could take care of that little problem if he would just come over. "Because Mary Elizabeth Graydon speaks so highly of you, and ..." she was nearly breathless now, "my goodness, you and all of your lovely friends were just such perfect gentlemen at the Cotillion. Why, it was almost like having real Charleston boys right here for the dance!"

"Honey, your father's nickname for you fits you well. The honey just rolls off your very charming little tongue."

Actually he realized that Honey was a beautiful woman who used every nuance, phrase and gesture as provocatively as possible in her quest to satisfy an extremely over-sexed body.

He knew that Honey could be trouble and he didn't want to be any part of it. Here we go, he reflected, she's calling me again, flirting, proposing much more of a relationship than dinner with the folks. My God, she's engaged to Mrs. Graydon's cousin! He grinned, I may be a boy straight off the farm, but I know when I'm being had.

Honey hadn't been one of the season's debutantes at the cotillion. Mrs. Graydon explained that the girl was so miserable with her fiancée` serving in the Army in England, it had been a nice gesture for her to have a safe escort (from John's supplied roster of young officers) at the party.

She had brought long low whistles from the young escorts

after the ball was over, and well she should have. Her figure was perfect. Long, lean well shaped legs made her seem taller than she really was. Her waist was small, her breasts were carried high and firm and her perfectly shaped head was held with aloof haughtiness. Honey's skin fit her name too, being sweet and rich, near to peaches and cream slathered with honey. Her hair, falling into a perfectly turned page-boy with just a thin strand artfully and sexily arranged to slide over her forehead, was the color of sage. It was musky with a yellow, mellow golden glint.

Honey was a rapt listener, she was clever and quick conversationally and being with her was exciting.

The first time John and Honey danced at the Cotillion, it was evident that Honey smiled and listened only until she could captivate her companion. Her quest seemed to be for a man, any relatively acceptable man who could brighten her needs with the activity of a physical relationship. Loyalty to her fiancée had no part in Honey's search for satisfaction.

John had held her off and it wasn't until several days after the party that he realized how wise he had been in doing so.

On the day after the party, as they enjoyed a highball together, Mr. Graydon, with a twinkle in his eye had offered, "John you should receive the Medal of Honor for your actions during the cotillion."

"Thanks, you know I enjoyed the evening."

"Come on John, we watched you, and the way you fenced with our Miss Honey was wonderful. Your defense was brilliant!"

Mary Elizabeth reached over and patted him on the hand, John, you were wonderful! We really do appreciate the fact that you were most protective of the reputation of a young woman you don't even know. You know, Honey has always been strong willed and I'm afraid she's a bit wild. Heaven only knows what she's gotten away with in the past. Her father dotes on her and will move mountains to give her anything she asks for, and he has the position to do just that. He doesn't realize that some of the things she gets away with aren't really very nice, we've heard some stories about her that we don't approve of at all."

"She's a provocative little thing, and a beautiful young woman." John smiled, recalling the suggestive things Honey had said to him. "As you know, she is engaged to marry a distant cousin of mine. He's strongly connected socially to the same circle her family moves in. He has a fine future in the family bank right here in Charleston."

It was obvious how important these things were to someone Charleston bred, as Mary Elizabeth was. John thought the whole thing was silly, but he wouldn't hurt the Graydons by letting them know that.

"It would be an excellent marriage for her. We all hope that before she gets herself into real trouble Robert will be back from the war to marry her and settle her down. She is so headstrong!"

As he listened to Mary Elizabeth he thought, if anyone ever settles that girl down it will be a miracle. I don't want to get involved with the little southern honey pot in any way. She is a magnolia blossom who could harm herself and anyone else she touched.

Honey's voice on the telephone brought him back to the present.

"Well Johnny Knowlton, don't you think for one minute that I won't call you again, hear? I want to know you better and if you won't call me, then I have to call you. How much longer are you going to be what you call, 'busy'?"

"I'll tell you what Honey, next week things could lighten up a bit, and if they do, I'll be sure to call you. He thought to himself, "Not if I can help it!"

"I'd just love that Johnny." She started to ask another question, thought better of it and added, "Johnny, I'll wait to hear from you. Until then I'll just think the most pleasant thoughts I can about being with you again." Her voice lowered to a sultry, come-hither purr, "Bye now. Call me soon, you hear?"

"Bye Honey. Soon, I promise."

He hung up the telephone and thought, "That will hold her for a week or so."

"Captain Knowlton, sir," A young clerk in the office was holding another telephone. "There's another call for you."

"Captain Knowlton speaking."

"John, oh John, come quickly, I need you!"

She was crying, but he could sense that she was holding herself as steady as possible. It was Mary Elizabeth Graydon.

"What is it, Mrs. Graydon?"

"It's Tommy ..."

Before her sentence was finished, John had his answer.

"I'll be there as soon as I can. Sit down. Wait for me. Are you all right?"

She was sobbing, "I'll wait, oh John, hurry!"

He drove too fast, using a car borrowed from the Colonel. The knowledge that the Graydon's only son was either missing in action or dead made him eager to get to this couple he had come to consider substitute parents. He had to be as much as comfort as possible for them.

As the months of their relationship had passed, the three of them, Mr. and Mrs. Graydon and John had grown closer each day.

John was an interesting companion for Mr. Graydon and

their common fascination with the large gun collection Thomas had acquired gave them many hours of mutual pleasure. John had convinced Thomas that target shooting could somehow fill the activities he had lost as far as field and stream because of his health. The fine old gentleman enjoyed every encounter that he and John shared, using the weapons that he had cared for so many years.

Mrs. Graydon on the other hand had come to regard and treat John as a second son. Having been without the affection of a real mother most of his life, John responded to her affection, returning it with no fear of the personal emotional injury he suffered in the past. He was sure that had not the strange circumstances of war, and his assignment here in Charleston occurred, he would never have met this wonderful couple. He knew that he was sharing the privileges of affection that very well might disappear at war's end when they had their own children back in the fold. However it was hard to think that way when these new friends accepted him so warmly. They offered him such honest, open friendship; he knew they would be friends for the rest of their lives.

As he turned the corner onto the Graydon's street, John realized there was more to the crisis than Mary Elizabeth had explained on the telephone.

Red lights turned on top of the ambulance parked outside the Graydon's gate.

My God! Maybe he didn't understand her, maybe it's Thomas! He choked at the thought as he realized with a rushing surge how much he loved the old man. Pulling the car to the curb he got out and ran across the street.

Virgil, agitated, showing strain and shock, was accompanying the two men who carried a stretcher. He spotted John and came to him.

"This is terrible Captain, first the telegram and now this," he gestured towards the still body of Mr. Graydon on the stretcher.

"Where's Mrs. Graydon, Virgil?"

"She's in there sir. She doesn't know yet."

"Doesn't know what?"

"That's what I'm trying to tell you Captain. Mr. Graydon is dead."

"Oh my God!"

John talked briefly with the attendants and assured himself that they would take care of Thomas.

Momentarily a cloud of violent memory passed across his thoughts. This is my punishment. Nothing I care for can remain. Then as quickly as the thought came, it was gone.

"Take me to Mrs. Graydon now Virgil," John took the man's arm. He could see how shaken he was, and wanted to care for this fine man as well, "Then I want you to go to the kitchen and have Alice give you something to drink. Sit down and calm yourself."

John swallowed the tears that welled up, gave his good friend Thomas a final salute and turned to run up the steps.

"Lock the gates before you go to the back will you Virgil, I'll find my way."

It seemed strange to be giving orders to Mrs. Graydon's servant, but he knew that in the hours to come, he was going to be on hand for many of the decisions made in her household.

Crossing the foyer, he stepped into the living room, remembering how it had impressed him on that first day. It's still beautiful, but strangely empty somehow, he thought. While there had been no change physically, the room was sober with a cold feeling. It would never again have the cheery warmth of Thomas Graydon, one eyebrow cocked, a twinkle in his eye as he related a local story over a carefully mixed highball.

Sitting on one corner of the sofa, wearing only a light wrapper, Mary Elizabeth Graydon looked blank. She held the black-edged telegram in her hands and her posture was close to catatonic as she slumped forward, staring at the wrinkled piece of paper, seeing nothing.

John reached her quickly. She looked up, dazed.

"It's all over, John," her voice faltered and faded away. She reached for him and he sat down beside her as she fell into his open arms. He held her while she sobbed, her tears soaking into his   shirt.

"Over. All over. My Tommy, my son. Oh, Tommy .. The sobs grew in intensity and the pain in John's own chest as he held this frail woman who had been so cruelly double struck with tragedy was sharp and poignant. He brushed back her hair, reached into his pocket for a handkerchief and wiped her face. He held her to him and when the sobs had become soft, mewing, hurt sounds, when exhaustion stopped even that, he rocked her gently.

Taking the telegram from her hand, the news of Tommy's death was verified with words of regret.

"Don't cry, Mary Elizabeth." It was the first time he had used her given name. "Don't cry. Try not to think."

She sat up suddenly. "How is Thomas?" Standing, she made an attempt to walk across to the foyer. "Thomas fell and, oh my, what kind of a wife am I? I thought only of myself. Oh, and our Tommy was so close to his father," she moved jerkily now. "Where is Thomas?"

John went to her and put his arm around her again, "Come sit down. Thomas is comfortable."

She allowed him to lead her back to the sofa and the weakness of grief overcame her again.

How could he add this last cruel blow?

He had to.

"Mary Elizabeth, dear Mary Elizabeth, Thomas is gone.

He continued to explain in a soft, soothing tone. He wasn't sure he was giving her the right information, but precise details could wait. Now it was only the telling. As softly and gently as he could, he told her that her husband of nearly forty years was gone.

"His heart just couldn't take the news you both found in the telegram."

Her eyes widened, she gasped in shock as her hands flew to her mouth.

"Thomas! Oh, oh...No!"

The scream turned to sobs that wracked her body over and over again and the large young man, usually graceful and articulate, clumsily clutched the small lady to his breast. The grieving pair held one another, rocking, touching comforting. There were no answers for this double tragedy and the survivors wept.

Chapter 11

SHIRLEY

February 1944

Charleston

The beginning of a southern spring made the day pleasantly warm, and the lovely gardens at the back of the Graydon house were dotted with late blossoms on the camellia trees. Pinks, ruffles and variegated forms of each variety nested among the dark shiny leaves, promising more beauty with each advancing day.

Shirley Graydon Knight sat in the gazebo with John. Their mood somehow matched the spring weather, a relief from the pall they had experienced together over the last days.

The only daughter of the Graydons had come from California immediately after John called her to tell of the deaths in the family. She and her husband had been with her mother through the funeral and the memorial service, and then Commander Knight returned to duty while Shirley stayed in Charleston to be with her mother and settle her father's affairs.

In many ways she resembled her father, showing his same shrewd wit. Her intelligence and ability with words made the similarity even more pronounced, and this likeness seemed to give her mother comfort.

The only other solace the frail, grieving widow seemed to accept was from John. She had leaned on him as if he were a member of her family, and in a strongly stated ultimatum, had made it clear to her daughter that he was to be treated as such.

Shirley accepted this edict without a problem. She had liked John immediately and recognized her mother's need and affection of and for him.

When she ran into any problems in the many business and personal arrangements it was necessary for her to deal with, she found that John was able to help, and she enjoyed working with him.

"Johnny, I talked with mama today and we want you to have Tommy's car."

He was pleasantly shocked, "But Shirley, that's not necessary."

Shirley looked at the man who had become such an important part of her family.

"In the short months you and I have been together through all of this, I feel as my father felt about you, and mother too. You've become as close to me as if you were my brother. I know Mama likes to think of you as her second son. It gives her comfort, somehow."

"Shirley, I don't want your mother to replace Tommy with me."

"No, I thought about that too, but I don't think that's what is happening really. I agree, to be a replacement would be unhealthy."

Shirley stood up and walked restlessly to another chair. "I think she was already beginning to regard you as something closer than just a friend before Tommy died. Then when daddy went too," her voice faltered, "I know that Dad," choking, she wiped her eyes. "John, Daddy wrote to me about you. He had been so lonely without Tommy and so disappointed at the debilitation of his stroke, he really spoke highly of you. He told me about all the time the two of you spent together, of your interest in his guns. The fact that you started him in yet another sporting endeavor with the introduction of targets as something for him to enjoy was so appreciated. He loved you John. Did you know that?"

"He opened new vistas for me too, you know. We talked the same language, enjoyed so many of the same things, and he is the first father figure I have ever been as close to. He meant a lot to me ... so does your mother. I simply accepted their kindnesses as a friend, I never thought about it as family, but I suppose the way we three interacted is the way family life should be. I loved him too and learned so much from both of them."

She reached for the paper on the table between them. "Here is the bill of sale, the registration and all the papers you need."

"I haven't ever owned a car before! This is wonderful!"

"There's method to our gift you know. Now you can get here quickly and on your own. That means Mama will have the company she's going to need when I leave."

"She'd have my company anyway, no matter how I got here, but you're right. Now she'll have it faster."

John didn't want to seem abrupt, he tried to curtail the boyish excitement he felt, but he couldn't. He rose from the white wicker chair with impatience and realized that Shirley understood. Grinning, he picked up the papers.

"Can I go have a look?"

"She's all yours!"

John was gone, down the path to the garage, nearly flying.

Shirley raised her voice to stop him.

"John whenever you need any help in dealing with mother,

helping her or explaining business details to her, I'll be behind you all the way." Shirley walked toward him, arms extended, "Please feel free to make this home yours at any time. Remember, you are considered family and friend all together. That's very important to Mama and me."

Realizing this was more than light chatter; he walked back up the path to meet her and with a deep sincerity said, "Shirley, you and your mother are my only family. You can't know how wonderful the acceptance your father and the two of you have given me is. I'll consider anything I can do for you or your mother a privilege. I'll try to be the strength your father gave to all of you. I love you both."

They met in the center of the garden path and embraced warmly. There was no self-consciousness; rather there was a new bond, a bond of strength between two people that would be stronger than blood for the rest of their years.

John Knowlton, Jr. had finally become a part of a warm and loving family, and he would give all that was in him to the relationship.

Chapter 12

JANICE

May 1944

Charleston

She should have known this trip south, when it was beginning to get hot, was going to be miserable. She hated this train, hated the dirty smelly passenger cars and she could hardly endure the heat. Being on this train was like being in prison.

There were many soldiers and sailors on the train and they were being shunted to or from military assignments. Unfortunately while they were on the train, they spent most of their time drinking, smoking and being generally offensive. She had been the object of one or another drunk serviceman's attentions several times and she didn't like any of it a bit.

As she sat by the open train window, the mohair of the seat pricked her legs and no matter how she tried to change to a more comfortable position, the scratch was there.

Air came in through the partially opened window by her seat. It wasn't fresh and carried the smell of coal dust. She felt as if she might never breathe clean air again or for that matter, ever feel clean again. Wild-eyed, she was desperate, like a caged animal, but this cage was moving.

Why did I do this, she wondered? Why did I, Janice Adams even begin to believe I could leave Harper where my life was so organized and my friends were decent. Why did I come here to marry John? Tears gathered at the corners of her eyes ready to spill over, but she stopped them with sheer strength of will as she mentally turned back the miles of this terrible trip that was leading her into who knew what?

She started the trip by traveling by car with her father to the depot in Crispin where she boarded the train for Chicago. That part hadn't frightened her because she had made the trip before. The rest of the journey though had terrified her. She hadn't been able to make her father understand how apprehensive she was. As a matter of fact, she didn't want to acknowledge her fears because if she had it would have been impossible for her to board the train.

Fear had knotted her stomach when she changed trains in Chicago. The next leg was to Atlanta and it had worked out. She kept to herself, paid attention to the time tables and followed directions carefully. In Atlanta she had only a short time to find the train to Charleston, and somehow she made it. She was proud of her accomplishments as a traveler so far, but anxious to end this terrible trip.

A drunken sailor was walking towards her, lurching with the motion of the train. She could see that she was his target again. It would be the third time he had bothered her and as she straightened to deal with him, she thought to herself, this will be the last time he bothers me! Turning her head, she looked out the window to avoid any eye contact.

When the sailor reached her seat, he leaned over the back of the dirty white headrest. His breath was foul with sour smelling whiskey and his clothing reeked of perspiration, cigarettes, and heavens only knew what else.

"Come on honey, be patriotic. Come on Sweetie, just have a

little drinkie with old Harold here." He touched her shoulder. She jerked away.

"You know honey, when we get to Charleston I may be leaving this good old Hew Hess of Hay for a dangerous mission. Come on, you could make my last hours so nice."

Janice shrugged his hand from her shoulder as she turned toward him and in a high pitched nasal voice that seemed to pierce even the sides of the old railroad car, she said, "Young man, you get yourself down that aisle," she pointed, "and don't you bother me again!"

The young sailor lurched back, a silly grin exploding over his face.

"I'll call the conductor," she said, "and if that isn't enough, when we get to Charleston," her voice gained momentum, "I'll see to it that my fiancée`, Captain John Knowlton deals with you personally."

She wasn't really sure she had the right to use John's name but she needed something to intimidate this boy.

The tipsy sailor lurched to the side and then straightened slightly. Somehow her assertiveness brought him back to some semblance of sobriety.

She didn't take her eyes from his face and she watched his thought processes as they passed through his sluggish mind. Suddenly she saw him realize that his pursuits were futile, that she would have the last word.

"OK honey, you're really missin' a treat not comin' along with old Harold here, but if your Captain is so God-damned...oops, scuse me, IMPORTANT, then I'll sure find somebody prettier than you." Under his breath he could be heard to say, "and that won't be very damned hard to do either." He staggered back down the aisle, bumping from side to side, producing a ridiculous picture as his head flopped in opposite directions to his lurching body.

Well! That's that! He shouldn't bother me again. She leaned back in her seat. The spine of the encounter left her and her head dropped weakly. Why am I here? This is so miserable. I want to go home.

John's letter had come as a complete surprise. They'd been seeing one another for years, but then he'd gone away to college. When he was back in Harper all his time was spent with his aunt. When the war started he went into the service. She hardly knew him. She couldn't imagine why he had asked her to marry him. There had never been any romance between them. For that matter, there had never been any romance between her and anyone.

Why me? She would always wonder about that. She was five years older than John. There had never been any intimacy between them. She suppressed a small shudder at that thought. She wasn't sure at all how she'd get around the embarrassment of that little detail that marriage assuredly expected. She knew sex...oh dear, what a revolting word...would have to be a part of her relationship with John and that idea didn't appeal at all. She thought about her encounter with the drunken sailor and how she had gotten rid of him and she smiled to herself. She could deal with anything and get rid of what didn't suit her. She would face sex when it came and deal with it as she felt it should be treated. That was all there was to it. Closing her eyes, she leaned back against the headrest.

John pulled into the station parking lot. His excitement caused him to miss the first available parking space, and he circled impatiently, looking for another slot for the car.

He had given lots of thought to asking Janice to be his wife. He hadn't been sure at first that she was the woman he wanted in his life, but as the lonely months passed, he knew he needed permanence. Marriage seemed to be his answer. He thought about Janice and she seemed to fill the necessary requirements. They came from the same rural home town background; there could be no secrets about the past between them. She was a decent girl and fit the necessary requirements to be a good wife and mother. They would establish their own home. After all, he thought, a completely normal home was something he had never lived in.

He had watched the fine relationship between Mr. and Mrs. Graydon, had seen the love and companionship between Barbara and Hank grow, and felt the need for the same type of relationship for himself.

As 'uncle' to Hank's young baby, the pull and the need for a child of his own had become strong.

Fellow officers and Mrs. Graydon had arranged many dates for him here in Charleston, but somehow he couldn't attach himself to any of the women he'd met. The Graydon friends were from another world; true the world he was living in now was different too, but he came from such an incomparable background, he was sure he wouldn't be able to fulfill the needs of the Charleston girls. The dates that were initiated by fellow officers fell into several categories. There were the nice girls, and then there were the wild ones. There simply hadn't been anyone that met what he felt were his needs, or that seemed to be the type that he could live with for the rest of his life. That was when he began to think about Janice, someone from home.

The Last Magnolia

He planned to take leave, go home and spend some time with her, getting to know one another again. If all worked well, he would propose and hopefully bring her back to Charleston as his bride. The time table seemed short, but this was war, and fast marriages were happening every day.

All leaves were canceled. His growing obsession to have someone waiting at home for him while he was flying in the war intensified as rumors persisted that he would soon leave for the war zones in Europe.

He wrote Janice and asked her to come to Charleston to be his bride.

Her acceptance seemed to fill all his needs and now the day of her arrival was on hand. They would be married tomorrow.

Pulling his little car into a spot, he turned off the engine, stepped out of the car and headed for the depot.

He hadn't told Mary Elizabeth about Janice or his plans for a proposal until Jan's acceptance arrived. Then as he shared a late supper with his good Charleston friend, he explained about his coming marriage.

Mary Elizabeth, somehow smaller, and weak, surely no longer the commanding personage she had been before the double loss of her husband and son, was surprised, then upset when John explained his plans.

"John dear, why didn't we talk about this?" She obviously felt left out.

"I couldn't bother you with my problems. You have too many other things to think about. Now don't worry, you're going to love Janice and approve of her, I know. She's a quiet, very proper lady and she'll be a good wife for me."

Mary Elizabeth shook her head as she looked at this young

man with motherly adoration. He was all she had to smother with her affection, but she felt a stab of foreboding. There was something wrong here. What was it? She couldn't put her finger on the missing equation but it was there. Am I jealous, reluctant to give him time with anyone else, she wondered? If she had just thought a little further she would have realized that the word love had never been mentioned.

"When will you be married?"

"Jan will arrive the first part of May and we'll tie the knot."

Being careful so that he wouldn't sense her misgivings, she made a request.

"Will you please me by having your wedding here? I would be so pleased to use this house as your marriage chapel. It would have to be small and quiet, but I would like to have your wedding here." Tears spilled over and rolled down her cheeks. She would be as kind and accepting as possible no matter the qualms she was feeling over this marriage.

"Oh, don't feel you have to do that. We'll just be married at the base chapel, and I want you there!"

"No!" You'll be married here in the house that has meant much to you while you have been in Charleston… she walked to the window, "I'll start planning now."

It was the first time John had seen her assert herself since the tragedy, and he thought that possibly it could be a turning point, it could be a beginning for the healing of the scars of deep grief.

"Jan will be pleased, and I'll be honored," he kissed her softly on her cheek, "to have the privilege of being married in this lovely old house. Thank you Mary Elizabeth."

The conductor announced the station and Janice began to freshen up as much as possible. It had been nearly two years since she had seen John and she wanted to look her best.

She powdered her nose, ran her fingers down the sides of her legs to straighten the seams of her stockings and stood so her hands could press out some of the rumple and wrinkles in her traveling suit.

The sound of steam being released from the engine along with the smell of coal smoke and the dirt and litter would soon be left behind. That made her happy and a short surge of excitement rippled between her shoulder blades as she watched the boarding platform come into sight.

Janice Adams was a small person, just over five feet and quite thin. She was dressed neatly in trim, but obviously homemade clothing. Her face was tightly pointed and its smallness seemed to magnify her petulant expression. There could be cruelty in that face too, and what led one to see that possibility were her eyes. They were a light, ice blue. The lids were nearly lashless and their sharp appearance was accented by the way Janice looked piercingly into every situation, making her own narrow evaluations. Her mouth was small, thin and generally turned down.

She was perfectly attired for a young woman traveling. A short-sleeved linen jacket fit down over her hips to top a short, shirred skirt in a brown rayon print. Her shoes were neat, if a little smudged, brown and white spectators and she carried a large imitation leather handbag.

The train came to a stop with steam and brakes joining in a squeal of harmony. Janice lurched slightly and then bent to gather a few small bags from under her seat. She looked out the window. How would she find John? Her fear of being alone and lost in a strange place took hold again, but the fascination of watching the crowd on the platform made her forget herself.

There he was! She had forgotten how handsome he was and the uniform added to his good looks. All of her fears dropped away and she felt a great surge of pride and a sense of elation. Love. This must be love! There is the man I have come to marry and he looks wonderful!

Many of the crowd was milling around John, but still he seemed to stand alone. His arms were folded and he was perfectly assured as he scanned the train's windows. He was watching for her! Janice's elation mounted and she stepped into the aisle quickly, nearly knocking an elderly woman off her feet as she hurried to follow the line in front of her of passengers getting off the train.

"Janice! Over here!" Johnny strode toward her and picked her up around the waist to hold her as if she were a little girl.

"Jan! I've waited so long for this!"

She caught her breath. What excitement. It's almost like a movie and I'm the star. I'm in the movie!

"How did you know I'd get off this car?"

"Just luck I guess. Here," he pushed her back from him a little further, "just let me look at you. You made the trip all right? Did you have any trouble in Chicago or Atlanta? Are you tired?"

His excitement communicated itself to her, and she didn't even try to answer the questions. Now she was happy and glad she had decided to come. What a wonderful man John was, her father had been right. He would make a wonderful husband.

"Enough of your questions," she laughed, trying to catch her breath, "oh John, it's so good to be here with you."

John beamed. He had known this would be right and her happiness, united with his, proved that he had made the right decision. He was marrying his own kind, a home town girl. He stood with pride as he took the bride-to-be by the arm to lead her to the baggage counter.

"You're going to really like Hank and Barb. They have an apartment above ours so you'll see lots of them. Wait until you meet little Hank, my Godchild. Now there's a boy! I'm Uncle Johnny to him, so I suppose you'll be Aunt Jan. He's going to love you too!" Walking quickly, Janice tried to match his long strides, but it was impossible so she trotted in short little steps by his side, nodding, listening and dodging other people so as not to lose him.

"You'll get to spend a lot of time with Barbara," he continued to lead her through the crowd, "she'll show you around Charleston. She's really quite a gal; I know the two of you will be good friends."

Janice pressed her lips together until you couldn't see a mouth at all. Naturally, she thought, I'll have to meet these people today. I had hoped I could be with John alone for awhile, but I might as well go along with his plans, the sooner they are over the better.

Bags retrieved, John carried the two heavy suitcases and led the way to the car.

He drove easily, his left hand on the wheel as he held her tightly with his right arm.

"Hank and I have been together since our preliminary training and he and Barb have been married since we finished transition. They're going to stand up for us."
She wasn't comfortable being held against him this way. She wanted to sit up straight. The buttons from his jacket pressed into her chest.

"John, when are we going to be married?"

"That's another surprise Jan, I have so much to tell you, he looked down at her fondly and she wriggled with her discomfort. He let her go. "Was I holding you too tight? I'm sorry. It's just so darned good to have you here."

Straightening in the seat, she patted her skirt down, wrapping it under her knees.

"No, it's all right. It's just so beastly hot. Is it always this way?"

"You'll get used to it. It's awful at first, but in no time at all you'll hardly notice it."

He turned a corner and continued a steady patter of conversation, pointing out landmarks, negotiating traffic, "I'm anxious for you to meet Mary Elizabeth Graydon. I've written to you about her Jan. She's one of the loveliest ladies in Charleston." His eyes shone and his words came faster as he described the closeness he felt for the other woman, "She's made me so welcome. I'm sure I wrote to you about her loss...both her husband and her son. That was such a bad time for her."

Jan nodded, watching the buildings that seemed strange in color and structure to her as she half listened.

"Mary Elizabeth is going to have our wedding in her house! Wait until you see it Jan. I wish your father could be here to marry us, he would be so proud."

She leaned back, the oppression of the heat curtailing her happiness to be here. She felt curious and strange about everything she was hearing.

"She gave this car to me Jan. But more than that, she's been my friend. The way she has accepted me, and let me be a part of her life, it's really the closest I've come to being a family member.

I'll always love her for that."

"From the sound of your letters, you've been awfully good to her too. If you ask me, she owes you a lot."

"Oh no! I haven't done nearly enough for her. She's such a good woman. Wait, you'll see. I know you will come to regard her as highly as I do."

She watched the street signs pass by. She was uncomfortable about this other woman in his life. She didn't need doubts at this time, things were just too strange. To rid her mind of fears, she turned to closely scrutinize John.

She liked what she saw. Maybe I do love him. Maybe I'm pleasing myself as well as my father. I think just maybe I'm going to like being with this tall handsome man for the rest of my life.

They had put her bags in the apartment; she had freshened up and then gone upstairs to meet Barbara and Hank. Now as they were about to leave, Barbara stood at the curb, holding her baby on her hip.

"Johnny, you two have a great lunch now. Be sure Janice has the She-Crab soup," she turned to Janice, "Don't miss that Jan, it's one of the specialties of Charleston and absolutely delicious."

Well, I've met them and I'm not that impressed, Jan thought. But after all they are John's friends; I will be nice to them.

"Thanks for reminding me Barb," John knew his friends wanted this relationship to work out for him, "we're stopping at Mary Elizabeth's after lunch. She is so excited about your arrival. I hope she can contain herself while she waits for us to get there."

They pulled slowly away from the curb, John handling his little car as if it were precious goods.

"You really have things well planned don't you John? Tell me Captain organizer," she attempted to add a flirtatious lilt to her voice, "where are we going on our honeymoon?"

John laughed, "Well that's been planned too as a matter of fact. Mary Elizabeth has turned her summer home on Kiawah Island to us."

Sick and tired of the name of Mary Elizabeth, Janice threw herself back into the seat...just how much more am I going to have to be grateful for, she wondered.

"It's a beautiful old home Jan, right on the beach. We'll have sun and sand and I'll teach you how to…."

"On the beach John? Do you mean the ocean? You probably don't know this, but I'm scared to death of water, and I'm not at all sure I even want to see the ocean!"

"We're going to be doing lots more things than sitting in or by the water, it's our honeymoon honey," he reached over and patted her affectionately on her knee and his voice was suggestive, "we only have a few days."

She shuddered and pulled her knee away from him.

I can't go through with this. I hardly know this man and he's thinking and touching me and talking intimately to me. I know what those looks mean. I know what he's thinking, and I don't want a thing to do with any of it.

Unaware of her sudden withdrawal, John went on,

"Here it is. This is one of Charleston's oldest eating establishments. There'll be nothing but the best of the city for you today, Jan."

Looking at the building she thought, well we'll get on to another subject anyway.

The restaurant was impressive, the food expensive. Janice loved the waiters and their very special attentions, but the menu had things she had never heard of before, and John's insistence on choosing for her had turned into a disaster. The flavors and difference in texture, taste and appearance were revolting. She tried to eat enough to please him, but as far as she was concerned, this would be the last time she ate any of this kind of food."

She did enjoy John's company though. He was by far the most handsome officer in the long narrow room and he knew exactly what to do. He made her feel as if she were the most important woman in the world.

When they were ushered to their table she was aware of heads turning to watch them and then she realized that some of the people were nodding at John as if they knew him. He returned their greetings and she wondered how he knew so many of these strangers.

"Let me order a cordial for you Jan, I think you might like it." When it came, she hated it. Sticky, sweet and mint, she could hardly stand to sip it. The only thing she enjoyed was the fact that she was in the company of such a handsome man in an impressive place, and he was hers.

"Johnny Knowlton!"
The voice, softly accented, carried across the room and a smartly dressed, very beautiful blonde woman followed that sound towards John. As she arrived at their table her voice became an unmistakable caress, "How wonderful to find you here!"

John rose, "Honey! I thought you and your family were at the beach house."

"Oh Johnny Darlin', I can't be down there all the time, now can I?" She chuckled a deep, throaty sound, "Charleston needs me right here in town!"

The beautiful woman turned and rudely scrutinized Janice.

113

Her eyes scanned the nondescript woman and her instant opinion registered clearly as, "no contest."

"John honey, introduce me to your little friend." her request was cunning, catlike.

Janice felt smaller than she really was and terribly uncomfortable. Who could this be, this beautiful woman who was so confidently friendly with John?

"Honey, I want you to meet Janice Adams, my fiancée`. Jan this is a good Charleston friend, Honoria Bascomb."

Janice smiled and reached to take Honey's extended hand. The contact was limp and hands barely touched.

"My goodness, time does fly," Honey said with saccharine dripping from her words, "your fiancée`!"

No more caress from the southern damsel. "When will you be getting married Johnny?"

"Tomorrow," John beamed, "at Mary Elizabeth's. Jan just arrived from back home today."

"Back home? My goodness life is full of little surprises."

T his woman is hurt, Janice thought. What could have gone between her and John?

Actually, Honey was furious, and her upscale southern upbringing wouldn't allow her to show any of the anger. Rather she continued to include both John and Janice in her conversation, but that ended quickly. Backing away from the table, anxious to make an exit, she said, "I do hope I see you again real soon Janice...it is Janice isn't it?" Honey's eyes moved from Janice's head to her toes one more time, sizing her up and judging her quickly.

Janice smiled and before her affirmative nod could be detected Honey continued, "I'll try to get in touch with you so I can show off some of our beautiful Charleston."

"If you're going to be at your folk's beach house we'll see you sooner than you think Honey. Mary Elizabeth has arranged for us to have her house next to your folks for the next few days."
The expression on Honey's face showed sarcastically that this was all she needed, but aloud she said with soft southern charm, "We surely will try to get together Johnny. I'll be giving my usual few hours to the Red Cross, but I sure will try to be at the beach while you all are there." She left, moving out of the restaurant, nodding at acquaintances as she moved.

"How about another cordial, Jan?"

"No thanks," her lips pinched together.

"What I'd really like to have is some information about Miss Bascomb," her suspicion was evident in her tone," she's really a stunning woman isn't she? How well do you know her?"

John caught the obvious inflections and realized that Honey had gotten her devious message across due to her surprise at meeting Jan. Honey had finally acknowledged the final ultimate defeat in her persistent tracking of him. That defeat brought out the bitch in Honey.

"Honey's a mutual friend of Mary Elizabeth Graydon and me. She's engaged to be married to Mrs. Graydon's cousin and I've seen her occasionally."

Jan decided to drop the subject. Getting into it would only peg her lower on the ladder because the Bascomb girl was obviously a socialite. Jan was not.

"I guess we should get over to meet your Mrs. Graydon now, John. I'm anxious to meet this paragon," her face assumed the pinched expression and snippily she continued, "she's been the greatest topic of interest in Charleston since I got here. Judging

115

from everyone I've met so far your 'Mary Elizabeth' is the greatest of all to you, isn't she John?"

"I want you to like her."

"I surely will try, but let me tell you this," Janice threw away all the insight and wisdom of a few moments before, "I don't think I can ever like Miss Bascomb, and if being on a honeymoon with you is going to include her, I'd just as soon skip the beach house. I don't like the water anyway."

John felt a sudden finger of ice poking into him and he warmed it by telling himself she was tired.

Chapter 13

JOHN AND JANICE

July 1944

Charleston

She finished cleaning the rug with the antiquated carpet sweeper that had come with the apartment. She moved so slowly because the heat, the dampness and the July air were stifling and she hated it. Well, it's clean she thought, as clean as it is ever going to be.

Things were so different from what she had imagined they would be. Life in the two room apartment was stifling. She wanted to be back in Harper, back with familiar friends from the church, back where she was needed.

Just exactly what was she? Just Mrs. John Knowlton, wife of an Army Air Corps Captain, a camp follower, nothing more. She was trapped in two rooms with a tiny Pullman kitchen and nothing to do but clean, cook and wait for her husband to come home.

Her wedding, planned and organized for her had taken place too quickly. She remembered the coolness of the beautiful Graydon drawing room and of the kindness that was offered by John's wealthy friend. The memory of the beauty and care that had gone into the wedding softened her expression. She nearly looked happy as she retraced her days back to a bright spring day. Then her joy was replaced with her mean spirit.

The Last Magnolia

There had been three 'honeymoon' days at the beach. They were horrible. The sound, the constant roaring surf, the grit of the sand and the inescapable humidity were more than she could bear.

Worst of all there was John. Now he was her husband and he really took advantage of that by demanding all the privileges he felt the marriage ceremony had given to him. She had known she would have to be of some service to him as a wife . . . physically that is . . . but to have him become such an animal was more than she could take. Sex. It was awful. Dirty. Degrading. The idea that people could touch each other in those very private places disgusted her. Those parts of her anatomy should be revealed only to the person to whom they belonged and then only to be kept clean. John had shocked her with his knowledge of her body and what he expected of her. It all came down to this. He was an animal and she was a lady. Sex had ruined any of the thrills of being married to such a handsome man.

She had tried not to listen to him; she really couldn't look at him as he patiently explained the love act, and how he would help her enjoy it with him. He had been surprised to learn that her father hadn't given her information about love making, or that she hadn't talked with friends about it.

Her father! Talk to her like that? Absolutely not! He was a gentleman. Surely he had never allowed himself such degrading dalliances. She was sure her father thought sex was dirty too. And to think her friends would discuss things like that? What kind of people did John think she had for friends? She sat and held her head in her hands. How had she gotten into this mess?

The memory of that first night replayed itself.

She supposed he had been patient; he did seem the soul of

118

kindness. He tried to help her and she did try to enjoy it, but it was so . . . so . . . dirty . . . that's all that could be said about it. She was revolted and he was disgusting. Surely love could have nothing to do with that terrible act.

Since the stay at the beach, she had avoided his attentions with every excuse she could use. Finally, last night was the last straw.

John had become impatient with her and they quarreled. When the fight ended, she made it quite clear that if he was going to demand that revolting act of sex from her, he would just have to forget about sleeping in the same bed. She would, she told him, make herself available to him several times a month. Beyond that, she would take nothing more from him as to a physical relationship. They could have a fine marriage she assured him, based on companionship and a home in Harper among the nice people they had grown up with. She simply wasn't going to put up with the filth of him on top of her with his heavy breathing and happy release. Those were things she would never enjoy and he could learn to love other things about her.

Mrs. John Knowlton, that would be her role, that of a perfect Christian lady. Clean in mind and body. She would not be a common harlot in the bed of her husband.

Janice had been able to suffer all the indignities she defined through the past months because of her plan for the future.

When John was sent overseas, if he was sent and at this point, she hoped he would be, she would go back to Harper. There she could pick up where she left off. She could live with and work for her father. She would find a small house, fix it up and when John returned after the war, they could settle in.

This dream had become so important to Janice; it was all she thought about. It seemed to preserve her sanity, she decided. Janice didn't discuss these plans with John, she wasn't sure exactly why, probably because she was afraid he might disagree, and then there would be nothing left to go on.

John had been cool when he left this morning. Their argument, and her ultimatum about the bedroom hadn't pleased him, but he seemed to have given up in his persuasions.

She didn't want to lose him as a husband. He was a nice person to be with, and he certainly gave her everything she wanted, but what she wanted most was to be back with her kind of people and John with her, back in Harper.

Oh God! Charleston is so filled with Southern people, she thought. I hate them. I hate their mealy mouthings, their snide politeness. She knew they called her 'Yankee' behind her back and she didn't care. She wanted nothing to do with them. For that reason, when John suggested that they go somewhere, she declined. There was nothing she wanted to do in this miserable city, and no one she wanted to see.

Oh my, how that would change when they went home. She'd get John back to the good people, then he would forget all about his uppity friends and sex and all the other things that being in the service had taught him.

A small tap at the door broke her reverie and she crossed the room to open it.

"Hi, Jan!"

Barbara was in the fifth month of her second pregnancy and beginning to show. She walked into Jan's living room slowly as if a curtailment in action would give her the reprieve of being cool.

"The nicest call just came in, and it includes both of us. I thought on a day like this, you would welcome the invitation as much as I do."

"Who from?"

Janice didn't like Hank and Barbara. They were too easygoing, and took too much for granted as to friendship as far as she was concerned.

For some reason Barbara had taken it on herself to make Charleston wonderful for Janice and so Janice avoided as much contact with her as possible.

Actually, Janice harbored a strong resentment toward the friendship that existed between the Baileys and John. They seemed to have things to talk about that didn't include anything she was interested in, and she felt left out.

John had explained, to try to make her a part of their fun, but she really didn't care and she had almost put a stop to seeing Hank and Barbara entirely.

She could see there wasn't to be any escape this morning though. Here was Barbara, sitting in her living room with another message of 'great importance.'

"Mrs. Graydon just called," Barb shifted her weight in the chair, "she'd like you and me to come to lunch this afternoon."

Mrs. Graydon again! Janice stiffened. You'd think she was a queen or something, the way everyone bows to her every wish.

That was another friendship she was trying to end. John was entirely too close to that woman. It almost seemed indecent, the way the lady relied on John for everything. You'd think they were related or something.

"Oh no, I don't think I can go out today. I have cookies to bake and the apartment to clean . . ."

"Come on Janice," Barbara's tone was tight, "you can bake any day of the week and your apartment is always clean. I have the car today and can drive us over. Mrs. Graydon needs a bit of company and frankly, I could use some of the coolness her house offers."

"No Barb, you go ahead; I promised John his favorite cookies tonight."

"Well, he'll be a little late getting home to eat them. Mrs. Graydon has asked he and Hank to stop for a drink on their way home from work and John has accepted. They plan to meet us there."

"John has no business making arrangements behind my back!" Janice started for the telephone in the hallway, "I'll just call him and tell him to come right home."

Barbara watched the tight, unhappy, disgusting woman. She and Hank didn't like Janice any more than Janice cared for them. They were sick at heart that they hadn't talked John into waiting before jumping into this marriage. Since Janice came to Charleston, all of the spirit and fun and goodness that were John's had gone out of him. Janice had, in only a few short months, drained their good friend of happiness. They felt powerless.

Barb was tired of trying to be nice to Janice. The only reason she had come to tell her about Mrs. Graydon's invitation today was to get her out of the house and at the same time to try to help Mrs. Graydon and Janice understand one another. She felt this was so important to John. How can I help Mrs. Graydon like this woman when I can't stand her, Barb wondered?

The plan wasn't going to work, and frankly, Barb's thoughts continued, I'm sick of trying. She got up, "We'll miss you, Jan." Walking to the door she said over her shoulder, "You be sure to call Johnny and tell him to come right home to you . . . I'm sure he will." Silently she hoped he would stop for a drink with her and Hank at the Graydon's house.

"Thank you very much for coming, Barbara," Jan's inflection was barely civil. She was surprised that Barb hadn't made more effort toward her going to the luncheon. Actually, she was surprised and a little bit disappointed when she thought about it a second time. The cool Graydon house surely would be better than this tiny hot apartment, but she wasn't going to beg.

"I'll see you later. Give Mrs. Graydon my best."

Barbara turned as she started up the stairs and wiggled two fingers at Jan, almost too cute it seemed, and probably deliberate. "Bye. I sure will."

"That's that," Janice said as she shut the door. Maybe one of these days she'll get the message that I don't want anything to do with her. When I get Johnny back to Harper, we won't have to put up with Barbara and Hank anymore.

She knew about all the silly talk about going into business with the three of them. Their plan didn't worry her in the least because she knew they didn't have any money to do what they planned. When she and Johnny moved back to Harper, those plans could be forgotten.

"Jan, it's me, Barb." The tapping on the door was loud, interrupting her thoughts. "Now what does she want?"

"Yes?" She didn't open the door.

"Hank just called. The orders are in for him and Johnny."

She pulled open the door, "Orders?"

"Yes, surely Johnny has talked to you about the possibility that he could be sent overseas?"

Janice came alive. She was bright, her face radiated, she seemed nearly friendly.

Making an attempt to hide her elation, Janice assumed a

complacent mask-like countenance.

"Yes of course, John has tried to prepare me for the worst."

Now, she thought, I can go back to Harper!

Barb on the other hand, was steeling herself. She had promised Hank she would be good about the day the orders came. Now that day was here. Hank was going into combat, she had one small baby and another on the way. She would be alone.

When Hank called, she kept her voice strong and accepting, "OK honey, how much time do you have?"

"About enough time to get back to the house and have you bring me and my belongings back to the field. Can you handle it honey?"

"Of course I can, come home fast darling!"

They had made their plans. She would stay in Charleston until the new baby came and then would return to Texas and her folks to wait for him to come back. If he came back . . . no, she couldn't think like that. Definitely when he came back.

Here, in Charleston she had friends who would see that she was taken care of while she waited for the baby. She knew John had felt Janice would fit into their plans, but at this point, she didn't give a darn. She didn't feel close enough to Jan to care whether the woman stayed or went, but she would do anything to make things good for Johnny.

Barbara watched Janice, who stood deep in thought, a smile on her face.

By golly, I think she's glad Johnny's leaving. Damn! Why did he marry her? What had possessed him? He brought a woman he hardly knew to Charleston and then married her! She and Hank should have tried to stop him, but he was so intent on having a wife, a family of his own. What a shame.

"I'm going to go pack Hank's things. They'll be here in a few minutes."

"Thanks for coming down Barbara," Janice was being too nice, "how long will we have?"

Barbs' answer was curt, "Only long enough for them to leave again, and then they'll be gone," a small sob gathered in her throat, "for Lord only knows how long." She turned and bolted up the stairs to her apartment.

Janice smiled and turned into her own apartment. "Oh well, I guess I had better get John's things ready too." She rushed into the bedroom. Pulling his things out of the drawers, she reached under the bed for his B-4 bag. She packed everything that was his, running into the bathroom to take his toilet articles from the medicine cabinet and then she piled everything, one on top of the other, into pockets and compartments of the bag with no thought to her usual organized neatness.

Harper! Happiness! These were her only thoughts. Finally she could go home and be with her father again!

Johnny took the front steps two at a time. His excitement at finally being sent into a war zone to fly and fight was only tempered by the fact that, in spite of general arrangements made in advance, he would have to try to make final quick preparations for Janice.

The door to their tiny apartment was open and he walked into the shining perfection Janice always achieved with her constant cleaning.

Janice, despite the heat she hated, was putting a tray of cookies into the oven and he crossed to put his arms around her waist.

She stiffened and turned, "John, you could have caused an

accident." Pulling away from him, she put the cookie sheet on top of the stove, "I could have been burned."

"Jan, I'm sorry . . . oh what the hell. My orders have come!" The excitement in his voice couldn't be reduced. This was what he had been training for these first war years.

"Yes dear, I know. I have your bags packed." The false note of regret in her voice didn't match the satisfied cat's grin on her face, "I realize I have to be a good service wife. I know I have to keep a," she grimaced, "a stiff upper lip. Don't worry dear, I will." She couldn't let him know how wonderful she felt, how happy she was to be able to leave this hell hole.

John took her by the hand, "Come here honey," he tried to lead her to the bedroom, "I don't have long. Let's forget all the unhappiness last night. Let's clear the air. Make love to me. Let me make love to you. Let me take a piece of us with me. Please?" He looked at her tenderly, pulling her toward him.

"What in the world do you mean? Make love in the middle of the day?" She pulled away from him. "You expect me to go into the bedroom and do that now? Now, when you're leaving me?"

She was working into a good surge of rage now, and planned to stoke that fire over and over again because she knew she wasn't going to bed with John or anyone else ever again if she could help it!

"You just want to flop and run, is that it? You've made me nothing more than a common camp follower, bringing me to Charleston. Now what do you suppose is going to happen to me while you go to gay Par-e-e-e or wherever it is you're going?" She tore her wrist from the grip he had on it. "No!"

John reached out for her again. He was broken and

126

completely defeated in all of his attempts toward a loving relationship with this woman. He led her back to the sofa and she resisted every step of the way, but he was firm as he sat and pulled her down beside him.

"All right Jan, but there are some things we should talk about," his voice dragged, "Barb and Hank have made some plans that can include you. I think I should tell you about them. I am your husband, and feel a responsibility for you."
She folded her arms like a petulant child and listened, against her will.

"Barb is going to stay here," he went on, "have the baby and wait until it's old enough to travel. I think they would like to have you stay here to help her with little Hank."

Janice jumped up from the sofa.

"Help Barbara? Take care of her brat? Forget it, John. I'm going back to Harper as soon as it is possible for me to get a ticket and get out of this hot house!"

"But Jan, I thought maybe you'd like to stay here, maybe find a job. I can leave the car for you." He looked around, "This is a nice apartment. You'd have the base for all of your needs".... His voice faded as he realized she didn't want any of what he offered. Still, he had to be sure she knew he had tried to arrange things for her. "Mrs. Graydon could be so helpful to you and you would be good company for her. She's so lonely."

Janice jumped to her feet and whirled toward him.

"Mrs. Graydon! Barbara! Hank!" She screamed, "I am sick, SICK TO DEATH John, of all your great and grand friends. Believe me, when we get back to Harper and settled down in our own community, I don't expect to hear any more about those three, 'friends,' as you call them." Janice paced back in forth in

The Last Magnolia

front of him, "You can take your fancy Mrs. Graydon, happy old
Barb and that Hank, and oh, that damned baby too."

Janice had worked herself into a frenzy. John had never seen
her like this before.

"Oh! And your car too! I don't want the damned thing! I'm
going home . . . HOME . . . do you hear me? The next time you
see me I hope this silly war is over and you've come to your
senses. I've had enough of this so-called glamour and your
friends. I want to go home where we both belong, and that's
exactly what I'm going to do just as soon as you walk out that
door!"

He felt as if he'd been hit in the pit of his stomach.

"Lower your voice Jan."

He couldn't believe this woman, disheveled from her
outburst, perspiration standing out on the extended veins on her
forehead and neck, "if you want to go home, do. There isn't
enough time for me to help you. Here," he threw money toward
her on the floor, "this should clear things up here in Charleston
and get you back home. You'll get a monthly check from me for
your support." He turned in disgust and walked into the
bedroom. Zipping the compartments in the bag he swung it to
the floor and picked it up.

"This is goodbye for now Jan. I'm sure you'll manage
everything," sarcastically he added, "you seem to have your plans
well made."

The realization that he was leaving suddenly got her
attention.

"Where are you going?"

"If you don't want the car, I'm taking it to the Graydon
house. Virgil will take care of it until I can come back and," he

128

walked to the door, "I want to say goodbye to Mary Elizabeth."

Her fury was renewed, and the next barrage began.

"Say goodbye to Mary Elizabeth! Of course! You can say goodbye to everyone but me, can't you? You're always running to that perfect society queen, aren't you?"

The perspiration on her face made her look slick and shiny and her eyes bugged out of her small face. As she screamed to spit out her words, white clusters of spittle settled at the corners of her mouth, ready to spill over and run down the sides of her chin.

"What is it between the two of you, your Mary Elizabeth and you? Are you some kind of a pervert who has to have a woman twice his age? I really wonder what goes on between the two of you, the way you take on about her."

Dropping the bag, John stepped in front of his wife and with the open palm of his hand he slapped her cheek.

"Get yourself back to Harper, Janice. You belong there, I don't."

He picked up his bag, walked to the front door and to the car.

She watched from the window, holding the stinging cheek. "Good riddance." She smiled.

John climbed into his car slowly. His mind flashed back to his failures with other women. His mother . . . but he shut that out quickly. There was something there that couldn't be approached. His grandmother . . . now Janice. Why was he being punished? The thought that he wasn't at fault didn't seem to enter his mind. Exercising the control he had instilled in himself as a young boy, covering a memory he had pushed into darkness, he carefully pulled away from the curb.

Chapter 14

HONEY

August 1944

England

She couldn't believe her eyes! A face from home this very minute, right here in the lobby of the Savoy!

She spent as much time as possible here and had met lots of new faces, but harkening back to her proper Charleston upbringing, it was really very important to have people from home in her collection . . . and here he was!

Walking rapidly, squeezing between the uniforms that filled the lobby she wondered why she was so excited about seeing him. He really wasn't from Charleston at all but then, she reasoned as she walked, he does know my family and some of my friends. She accelerated her pace as she approached the tall broad-shouldered officer standing at the bar. Then she remembered, damn! He's married and he's such a straight shooter, he probably won't even remember me.

"Johnny! Johnny Knowlton!" The soft southern voice carried the soothing caressing tones she used so effectively. Without raising her voice she had commanded the attention of not only John, but everyone else near the bar, "You look absolutely wonderful!"

John jumped, and then appreciated the moment with a hearty laugh because without even turning he recognized her voice. He swung around and yes, he was right. There she was in all her blonde feminine glory.

"My God! Honey Bascomb! What are you doing in London?"

Honey smiled, her eyes sparkling with intrigue and provocative mystery. She threw her arms around John and then stepped back and extended her hand straight towards him, fingers curving down only slightly. John thought, damn, I don't know whether to kiss her hand or shake it. He shook her hand firmly, pulling her back toward him.

"Johnny, it is fated in heaven that we should meet like this," her voice was husky and full of promise.

She was beautiful. Her grim gray uniform obviously had been tailor-made to fit every curve. The perky Red Cross hat was set just right, at a jaunty angle, certainly not the regulation set for this duty-designed chapeau. Her stockings were sheer and silk, suiting her extravagant tastes. There would never be the thick heavy rayon other women wore during this war. No sir, Honey Bascomb would always be able to support the black market when it came to her God-given southern needs.

"Well dear, as you know, I just do have the most awful luck. My life is just one terrible experience after another."

John held her away from him so he could watch her antics and laughed as he thought, she didn't look as if she were suffering. Pouting prettily, Honey went on, "Here we are John, two kindred souls," her eyelashes lowered and then fluttered open to reveal beautiful eyes that scrutinized him carefully, "together . . . and alone."

Well, almost alone she realized as she glanced at the many uniformed people who filled the lobby of the hotel.

The Last Magnolia

"Well," she whispered, "almost alone." Her exquisitely long eyelashes fluttered suggestively again and her gaze was for him and him alone. She reached up and kissed him lightly.

"You are really just something you know. Instead of giving a dear old friend a lovely little kiss, you shake her hand and act as if you aren't surprised in the least at seeing her on foreign soil."

"Why Honey," John decided to play her game, "I can see you're in the service of your country, but I just didn't realize that the American Red Cross had set up offices in the lobby of the Savoy during the cocktail hour."

He studied her from head to toe and back up again. She's still a beautiful woman and still dangerous as hell was his assessment. He grinned. I should have taken her up on her offer when we were both in Charleston, for sure.

"So I repeat my question, what in hell are you doing in London?"

She had observed him as he completed his scrutiny of her and, knew he liked what he saw. As far as she was concerned, he was better looking than she remembered. Lean, virile and tanned, he fascinated her. She wondered if he was still so honestly straight and proper.

"Well to begin with, I finally got out of that awfully dull old Charleston."

"Yes, I can see that."

"Oh, you stop that now!"

"There's a table!"

He took her arm and led her to a small corner table.

"I want to hear your story, but first let me order a drink for you. Bourbon? Good. Now, let's have your story, Honey."

Drawing in her breath sharply, she plunged into her tale with the affectations only she could employ.

"Oh Johnny, you don't know . . . you just can't realize how devastatingly awful Charleston is for a lonely young woman. My Mama and Daddy were so afraid I was going to meet someone who couldn't fit into their idea of what was right for our Charleston circle." Honey took a deep breath, "I was a virtual prisoner in the home of my girlhood. Then Bobby," another great breath, "oh, you didn't ever meet my Bobby, did you? Well Bobby was sent here to London, so I couldn't even count on him getting home on furlough. Oh Johnny, you just have to know how lonely I was. Just desolate." Her words drifted to a sigh.

Wryly, he remembered stories of her so-called desolation among the other officers in the squadron, and he remembered her efforts to date him. Somehow sympathy wasn't something he could dish out for this sexy blonde adventuress.

"You and Bobby are still engaged then, I take it?"

"Oh yes, Bobby and I are engaged, and that's a big mistake."

"A mistake?"

"Oh, you know what I mean. I was just so tied down. If I could have gone ahead and married Bobby and we could have been with a crowd of newlyweds, with our friends back in Charleston, it would have been all right. Why, if we'd been able to do that, by now I'd be well along toward motherhood and providing one of the at least two required descendants for Bobby's family. That would have satisfied the entire city of Charleston, and kept me busy, I guess."

She took a sip of the drink in front of her, then raised her glass. "Here's to us, Johnny Darlin`."

He matched the tilt of her bourbon, clinked glasses and took his first sip of scotch.

"Us, Honey. Now go on with your story."

She was so intent on herself and her problems, she failed to catch the slight cynical tone that matched the grin on his face. "Oh yes. Well, I volunteered for the Red Cross downtown in Charleston. It was such an easy way to get out of the house. Why, it wasn't long before I was working every day of the week and that's when I got this perfectly wonderful idea."

She reached into her bag for a cigarette, opened a lovely lizard case, extracted a cylinder of tobacco, closed the case and put it back into her bag. The entire act was swift and seductive since she never took her eyes from John's face.

John took matches from the ash tray on the table and lit her cigarette.

"What kind of an idea?"

"Well, I got to thinking about Bobby, very busy over here and me, very busy but bored stiff and lonely back there, and I talked with some of the Red Cross people and what do you know?" She took a long drag on her cigarette. "Why Johnny, I was sworn into the Red Cross officially and very soon after that, my orders came in for London!"

I'll bet they did, he thought. There is more here than meets the eye. Probably more strings were pulled by influential people for this assignment than for any others during the entire war. He was sure her father had been most instrumental in getting one more thing accomplished for his little girl.

"Wonderful, Honey. I'll bet Bobby was glad to hear your news."

"Oh my. Yes he was. Happy and glad and he met me when I got here." She added an aside, "Oh John, isn't it awful what the Boche has done to beautiful London?"

"I'd never seen London before, but it raises the hair on my neck to see what devastation war can create. My God, there are whole sections of this city crumbled and gone . . . and the victims . . . all innocent citizens. It makes me sick, but on the other hand, I admire these Londoners so much. The way they keep their heads up is amazing, considering the fear they live with night after night." Both of them were silent for moments as their thoughts returned unconsciously to their own missions in this war-torn country.

"Why isn't Bobby with you tonight?"

"And that sir is where all my plans were squashed. Just squashed. Life became horrible again. I was only here two days. Bobby and I decided to get married right away and he got orders. Just like that. Overnight!" Her eyes widened in surprised shock, as if the whole story was just beginning. "Overnight Johnny, and my Bobby was gone."

"Why I thought you were going to tell me that the two of you were married, living in a little cold water flat, pulling the blackout drapes and loving and living in England."

Honey's pout returned. "Well you were wrong, all wrong." She took another drag from her cigarette and a sip from her drink. "Bobby is in North Africa and here I am. I hate the Red Cross but there isn't any way I can go back home short of getting pregnant, and I sure don't want to do that. I'd have a time explaining it with Bobby gone."

Her voice lowered to almost a whisper. "I'm so lonely Johnny. That's why I come here with the girls as often as I can. This seems to be where the officers hang out, and after all, a girl with my background can't fraternize with just anybody now, can she?"

135

John tipped back in his chair and laughed. "Honey, you haven't changed a bit!"

He hadn't given it much thought, but this lobby was indeed a hangout for the officers. He came in every time he got to London between missions. Somehow the scotch, the noise and the good looking young women took some of the bite out of the existence that war forced them to live. It somehow made guns, blood, losses, death and destruction more bearable if that was possible.

"Where's your friend Hank?"

"I didn't know you knew Hank that well, Honey."

"Oh yes. You know, after you both left, I tried to look in on his wife. She's such a nice girl. Why, if I hadn't gotten my assignment over here, I'd planned to be with her when that new little baby was born."

Well. This was a side of Honey he didn't know. Was it possible that she could exhibit kindness and thought for someone other than herself? Maybe he should look a little further into this piece of southern fluff. His musing was cut short when the real Honey rose to the surface once again.

"And Johnny," she lowered her eyes, "your little old wife from back home isn't in Charleston any more is she?" The beautiful eyes held malice as they lifted to look him square in the face. "I really thought she'd wait for you in Charleston. Barbara thought she was going to stay too. After all, you two couples were just so close.

Johnny wasn't angry. It was kind of a relief to put the cards on the table with someone who had met Jan.

"Probably you, Honey, of all my friends, know better than I what a big mistake I made when I sent for Janice. I won't try to defend my decision. I'll tell you this . . . the marriage is all over.

Janice returned to Nebraska and when I get back from this damned war, there'll be a quick and simple divorce. Jan and I don't belong together. It's over."

Honey patted the back of his hand. "I'm sorry Johnny. I knew she was wrong for you the first time I saw her. Do you remember? At lunch?"

He shuddered, remembering his excitement that day. What a fool he had been.

"You outgrew girls like Janice a long time ago dahlin, you know that now, don't you?"

"Yes, I know." He signaled for another round of drinks.

"I thought you'd never ask," she said coyly, using those fantastic eyes again, as only Honey could use them.

Damn, she's a beauty and such good company. Too bad there had to be a Bobby.

Good. He's not married much anymore. Janice is gone, Honey mused.

Sirens broke the crowd's noisy pitch inside the hotel and the parade to the shelters began. Johnny picked up their drinks and she held onto his jacket as they joined the surge of people moving to heavy cover.

"Come on Honey, we've got lots of catching up to do and we can do it sitting in the shelter with our liquid refreshment."

"Why you're just the man I always imagined you could be Darlin`, we just didn't spend enough time together."
****

The sheets were damp when he woke. Damp with the moisture of London rain in August, and from the perspiration of their lovemaking.

He checked his watch. He had to catch the six-o'clock bus to the base. There was a briefing later in the day and he had to be at it. Five o'clock. Lots of time.

Rolling over, he took in the beauty of her. The bomb shelter of last night seemed a long way away.

She was awake.her hair was fanned out on the pillow and it looked like waves of gold. She was watching him with an amused, knowing expression.

"My God Honey, if I'd known what a tiger you were, I wouldn't have avoided you all of these years." He propped his head up with his hand.

She lay naked and fresh. Her small firm breasts showed pink nipples that had only a few hours ago responded to foreplay with tautness when he had begun their lovemaking.

"I do believe, Captain Knowlton Darlin, ` that you are the nicest thing in bed that I have ever had happen to me." She patted him on his naked thigh.

"Why did we let so much time go past us?"

He feigned shock. "Miss Honoria Bascomb, you're talkin' more like a man. Surely not like a lovely southern lady."

"Your southern accent stinks," she snuggled close to him, her warm flesh touching his bare skin, "come on old dear, we know what we both like. I don't think we have to play games with one another, do we?"

"Well Honey, I was just wondering about Bobby."

"What Bobby never knows, Bobby will never be upset about, now will he?"

"That's the spirit, mums the word. I just wish things had been different with Jan."

"How was she in bed John? She must have had some redeeming features."

Honey's voice held that small cruel note she used so well as she giggled lightly.

He moved away from her.

"Jan and Bobby are both people you and I shouldn't be discussing. This is us. Now." He smiled, "I can assure you that your talents and Jan's talents move in two very different directions. Different directions indeed! Jan makes a mean batch of cookies!"

They held each other in their laughter and he put his hand on her firm belly and gently began rubbing in small circles, letting his fingers range further and further around.

"Johnny, you know what can happen, don't you?"

He leaned over and kissed the center of the circle he had made with his fingers.

"What I know little magnolia blossom is, what's sure to happen."

Slowly his hand continued to make an ever widening circle. Gently, firmly working outward, then sensually upward, the hand continued to caress.

She lay very still and the chills began. First they thrilled across the area he was massaging, then the sharp, demanding signals shot down into her groin and began to work up hotly. Again her nipples became taut and rigid with the dark red of passion. She moved her torso toward him, pushing her naked, beautiful body against his.

"Now, now Johnny," her breath came in short gasps.

He pushed her away gently and began to massage her back with his free hand as he held her off, just nearly but not quite touching him. The massage continued in the same way her stomach had been touched.

139

She pushed herself closer to him. "No more. Now, come to me now!" Her words were nearly a moan.

John smiled, "I want you to beg me for it."

She thrust her body to him, pushing him into her and the slow, exploratory, thrusting motion began. As they moved, the pitch ascended. Higher . . . higher . . . more . . .

"John, oh my God, John!"

He held her tightly, moving quickly in her. Then he changed his rhythm and she moved faster beneath him, holding him to her with a fierce intensity. It was as if they could never have enough of the ecstasy of this unification, yet if they continued they would miss the crest they were creating for one another.

"Johnny!"

"Yes! Now! Oh, Honey!"

The moisture of their bodies held them together and then they released and parted. Their breath still came in heavy gasps.

"Oh Johnny Darlin`, it was even nicer than . . ."

"Honey, Honey. You raped me, you little minx!"

She laughed softly, too exhausted yet to move, "That, Captain Knowlton sir, was what I'd call mutual rape."

"I'm so exhausted," John pulled himself off of the bed, "I don't know how I'm going to do it, but Honey darling, I have to catch that bus!"

He stood, looking down at her, "You're a lovely little lady, and I'd be interested in repeating our last performance."

"Oh Johnny, we'd better!"

He walked to the bathroom of her small flat and she called after him, "Will you be back tonight?"

"I just don't know from one day to the next whether I can be with you or not. Just know this young lady, when I can leave the base, this is where I'll be. I know all about you and your hidden charms now, and don't you ever worry about my coming back. I'm the bee baby, you're the honey! You just be here waiting for me. OK?"

Her smile was feral.

"Why Captain Knowlton, you mean you've been avoiding these hidden charms all these years, and now you're going to start telling me where to be so you won't miss them?"

"You bet! Wait for me!"

Knotting his tie, he bent swiftly to kiss her and was out the door.

Chapter 15

SIS

September 1944

Over Germany

The morning flight was launched under a low ceiling. Less than a minute after lift-off, the B-17s disappeared into the overcast and within only a few minutes more, they had climbed through the dark gray shroud of morning mist and burst into dawn's clear sky.

As they climbed toward their initial rendezvous point, John could see other bombers from his squadron. Even further in the distance, many other groups and squadrons from other airfields in England were forming to head for their final meeting point prior to a combined massive sweep across the English Channel. Their ultimate mission was for another huge drop over Germany.

On orders for overseas, John had picked up a B-17 and his own crew in the states. They had ferried the aircraft together to England. As with all Army Air Force bomber crews, John had assumed he would fly with these same men until he had enough points to return to the states, or until the war was over. Finally, he thought, he was doing some real flying. No more instructors' jobs. He was in the war.

When he and the crew arrived at their final destination in England, he was surprised to find himself ordered into a briefing for a strategic mission. He was assigned as the commander of another, older aircraft whose pilot had been killed during its last raid.

This reassignment in itself was a difficult transition for John, as well as for the men he was to command. These war-weary crew members were grieving for their former leader. They had flown and fought all their missions with him and now it would be hard for them to develop the same camaraderie and loyal trust in their new leader, John.

Through the next months as they flew mission after mission, John and his new-old crewmen got to know and respect each other. While they lived and fought together, they became a close-knit team. Facing death over European skies had matured them all far beyond their years. As they developed individual self reliance, they became a well-coordinated team, able to adjust to the accidents of war and to support one another toward their ultimate end. Each man in John's crew, John included, knew he could depend on the other.

The old B-17 they flew in together was named, "SIS." Her nose was painted in a hot pink, and, as was the custom, she had been named by her previous captain. While other planes were named for lovers, movie stars and girlfriends, SIS was named after sisters. Her former pilot had been a brother to eleven, and he hadn't had the nerve to name his ship after just one of them.

When John took command of this pink painted, flack-flecked beauty, he chose to keep SIS just as she was christened.

She had flown missions since early 1943 and had come back to home base again and again with only repairable damage. This, considering the fate of hundreds of other flying fortresses, was a near miracle in itself and John and his crew felt the pink nose and the name were a sign of good luck.

The Last Magnolia

The day remained clear as they approached their target over central Germany after final rendezvous. For this daylight raid, bombs were to be dropped over a factory that manufactured bearings.

SIS brought up the rear of the huge formation. Throttles were pushed forward to maximum continuous power prior to opening the bomb bays of the lead ship. In sequence each following plane increased their speed.

As they came in on target, John heard the voice of his bombardier, Charlie Dawson report,

"Bomb doors open."

Within seconds, Charlie's voice excitedly called,

"Hit!"

Amid the intercom cheers from the other members of the crew, John jockeyed throttles and maneuvered back toward the retreating formation. SIS was lagging, with the flight leader and other flying fortresses already far ahead.

Puffy black blossoms filled the air all around them as heavy anti-aircraft fire from the ground filled the sky with flak. The black puffs looked harmless enough in the distance, but whenever a near blossom burst, the concussion caused turbulence not common to upper altitudes and SIS shook violently from the blasts.

As they headed her home as quickly as possible, relatively harmless fragments bounced off the skin of her wings and body. Then a closer bursting shell ripped a jagged hole through the skin of the rear fuselage.

The sound of flak ripping a part of their fort away and the terror of another possible crushing shot removed any thought of beauty or blossoms as the black bursts of flak continued around them, bouncing and penetrating the walls of their B-17.

Reports on the intercom were shrill as waist gunners revealed conditions to the rest of the crew.

German planes zeroed in on the scene and began a systematic attack on the formation. John and his crew were thrown into action, battling valiantly to save their own lives and their ship.

The FW-190's were relentless in their attack. Using their well-developed frontal approach, they were able to hit the B-17's most vulnerable spot, and the sight of those small fighters, guns blasting and headed directly for their nose was frighteningly awesome. John could clearly see the features of the attacking German pilots firing on the fort just before they made a half-roll and dove through the raking fire of SIS's .50 caliber machine guns.

Reports of damage to part of the oxygen system made it necessary for some of the crew to share emergency oxygen bottles.

A dive to a lower altitude would lessen their need for oxygen, but John and his men knew it would be suicide. To stay with the relative protection of the massive umbrella of firepower afforded by the tight formation of their fellow B-17's with their many defensive guns was the safest approach. As the air battle raged, SIS, crippled, but supported by a crew fighting with all they had, stayed with the formation.

Potential disaster was shown when the number four engine began to smoke.

God, John thought, if we lose an engine before we reach the protection of our own escort fighters, we'll be sitting ducks for these damned F-W's.

The Luftwaffe knew exactly what the range was of the

American Mustangs coming from England to escort the returning fleets of bombers to their home bases. They had learned to attack the bombers up to that limit. John and the formation were approaching the rendezvous where the Mustangs should pick them up.

As each minute of the battle ticked off, the universal prayer among SIS's crew was, "Please, God, let's see our P-51's."

Plunging forward, staying close to the pack of surviving super forts, John watched number four engine. It smoked, then began to lose oil pressure. He knew as soon as the engine froze, he would have no choice but to turn away from his course to England and head back toward Germany, landing gear and flaps lowered. This was the signal for surrender, one of two choices the pilot of a crippled plane could take. Either bail out or signal and be escorted by FW 190's to a Luftwaffe airfield.

Hell, he thought, after all of this, we have to offer ourselves as prisoners of war. Damn it to hell!
Because he felt his crew would rather risk a bail out, he started to ask for choices.

The report that one of his waist gunners, Billy Alberts, was severely wounded made the decision for all of them. Bail out was impossible if they were to save Billy. No vote was needed. They were a team . . . a crew who would remain together.

The atmosphere in the sorely wounded B-17 was despairing as men who had fought and survived all previous missions together now faced a future they would have no control over. Time was up. They had flown their last mission together. Silence enshrouded the old fort as each man seemed to experience his own epiphany.

Black specks in the distance rapidly grew into the shape of

the eagerly awaited P-51 fighters. They had another chance!

"There they are!"

The voice carrying the message reflected the jubilance felt by the whole crew as the Focke Wolfes quickly broke off from the retreating bombers and headed back to their German base.

A resounding cheer shook the battered old SIS as she headed across the channel with her guardian angels in the guise of American fighter planes.

John held her steady, beaming as he watched the Mustangs. "They should all have halos," he said to his copilot.

"Second and carried," came the reply.

Relief and a sense of security were shattered when the gauges showed the temperature climbing rapidly on number four engine.

The co-pilot, Bob Fellowes, hit the feathering button and the propeller ground to a stop.

So far, so good.

They continued their escorted flight across the channel and back to home base.

The number three engine didn't last the trip. A run-away propeller caused the loss of all its power.

Again, Fellowes reached for a propeller button to bring the spinning disk to a stop.

The feathering system had been damaged along with the propeller button needed to bring the spinning disc to a stop. The jig was up. Rather than stop, number three engine wind-milled to uncontrollable high revolutions per minute. They had a runaway propeller on their hands.

The B-17 could fly lightly loaded on two engines, but not with the drag of that uncontrollably spinning propeller. Their only hope to stay out of the channel was to maintain enough altitude to pass over the coast of England and glide into an emergency landing.

"Hang on boys, we're going to ride this one out," John yelled excitedly to his crew.

The experienced veterans who flew with him prepared themselves for the glide to terra firma.

The wet black mud of a turnip field became the last place SIS would ever land. The flights that had taken her to success in mission after mission during the war were over. John and his crew, who had valiantly fought with her as their fort, left her to trudge through the mud of the field. They carried their wounded to the nearest farmer's cottage where they would be picked up for the return to home base.

Less than eight hours from their take-off through a patch of English mist, these men had completed a major assignment in the mission of war. They had faced death, and been saved from what seemingly had been an inevitable fate, by fellow airmen.

Their battered old friend, SIS would never fly another mission, but her crew would carry her in their hearts, remembering her as their ultimate weapon during their personal war on Germany.

Chapter 16

HONEY AND JOHN

October 1944

London

She was waiting in the lobby. He was sure that was where he would find her there. He was tired and wanted to go straight to her flat. Still the feeling of togetherness he felt, in the same room with others who like he, had recently flown and fought in missions gave him an added stimulus to replace the letdown at the end of a combat mission.

From his vantage point he watched her, sitting across the lobby. Animated, beautiful, and young.   And he grinned and shrugged, momentarily his.

He had left behind desperate, fearful moments of war. Now better times, magic moments with Honoria Lee Bascomb, were going to be his.

He crossed the room with long strides and bent to plant a kiss on her soft mouth.

"Oh! You did come back! It was too long." Her little pout was as pretty as ever, "I asked a million questions about you, and no one would give me any answers." She stopped long enough to take a breath. "Johnny, I do believe you know most everybody who comes here."

He smiled at her tenderly, "Knowing you is the most important Honey." Reaching down he pulled her to her feet.

149

The Last Magnolia

"Let's get a drink and some dinner. I don't have to be back until tomorrow morning."

A sexy, sidelong glance was directed at him, and she took his hand to pull him along toward the exit,

"My place Darlin?"

"After dinner you minx."

The weeks they had shared had gone by too quickly, but it seemed like months. Good months as they caught moments together. Their relationship had become firm, honest and happy.

John was with her as much as he could be, and she arranged, as only Honey was capable of doing, to be free any time she knew he could be in town.

In bits and snatches, their only excitement was being together. They were able to discuss almost anything. While Honey came to appreciate John's intelligence and serious approach to life, he had come to love her feminine, flirtatious manner and her insatiable lust for sex.

They were good together, in or out of bed, and they knew it. The relationship was moving toward something permanent and, while neither of them had mentioned it, the thought of marriage was beginning to assert itself in their minds.

Dinner had been brief. Their need for a physical relationship surmounted other appetites, and they retired to her small flat early in the evening. The lovemaking, the sleep, the being together was over again. As John dressed to leave, he watched Honey as she sat at a small table drinking black market coffee.

"We never have enough time together, do we?"

Her peach satin wrapper was tied around the waist, but the top had come apart, and two firm, luscious mounds of breast showed.

The Last Magnolia

He walked over, took the coffee mug from her hands and gently kissed the rise of each breast.

"Johnny, you are a devil," she added huskily, "and I love it."

He walked back to the bathroom, leaving the door open while she continued to sip coffee thoughtfully.

"What's going to happen to us, Johnny? When will you be back again?"

"Boy, you're full of questions this morning, aren't you?"

"It's just that I'm beginning to wonder if this damned old war will ever be over, and when it is," she looked at him sadly, then shrugged, "I guess it's just insecurity darling. I'm beginning to love you too much."

"Oh Honey, don't. Not when I have to leave you again. There's so much for us to think about, to talk about. We didn't plan on love when we started this you know. Then there's Bobby."

"And with you Johnny, there's nobody. I don't like that. I want to be the somebody in your life."

He stuffed toilet articles into his dop kit.

"Don't you understand my dear, dear John? I want to know because I care so desperately for you. Are you coming back to me?"

"Yes. Yes, yes, yes, magnolia lady. I'm coming back to you. I don't want to miss the rest of my life with you. You see, I love you too Honey, but I want both of us to be sure. I don't want to make another mistake." He sat on the chair opposite her, "We come from such different backgrounds. You know I can't offer you what Bobby can. Besides that, I don't come from your very rigid wealthy Charleston society. I'm not sure I know all the rules."

151

"But Johnny, you're known and admired by all of what you call my 'society' because of Mary Elizabeth Graydon. Why, with her as your sponsor, you can do anything you want to do in Charleston and it will be sanctioned. I can tell you that for sure."

He lowered his head to avoid direct eye contact, "I want it to be right for you, Honey, don't you understand? I want you to be as happy twenty years from now as you are today. Get it?"

She put her coffee cup down and walked across the room, her wrapper opening to reveal her beautiful naked body.

"I understand all right Johnny. You're afraid I'll play around," her fluffy mules sounded a sharp, angry staccato as she paced back and forth in the small room.

"Oh Honey," his voice sounded sad, almost despairing.

She dropped the anger and irritability as she ran to kneel by his side, putting her arms around him.

"Oh I do understand! It's just that when you're gone, that understanding gets a little doubtful, and I get so scared." She pulled away from him, "You're right. To talk about us or the future, to settle anything now is silly. I'll just rise above my insecure days when you're gone. I won't think about all those planes that go down. I won't worry anymore and when you come back, we'll talk about us."

He reached into his kit, "I'll tell you what Honey. I'm going to give you an insurance policy. Something to make you absolutely sure I'm coming back to you. Here," he held out his hand. Lying across his palm was a large green toothbrush. "Here's my toothbrush."

Eyes wide in mock seriousness, she took the brush and burst out laughing, "Johnny Knowlton!" Between the peals of laughter, her voice was incredulous, "A toothbrush?"

"Now don't laugh, you little devil. My toothbrush is a very personal item. Now it has become a sign of permanence. Just think about it. When you put your toothbrush in a glass in your bathroom, you know you're coming back to use it again, don't you? Every day you use it, and you put it back in the glass, and you know you are coming back to use it again, right?"

She looked like a little girl as she nodded, "Right."

"OK, you take my toothbrush. Put in the glass in your bathroom along with your toothbrush. Now you have insurance. 'Come-back' insurance, if you will."

He pointed her toward the bathroom, "Now you know I'm coming back, and back again and again, to use my toothbrush. Get it?"

She held the brush up, looked at it, and then turned to kiss him lightly. Holding it between them, she recited, "This is the come-back toothbrush. It is yours. It is mine and ours. This toothbrush means we're going to belong to each other for the rest of our lives," she raised her beautiful eyes up to him. They were wide, light amber and questioning. "Right?"

He smiled at her tenderly, "Right!" To add emphasis to the declaration between them he asked, "Right?"

She was smiling, holding the toothbrush over her head and pirouetting, she repeated emphatically. "Right!"

John reached out to stop her spin, kissed her on the mouth, holding her tightly against him molding her body into his, "Of course, my little magnolia, I'm going to come back to do more than brush my teeth."

Holding her away from him, his eyes shone, his look devoured her. "Make a note of that!"

153

The Last Magnolia

Releasing her, he was gone before she could reply.

Chapter 17

APHRODITE

October 1944

Great Britain

I'm glad Honey didn't know I was leaving on a special mission, he thought as he watched the English countryside pass by from the window of the bus. We both would have worried about it too much. It's better that she hear about it now, when it's all over.

My God, what a fiasco! She won't believe me when I tell her, or if I'm ever able to tell her, anything about the past two weeks. If this stuff ever makes the history books, well actually, it shouldn't. This is a top secret that should stay that way forever!

He thought back to the last morning he'd had with Honey. Although his information was sketchy, he had known that his next assignment was highly classified. From what he had been able to fathom from conversation with his commanding officer, he wasn't going to get much more information until he reached his mysterious destination. He hadn't been able to tell Honey they would be separated, or for how long.

The time away from her had passed from days into weeks. Finally it had been more than a month before he was able to return to his old squadron today. Hopefully he would get back to her in the next couple of days. His classified mission was completed. Thank God.

The Last Magnolia

Now he could get back to the familiar routine of bombing missions. He had been filling in as a substitute pilot now that SIS was gone and hopefully he would assume command of a new ship soon. Getting to London occasionally for time with the woman he loved would be a big plus too.

He sat with his head against the dirty mohair seat of the bus. How in hell was he going to tell her, or for that matter anyone else, what the last days had held for him, of the terror he finally admitted to, of the strong opinion he had formed about the entire exercise? There was little he could tell, as he was limited by his pledge to secrecy. In many ways that was the best way to deal with it. No telling.

"Get yourself to Fersfield Airdrome, Captain," Those terse words came from his squadron commander and when he started to ask questions, the response of this officer he had learned to respect as a leader was quick, "I don't know what they're doing up there John. It's highly classified, with a lot of the big boys in this war zone to observe. Seems they are mighty interested in it. Big boys like General Arnold, Doolittle . . . more. With you waiting here for a new fort to command, and with your qualifications as a pilot, I have to send you. Look into it. Volunteer if you want. That's what they're calling for, volunteers. Good luck!"

At Fersfield, John had gone through his first briefing. Volunteer hell! There wasn't any choice! He was a pilot and he was a part of the mission, a hazardous assignment that, if successful, would be a World War II achievement without comparison.

As he was briefed, he was carefully scrutinized by the other pilots and crewmen who formed the nucleus of manpower for this mission called, Aphrodite.

The Last Magnolia

During his first days with the group, John learned officially as well as off the record, about the drone missions that had been in the works for the United States since August.

German storage bunkers, Watten, Mimoyecques, Wizernes and Siracourt, located in France had become a major concern. Intelligence reports indicated that the terrifying V-I and V-II rockets leveled at, and devastating London were coming from these sites in France. If additional reports were confirmed, rocket weapons were being designed that could soon be released at these same missile launching sites and aimed at the states, specifically New York City.

Mission Aphrodite was devised as a potential squelch, which, if successful, would conceivably destroy a major portion of the German missiles and possibly, at the same time end the war.

Why the Greek goddess of love's name was chosen for the mission was beyond John. Love had little to do with the destruction the mission's success would deliver, nor could love be associated with the violent, explosive deaths of pilots assigned to the mission itself.

Aphrodite was carefully planned to use stripped, war weary B-17 flying fortresses as guided missiles. These 'drones' as they were called, were controlled by other electronically equipped planes called, 'Mother Ships'; which would direct the explosive laden drones to the German Vergeltungswaffe Blockhause rocket sites on or near the coast of France.

The exercise, simplified, was expected to work like this. Qualified bomber pilots such as John, with a flight engineer as the only other crew would fly the bombers fully loaded with ten tons of explosives to just near the English coastline. They would turn remote control of the flying drone over to the nearby Mother Ship and bail out. Just before bail out, the pilot would push the arming buttons that would cause detonation on impact of thousands of pounds of Torpex, a British version of a German super explosive. This guided missile, when directed properly by the accompanying Mother Ship, was expected to crash, explode and destroy the target on which it had been centered.

As he learned the details of his expected involvement in Aphrodite, he also heard the stories of missions which had failed. There had been several injuries, deaths, and many aborted missions because of the English weather.

Morale was low. All crews had been trained and held in such a high state of expectancy, only to be prevented from flying their missions because weather would crowd in and hold them on the ground time after time. To top it all off, one blunder after another had made the entire plan seem irresponsible, yet it was one of the favorite war plans of General "Hap" Arnold, commander of the Army Air Force.

A joint service effort was brought about for Aphrodite when Navy PB4Y's were brought in to fly as drones along with the B-17's. The Navy had experimented extensively in remote controlled airplanes, and its expertise, really yet to be proven was brought into developing and refining drone technology.

Only a short while before John reached the outfit, the first Navy drone, piloted by a popular young Naval officer, and the son of a former U.S. Ambassador to England, Lt. Joe Kennedy, had been blown to bits in midair. His copilot, Lt. Bud Willy, the young executive officer for the Navy contingent at Fersfield, who went down in the same accident, was as well liked as Joe. So it was with cynicism, criticism and expectations of failure that John and his fellow pilots faced projected future missions. There was a grim lack of determination among them all.

A further blow was aimed directly at the project when it was discovered by invading Allied ground troops that the targets they had chosen were only German shams. There were no V-I or V-II rocket emplacements, nor were any other experiments being conducted in the concrete bunkers that Mission Aphrodite was directed to destroy.

When it was proved the targets at Watten, Mimoyecques, Wizernes and Siracourt were unmanned by the Germans and of no danger to the British or the U.S., the direction of the Aphrodite drones was changed to Helgoland Island in the North Sea, off the coast of Germany.

It was at Helgoland that German submarines were berthed. They were stored under the hewn-out cliffs so that regular bombing missions made destruction of them virtually impossible.

Aphrodite it was reckoned, with its tons of Torpex and TNT could, with one direct hit, totally immobilize this major submarine stronghold off the north coast of Germany. These were the missions that would involve John.

Weeks of intensified training followed for him and missions were formed and reformed, as pilots and their flight engineers prepared for their one-drop assignments over the submarine pits.

Learning to use a parachute at low altitudes from the B-17 drone was primary, and John learned with others, how to jump as safely as possible in the quickie training course.

He watched closely as wounded and crippled B-17's were stripped and gutted, left only with the essentials for takeoff and switching controls. With those instruments he and his copilot would turn the control of the explosive laden shell over to its Mother-Ship for direction to its final target.

There was much technology involved in the exercise. For self preservation alone John and his companions learned their lessons well.

Finally, late in September, weather was fine and John and flight engineer, Frank Schaffer, were on deck, the two man crew that would accomplish the drone flight.

That morning, the sky was clear and stayed that way. They had completed their pre- flight checks. All that remained was the dangerous take-off in a ship loaded with explosives. The flight to the northern coast of England was short, and then they would program the drone, bail out, and ride by land back to Fersfield.

The exercise seemed simple and fathomable, but the undercurrent of possible disastrous failure floated between the two men. Their personal fear, unspoken, yet shared, created a brotherhood between two men who had been total strangers only a short time before.

John pushed his throttles forward and the old super fort trundled down the runway, nearly waddling as an old fat woman might. She lifted off just as they reached the end of the course. Failure to do this would have been sure explosive death, so a well-concealed sigh was emitted.

Their mission was underway. When their load of Torpex crashed and exploded into the Helgoland Submarine pens it would be the first direct hit for Aphrodite and would eliminate a major portion of the German U-boat threat.

God, John thought, you learn to live with fear even if it is stuck in your gullet like mine is right now. You don't talk about it and you kid yourself into believing that your method of dealing with stress will keep you safe. You suck it all in, you hold yourself tense and straight, and you know that if you do it your way, the sucking in, the holding tight, nothing will faze you, you will be the survivor. We all believe ourselves infallible, but think about it. If individual self preservation methods weren't exercised by each of us, no matter what the technique, no one would be able to face possible disaster. There wouldn't be any soldiers, no wars, no human feats of strength and fortitude. We'd be a race of spineless beings.

His personal human survival instinct was the only way he could deal with this awesome fear. John swallowed hard, but Jesus! We could blow up right now!

Flying over England was fraught with problems other than controlling his plane and passing control over to the Mother Ship for her final guidance procedures after John and Frank had bailed out.

British flak had to be avoided at every opportunity. England had been fooled once too often by the Germans, flying reconstructed American or British planes over the United Kingdom to accomplish relatively safe bombing missions. The Germans felt relatively safe on these missions because the Brits didn't fire on their own planes or those of their allies. Now though, all planes flying over England were exposed to flak. Flying through the United Kingdom was a feat of danger all by itself as all planes were subjected to 'friendly fire'.

John had a backup of P-38 and P-51 fighters, and, of course, it was general knowledge among the Aphrodite pilots that the big shots were always around to observe when one of their drone flights took off.

Generals Arnold, Doolittle, Spatz and any number of big brass were liable to be flying above, below or alongside the piloted drone. Their presence added confusion to the already questionable mission. Their being there added danger as well, but no one made any attempt to argue with the big boys.

Keeping the drone absolutely level, flying by each check point, John found the plane to handle well with her heavy load. These old B-17's were indeed wonder warriors. He began to think ahead to the manipulations necessary for he and Frank to accomplish before they could turn the plane over to the high flying Mother Ship and jump.

As they approached the northern coast of England, radio contact assured John that all was showing well with the controlling ship and he began the countdown to jump time.

"Get going, Frank. We're on time. Go!" To himself, concerned with the danger of the mission, he said, "Jump light, Buddy."

Frank's billowing white parachute only seconds later was good news. Frank would make it. Now, what about him?

He worked quickly, pushing the switches he had been trained to activate and arranging the levers and knobs so the drone would be in complete control of the mother ship. He was ready to go. Had he done everything correctly? He finished the entire procedure by pushing the final button, the arming device that would detonate the explosive load on crash contact. If he had made a mistake, he would be flying bits and pieces of flesh in a matter of seconds.

Breath held, creating a tense, surging pain in his mid section, he slipped out of his pilot's seat as swiftly as possible. There were no more questions to ask, no backward glances, only the desire to live urging him on. He jumped.

It was quick. He was out of the ship, plummeting toward the ground and the breath within him released as he was freed from the chamber of explosive possibilities that rumbled into the distance, guided by a hidden aircraft somewhere in his vicinity. There were no backward glances. So far, so good.

The painful tearing snap that jerked his body in an unmerciful pull was welcome because he knew that the parachute that would float him down to earth had snapped open. Still in one piece, John felt a profound sense of relief. While he didn't favor flying via a parachute, he began to enjoy the rest of his trip, supported by the beautifully billowing sheet of white silk above him.

He looked down toward his eventual landing site, and feelings of security and relief cooled when he realized he was heading down too fast for a landing in an apple orchard.

Still green with leaves, spots of red showed through the branches, to show a good harvest and John watched with detached fascination as, the closer he came, the redder the apples were against their green background. He tensed to wait for the jolt of his hit on an inevitable tree.

When he hit he was surprised. Other than scratches on his face and hands, and an uncomfortable spike or two in his backside, he was unscathed.

Nearly immediately, on an adjacent road, an Englishman on a bicycle approached and the end of John's mission was announced when apples fell to the ground beneath the tree he landed in. Wryly he reached for an apple, took a bite and proceeded to unstrap the parachute and join the man who watched quizzically from beneath the tree. "I say Yank, could I be of some help?"

Grinning as he jumped down from lower branches and hit terra firma, John shook the man's hand and asked for help in getting transportation back to his home base. His primary thought as he brushed himself off was whether or not he had actually flown the first drone that would hit its target. He hoped so. That news would have to wait until he got back to Fersfield. When he was brought in, Frank was waiting for him.

"What's the good word, Frank?"

"Hell John, we're just another of the 'almost hits' in this damned outfit!"

"What happened?"

"I know you're disappointed Knowlton, God knows, so are we." These words came from Joe Knutsen, the captain of the mother ship, "We pulled her along fine, all was working well and then damned if she didn't take a dip and dive into the sea!"

"Must've been a hell of a splash," John injected.

Knutsen didn't pick up on the humor just shook his head sadly as the three men walked together into the debriefing.

By God, we're all alive to tell the story and that's what really counts when you get to the bottom line, John thought.

Chapter 18

JOHN AND HANK

November 1944

England

The squeal of brakes as its driver brought the bus to a stop interrupted John's memories.

Raising himself slowly from the uncomfortable seat, he reached above for his duffel bag. He was home free, alive and on his way to Honey.

He had tried to call her several times from Fersfield in the past weeks to let her know he was coming back. She hadn't been available and, because of this, his need for her and his growing love for her was intensified. He needed to see her, to touch her, to be with her, to erase the events and knowledge of the past weeks.

"Knowlton, where in hell have you been?"

Charlie Dawson, John's bombardier from SIS clapped him on the shoulder.

"Charlie! You're a sight for sore eyes!"

He felt as if he had known this man all his life. They had flown so many missions together, that seeing the familiar face erased the events of the past weeks from his mind. It gave him a feeling closely akin to normalcy.

Charlie was pointing towards the runway. "See that fort coming in?"

John turned his attention to a severely injured and shot up B-17 attempting to land.

"Yeah, looks as if it's had it . . . My God! That's the Barb! That's Hank's ship!"

Charlie's eyes were veiled, "As far as they know, Hank's the only crew member still talking and he's badly shot up."

John was on the run. He had thrust his duffel bag at Charlie and taken hold of the bike his friend had been riding. Pedaling down the runway as though the bike had wings he approached the now quiet B-17, swung off the bike and started to run. He could see the ambulance at Hank's plane. The fire trucks were there, but it looked safe as far as fire was concerned.

He reached the side of the ambulance just as the litter carrying Hank was lowered.

"Hey old man, this is sure some lousy way to try to get home early!"

John bent over his closest friend. There was blood everywhere and Hank was a pale gray, but conscious. Reaching up he took John's hand, the grasp was very weak and frightening.

"Thanks old buddy."

"Thanks for what?" My God, he had to make it. He didn't look good.

John turned to the ambulance driver, "OK if I ride along?"

"Sure sir, get in the back."

John jumped in behind the stretcher and watched as the medics, working quickly, tore away what was left of Hank's flight suit.

What he saw sickened him. Hank's guts were torn to shreds.

The fear of loss hit John in the pit of the stomach and he swallowed his own gall.

"Johnny?" The voice was weak and the speech was beginning to slow from the effects of morphine.

"Yeah, Hank?"

"Take care of the boys and their mama, will ya buddy?"

"You'll take care of them yourself my friend, I'll just stand by."

"Do you think old Barb is going to mind this banged up old man?"

He couldn't touch his friend, but John answered as if he were holding him, "Mind, hell man, she's going to welcome you with open arms." His voice was low, nearly a whisper. John ran his right sleeve across his face to wipe away tears that he seemed to be unable to control.

The medic signaled him to be quiet.

"I've seen lots of wounds like this sir. We have some fine surgeons at the base hospital. They'll patch him up good." The young man patted John on the shoulder.

John smiled weakly, thinking, consoling an officer is service above and beyond the call of duty for this young medic.

"Thanks son, I'll wait at the hospital for a report. Tell the doctor will you? Tell him I'll wait right outside the surgery."

"Yes sir, we'll let you know."

****

Dark circles ringed his eyes. His uniform, rumpled and stained, still carried traces of Hank's blood. John had been waiting outside surgery for more than eight hours, sometimes dozing, but coming awake with a start when there was the slightest sound of movement. Now he was awake again, concerned, still waiting for word on Hank.

What if he was gone? What if they hadn't bothered telling him? Had he missed something when he was asleep?

The swinging doors creaked, and a man evidencing the same fatigue John felt came toward him.

"Captain Knowlton?"

John was on his feet, "Yes sir?"

"Your friend in there, Captain Bailey is one hell of a soldier. He was ripped up pretty badly."

John grabbed the doctor's arm, "Is he all right?"

The surgeon smiled, "All right and will be ready for an air-evac to the states in about a week."

John slumped with relief, then straightened to shake the doctor's hand.

"Thank God. Oh, thank God . . . Thank you!"

"It's OK Captain, that's what we're here for. Now you get some rest. That's what Bailey's doing, and what I intend to do."

John walked out of the hospital. His friend would live. The war was over for Hank and he would live! He headed for the room in the bachelor officer's quarters that he shared with Hank.

When he reached their room, he noticed the pile of mail Hank had kept for him, and passed it by to sink into his cot where he slept instantly.

Don't Sit Under the Apple Tree and the Andrews sisters from a blaring radio woke him? He sat up . . . apple tree? Oh, yeah. He grinned, remembering his unceremonious landing, then memories of the previous night hit him.

Surgery. Yeah, he's OK. Going home. I'll write Barb today.

He swung up and put his feet on the floor as he sat up. His eyes lit on the mail, and the small box tied with string that topped the pile. Picking up the bundle, he put the little box aside and leafed through the rest.

There was another letter from Janice. Her letters were always full of Nebraska and her plans for his homecoming. She wrote as if everything was just fine with them, wrote as if she received letters from him.

She didn't.

What was the matter with her, he wondered? He harbored no illusions about his coming home. She was his wife now, but that would be finished quickly. The marriage would be ended with a divorce as soon as got back to the states. He tossed her letter aside without opening it. Then, because the box intrigued him, he put the other letters on top of the rejected one.

He was pretty sure it was Honey's writing. It was bold, square, written with a left-handed slant. What could the magnolia blossom be up to now, he wondered? Tearing off the string he stopped, holding the box in his hands.

When they said good-by over a month ago, my God, it seemed like years with all that had happened; he promised her that they would talk about what the future held for them.

He loved her, he knew that, and she loved him. Together they had been compatible in every way. The war was winding down now and they needed to give one another some answers about their future together.

He turned the paper-wrapped box over and over in his hands as he concentrated, picturing her.

Was her love enough? He wondered if she would consider marriage. She was right when she said Charleston society would accept the two of them as husband and wife, but what about Bobby, her fiancée`? John didn't know how to handle that problem.

If he married Honey, he felt their only future was to stay in the Army Air Corps at war's end. He had risen fast and was due to get his promotion to Major soon, so they would have a decent income. He could offer her the life of an officer's wife. She might like it, he just didn't know.

Then there were the plans he'd made with Hank. He couldn't see Honey struggling as he and Hank and Barb knew they would have to struggle if they started their own business.

He loved her so much, and probably would have to give up the dream he and Hank had built on for all those years. He hoped not. There had to be an answer somewhere.

He tore open the paper. Wrapped around the box was a piece of crisp, white writing paper and as he unfolded it, he read,

"Johnny darling:

When you read this, I will be back in Charleston. I'll be filling the dutiful needs of my family. I will be Mrs. Robert Caton Carson, and should be well on my way to breeding those two children required by the Carson's to keep Bobby's family tree growing. Bobby came back and I know where my duty lies. I'll always treasure our beautiful moments darling. Here is your, 'come back' toothbrush. Thank you for all you gave me."

The note was signed, simply . . . "Honey."

Jesus! What a woman! He opened the box and inside was his green toothbrush. Not enough insurance I guess. He smiled ruefully, feeling half sick. He knew he could only thank God that Bobby had come back.

He crumpled the box, the brush and the note together with the string, wadded it into a tight ball and threw it with heavy force toward the wastebasket.

The Last Magnolia

Love. It's pretty sure I don't know much about it. Hell, what is love? Is this to be my punishment? A small flicker of dark memory began to rise to the top of his thoughts, but he was able to suppress his deeply buried sub-conscience urge of memory once again. I guess the lack of love is what's slated for me for the rest of my life. What the hell, who knows . . . love is nothing. Not one damned thing. He turned to the stack of unopened letters thinking, well Hank and I sure will go ahead with those plans now!

Chapter 19

FAMILY

November 1944

England

She was gone. She had died peacefully in her sleep.

A letter from the family attorney had added that personal aside to make it somehow easier for John to accept.

He put the letter down for a moment, brushed his eyes, then picked it up to read on.

"Her husband's death, the loss of her son Thomas Jr., the absence of her daughter, Shirley and then John's own transfer overseas had seemed to take the need for life out of her. She had simply given up because of her lonely unhappiness. She was a woman who needed the warmth and closeness of a loved one, and all of her loved ones had gone. Death," the family lawyer went on, "seemed to be her final blessing."

John put the letter down without finishing it.

Nothing she had written to him had suggested unhappiness. Indeed, she had kept him abreast of the affairs in Charleston, the things that happened to her day by day. He hadn't suspected in any way that she had hidden her lonely sorrow. Her letters always projected plans for when he came home. He was always included in her arrangements for Shirley's homecoming. Everything was well organized and cheerful in her letters. They sounded so like her. How could he have missed the messages of despair she had hidden behind the lovely penmanship on that sheer blue paper?

I'm not really up to this, not all of this, John thought. The near loss of Hank less than twenty-four hours ago, preceded by the most remarkable Dear John in history from Honey, now this devastating news of death. It was really more than he wanted to deal with right now.

Mary Elizabeth Graydon. The woman who had come to mean more to him than any other woman was dead.

She had been young in spirit and mind, and he had looked forward to being with her again. He wanted to give her what he felt a son should give of himself to a mother, devotion, companionship, love and support. The things he never had the opportunity to give his own mother, or Kate. Then he wanted to give even more to Mary Elizabeth who had lost her own son. John yearned to surround her with the comfort of love and affection.

She had given so generously of her spirit and had accepted John as a family member. By becoming the mother he had rejected when she deserted him, Mary Elizabeth had given him the comfort of her total acceptance. For the first time since his loss of Kate, he felt as if he belonged in another woman's world.

When John, who had experienced total rejection at such a very early age, received and accepted her gift, he had become somehow healed. His grim beginnings were pushed aside and he responded to Mary Elizabeth Graydon with the love of a son. It was as if they had been in need of one another for a long time.

Mary Elizabeth had been his advisor, teacher, and companion. She had shared the fine relationship between herself and her husband with him. The three bonded together in a friendship that was rare.

The Last Magnolia

John had thrived on this relationship. He had returned each favor, each kindness, equally whenever he could, making every effort to please her and her family.

When her son died, then her husband they became in different ways, victims of war, John had tried to fill the voids created by their deaths as best he could.

She responded by learning to lean on him.

When he left her, less than a year ago, she had seemed on the way to recovering from deep grief.

John had established a bond with Mary Elizabeth's daughter Shirley too, and that had pleased the elderly woman.

Now in his grief, John reviewed many of his moments with Mary Elizabeth. His memories moved from incident to incident as flashbacks of his relationship with the Graydon family renewed themselves.

Dear Mrs. G. His life had really begun anew with her and now she was gone. If he allowed his grief to come to the surface, it would tear him apart. He had to remember only their good times and dwell on the loss later.

She had been a fine teacher for the Nebraska farm boy, and he had responded by being a dutiful substitute son to her. This combination had strengthened both of them, and formed a strong relationship.

John stood up and shook his body as if to rid it of the weight of grief he felt. Crossing the room he went to his locker, opened it and brought out a bottle half filled with scotch. At the small sink, he measured three fingers of the light brown liquid into a glass. With a quick toss, he poured it all down his throat.

The liquor took his breath, and he gasped, then let the pleasure of its warmth desensitize him. When the last sensations were gone, he threw water on his face and poured another drink.

Why, he wondered, had the gods chosen this fate for him? Why could there be no loving relationship with any woman in his life? If there was an answer, he refused to allow it to surface and, steeped in self-pity, walked back to his cot.

Damned if this rejection by women would ever happen to him again! He was firm in his unspoken resolve. There would be no more loving liaisons with women in his search for love and affection. He was through. From here on women would be all for the fun of it, for the hell of it.

He picked up the letter from the lawyer. He read on and a tender smile crossed his face.

Mrs. Graydon had left him the magnificent gun collection that he and her husband Thomas had spent so many hours enjoying together.

What a generous and thoughtful legacy, he smiled. So like Mary Elizabeth. John had expected nothing, but this gift, of all things, showed her insight into his personal choices.

He took a deep shuddering breath as he tried to hold himself firm, but the tears of loss came anyway. His sobs were all that were heard in the tiny barracks room, and they continued for a long time until finally he gained control of himself and sat on the edge of the cot. Reaching for his glass he took another drink and wiped his face.

There was more to read and, with a deep breath of resolve, he continued, eyes scanning the pages, then rereading with a close scrutiny, the attorney's words.

It was unbelievable! This couldn't be happening! There had to be an error. John took another deep breath of shock. It was too much. His eyes continued line for line down the printed page and he learned he was to receive the share of her estate that was to have been given to her son, Thomas Graydon Jr. John was inheriting as if he were a son of Mary Elizabeth Graydon.

The pages of detail went on and on. There were trusts, there was money, there were investments that would pay large dividends and there was property.

He couldn't believe any of it. Putting the letter down again, he let the figures he had just read arrange them in his mind.

He had been aware of all this wealth when he worked with Shirley at the time of her father's death, but to own a part of it himself had never entered his mind. All of this was to be his? Shirley wouldn't go along with this. True, they respected and thought a great deal of one another, but this was Graydon money. Surely she wouldn't let good Graydon money transfer itself to a soldier from Nebraska. This was all impossible.

He picked up the letter again and found a slim gray envelope attached to the back of the last page. His name was written across the front.

"John dear,

What mother did in her last will was accomplished before I ever left Charleston. I tell you this because I want you to know there was no surprise for me in accepting the fact that you share in the Graydon legacy. I really think John that, had Daddy lived, he too would have done exactly as she did. They both loved you so much. As you remember, I welcomed you as a brother long ago, and surely you proved your worth as you cared for mother during those months after our loss. Please know that you are indeed my brother and you and I will continue to work together in the interest of our estate for many years to come.

Come to Charleston when you come home. We will talk then.

The Last Magnolia

Welcome to the family.
Shirley.

He was a wealthy man. This was too much to assimilate right now. Realizing that, John took another drink from his glass.
Now all he had dreamed and planned for could be possible. He'd prove to Shirley and the dear memory of Mary Elizabeth that he could and would handle this bequest efficiently. He would become the success that this money would allow him to be.
****

"Hank, you leave tomorrow, and there are things we have to talk about. Are you up to it?"

A week had passed since Hank's surgery. He was weak, but improving daily.

"If I don't have to move, cough or laugh, I can listen all I want," Hank held himself gingerly, but the old Bailey grin was splashed across his face.

"You may want to move when you hear my news, but in the interest of being pain free, contain yourself."
John told Hank about the Graydon inheritance.

"My God man, you're rich!"

John smiled, "Get ready for this friend, WE are wealthy men!" He touched his friend gently.

"This means we can set up the air service now, do you realize that?"

"God, maybe I'd better get up and dance a jig. This is unbelievable!"

"Hell man, don't do that. I need a whole partner, not one who's liable to leak from one or another of those patched up holes of yours."

177

Hank turned his head carefully, "But you'll be in Charleston. The only place to build this air service is in the Pacific Northwest. Just think about it John, you know that's what we decided."

"That's where it's going to be"

John explained his plans briefly,

"Hank, you get to that Texas hospital and recuperate. Then you and Barb take the kids and head for Spokane. By the time you get there, we will have put all the plans together and the two of you can start the business. We'll make it small to begin with, I think." He jotted notes on a pad held in his hand. "Start with a couple of planes and some hanger space. It's all down on paper; God knows we've worked on these plans long enough. Now we have the money to make it work."

Hank was tired and weak, but his old grin showed his approval and enthusiasm.

"OK John, we'll do it. You're sure we have the money?"

"Yeah Hank, we have the money. I'll finish my points here and get back to you fast."

A gentle handshake sealed the partnership. As Hank drifted off, John roused him one more time.

"Hank, look. We'll be even partners all the way, but could we call it, Knowlton Air Service?"

Hank's eyes were nearly closed. "You take care of that good buddy. Whatever you want John . . ."

Chapter 20

JANICE

June 1945

New York Harbor

Arms on the railing, he watched the nearly frenzied crowd of women, children and families as they stood waiting for their loved ones, then he spotted her. How could this be, how in the hell could she have found out he'd be on this ship? He looked again to be sure. There wasn't any doubt. It was Janice. She stood among the crowd of women and children watching the men with him on board, waiting for the gangplank to be put down. What in hell was she doing here? She was the last person in the world he wanted to see now.

Thinking back, he tried to find some connection to what he was seeing on the dock. He had finally written to her. It was the first letter he had sent since they parted so stormily in Charleston.

He explained to her in the letter that he would come to Nebraska for a short visit. He told her he had things of Aunt Kate's to pick up, and while he was there, he would begin divorce proceedings so both of them could get on with their lives.

Why would she, after receiving a letter like that, come to meet his ship?

John had worked out the new life he would have so carefully. He had been in touch with lawyers from the Graydon estate, and had advised them he would be in Charleston early in the summer to take charge of his new responsibilities.

Now, it seemed as he watched this woman who was still his wife, all plans were up in the air again because of the skinny bitch standing on the dock, waving a handkerchief.

Hank and Barbara were in Spokane where they had already laid the groundwork for Knowlton Air service, and as soon as John's business in the south was finished, he was going to fly directly to the northwest.

He turned from the ship's rail and headed for his stateroom. The gold leaves on his shoulders were bright. He'd been promoted to Major only weeks before he completed his necessary missions. He applied for surface travel back to the states to have some wind-down time before beginning what promised to be a busy, satisfying life involving airplanes, friends and business that he knew would thrive.

VE Day had held him up a bit, so he spent his last weeks in England doing little or nothing. He was restless and bored after the long trip across the Atlantic, and was anxious to get to Spokane. Now he had to get rid of Janice. Damn! What was she here for?

Entering the stateroom, he found his duffel bag and B-4 as he had left them, ready to go. His gut reaction was to pick them up and get off the ship without Janice's seeing him. He didn't want any of her confrontations on a day like this. This was the day he was home from the wars, the day when he would put his feet back on American soil for the first time in over a year, and he had plans. Big plans that didn't include Janice.

He realized he couldn't just get off the ship. He shrugged on his jacket and stood in front of the mirror to button it. As he wrapped and knotted his tie, he performed a quick scrutiny of himself.

I won't be wearing this uniform much longer, he grinned with the confidence of a man who knew where he was going, and how he was going to get there. The grin was replaced with a frown as out loud, he asked himself,

"How in hell am I going to get rid of her?"

At twenty-four, John had reached full maturity. The years of struggle as a lonely boy and the grim experiences of war showed in the characterization of his well-structured face. His light brown hair touched with flecks of auburn, topped a wide intelligent forehead. Rugged complexion carrying the light tan of an outdoors man, gave the impression of healthy virility. His eyes were the same almond shape his mother's had been, though they were a darker brown, flecked as if to match his hair. Those eyes watched everything and everyone around him with alert, intelligent interest. It seemed as if, when he needed to file an impression, there was an imperceptible lowering of his heavy blunt-lashed lids as the subject was listed for later perusal. Above those lively eyes, heavy coarse brows nearly arched but stopped at the corner of each orb to complement the square of his jaw and confirm the ruggedness of his entire makeup.

Military bearing was exhibited in his six-foot stature, wide heavy shoulders that tapered to a narrow waist, while his legs showed powerful musculature.

He smiled at himself in the mirror as he checked and approved each detail of his Army Air Corps uniform. Straightening his cap, he brushed lint from his sleeve and took one last look around the room before picking up his luggage. With a long patient sigh, he headed, like a man destined for the gallows, up to 'A' deck and the gangplank.

The Last Magnolia

The sun shone brilliantly on the pier, the air was warm and there was a spring-like perfection on this wonderful June day to welcome the fighting men home.

People were wearing light clothing. The crowd's contrast to war-torn London with its fog, rain and gloom was exhilarating. Bands were playing, confetti was flying. Excited onlookers were waving and cheering. It was good to be home.

John had finished his last mission just two days before VE day. He learned that his port call would be delayed, so when they asked for volunteers to fly into France to help with medical evacuations, he agreed to go. He felt sure of what the future held for him. A few weeks, more or less, wouldn't make any difference to the beginnings he was looking forward to. He could spend the extra overseas time being of service to others who hadn't been as lucky as he had. It was during this period he sat and wrote to Janice.

She must have gotten his letter. Why was she here? Maybe her father had been the instigator again. John couldn't figure it out, and all he could see for sure was Janice. She was out there, acting as if she was glad he was home, waving and jumping around like the others in the crowd, giving the impression that they had parted as friends and lovers . . . and worst of all that she wanted to carry on the same scenario.

He would have to straighten her out. Fast.

One of his cabin mates, a young Naval Lt. Commander from Michigan slapped him on the shoulder.

"My Girl is out there John!" He was flushed, and wiped his lip with the back of his hand. His eyes were shining.

"I feel like a kid again. It's been three years, and you know, I don't think she's changed a bit." The young man grinned, "I have though, God I hope she can put up with an old man like me."

He clapped John on the back, "Well Major, it's been great knowing you on this cruise," he moved to the gangplank, shouting the last over his shoulder, "I want to get to her as fast as I can . . . if you're ever in Pontiac, look us up!"

"So long Gene, good luck!"

John smiled bitterly as he thought back to that hot March day in 1943 when he'd met the train carrying Janice, his bride to be, to him. It was the day he had anticipated as the beginning of what he thought would be a life leading to days like this, filled with the excitement and love exhibited of a reunion with the woman he loved. Like his friend Gene. That was when he thought love between him and Janice would bring the same emotional reunion his rapidly retreating friend was going to experience the minute he stepped off that gangplank. Instead, he was filled with disgust and a desire to run and hide from the woman who waited for him.

Well damn it, he had to face her. That was all. He'd just get her back to Nebraska, get the divorce under way and then go on to Charleston.

She couldn't anger him. He couldn't let her do that. Her presence meant only one thing. She was a hurdle he had to jump over before he could join Hank and Barb.

As he strode down the ramp, she was waiting right at the bottom. Throwing her arms around his neck, she cried with excitement,

"John! Oh Johnny, it's been so long!"

He stepped into the crowd, pulling her with him, still carrying his bags.

"What's this all about Jan? I thought you'd decided to stay in Nebraska."

"Stay in Nebraska? Oh no John. I couldn't let you come back to the states without meeting you. I have so much I want to say to you." The noise of the crowd nearly drowned her words but her shrill voice reached above other sounds, "I'm living up to my responsibilities as your wife."

She was speaking as if someone else had put the words into her mouth, and she was intent on finishing her well-rehearsed speech.

"There's so much I have to straighten out for us." She pulled on his sleeve as she spoke, never really looking directly at him, "Come on dear, my father has made reservations in a hotel for us. They were hard to get, but he took care of it."

It was her father then, just as he suspected.

She had stopped for breath and, still refusing to meet his eyes, looking over his shoulder, she announced with great excitement, "John, we're going to have a second honeymoon, right here in New York City!"

He was dumbfounded. My God! She was acting as if they had a marriage. What in hell was she thinking of? She can't change things. I won't let her erase those last terrible months together. How can she forget? She was as miserable as I.

He had been lonely since Honey left, lonely and bitter. There had been several other women, English girls, but nothing serious. He had sworn to himself that he would never be trapped again by the madness of love.

Backing away from her, as far as the crowd of noisy, happy people would allow, he finally injected his own words. "Jan, I don't understand this. You don't sound anything like the girl I left behind in Charleston."

"Oh, John, that was such a shame. I've grown up since you

left. I missed you and worried about you so much, and I've had all this time to realize what a terrible mistake I made." Her words continued to sound prepared, not her own, but from another person. The fact that there were tears in her eyes was the only thing that might lead him to believe there was some sincerity in what she was saying.

"John, I want to be your wife. . . . I thought. . . . "the tears began to roll down her cheeks . . . ."I thought. . . . " her words faded, "Johnny, you don't want me here do you?"

No dammit, he didn't want anything to do with her. She belonged to Harper, Nebraska and that was where he was prepared to pay whatever it took to keep her.

Stop it. John disciplined himself silently. Listen to her. You can't be cruel.

"Let's get a cab if we can. I'll get my bags stowed, and we'll have a drink. Let's try to begin that way, with a cocktail and a little talk."

She dabbed her face with a handkerchief, "Just give me a chance. One chance, that's all I ask," she smiled, "I'll do whatever you want me to do. I just want us both to be happy and I can prove it. When you see what I've done and hear the plans I've made. Oh John, just try to be happy with me. You'll see, it will work."

He left a screaming, nagging cold wife and he'd come back to this? Here she was, making promises that sounded too good.

He was a fair man though. He'd try one little drink and some talk, but, he cautioned himself. Knowlton, you have places to go and things to do . . . she doesn't fit into any of it and you can't allow yourself to be trapped with more unhappiness.

185

Chapter 21

JANICE AND JOHN

June 1945

Nebraska

He woke with a hell of a headache and a terrible taste in his mouth. He couldn't remember feeling this bad in a long time. He'd always known when to stop drinking, so how in hell did he end up with a hangover like this one? To ease the pain in his head, he

remained very still as he rehashed the events of the night before. As realization began to sink in, he turned his head slowly.

It was a double bed, and there she was. Still asleep, her thin brown hair was as mussed as a tight permanent would allow it to be. Her breathing was heavy and deep.

My God, one small drink had brought her to bed with him? Or were there more? Yeah, there had to be more, the way he felt right now. He didn't want to move and wake her. He had to think it out.

He sure as hell hadn't meant to go to bed with Janice, wife or not. He wanted out of, not into her bed. He grinned wryly to himself at his sick humor. Moving his aching head back to a straight position on the pillow, he gazed at the ceiling. He reviewed the hours before.

Debarking. Cocktails. Words. Oh shit!

She stirred, rolled away from him and then, as she came awake, realized where she was, and turned toward him.

"You're awake?" She moved closer to him. He didn't offer her his arms, but turned his head painfully. The ache was like a sharp knife as he looked at her.

"You really wanted this Jan?"

Timidly, she put her hand on his chest, "Oh Johnny, I told you and told you I did."

He didn't remember any of it.

She rolled back over, "I'm afraid we both had a little too much to drink during our celebration. Now," she ran her fingers through her hair, "I'm famished."

"Did we eat last night?" He couldn't remember food, "I have a terrible headache."

She sat up and moved from the bed, "I'll get you something for your head, and then I'll call room service. We'll have breakfast up here, all right?"

He got out of bed as she talked, and was already in the bathroom. The aspirin was in his dop kit and he shook out three, tossed them into his mouth and washed them down with a glass of water from the tap.

She was still talking.

"John, do you realize this is the first time you and I have been in a hotel room together?" Her voice was light, coy, "I almost feel sinful."

He dropped the glass on the tiled floor.

This is too much. I can't play this kind of a game. He reached down to pick up the broken pieces of glass, and there she was, at his feet, on her knees, picking them up.

187

"Jan, you don't have to do that . . ."

"Of course I do darling. You don't feel well and that's what a wife is for, to take care of her husband."

He shrugged and walked back into the bedroom.

She continued, "John, I'm going to be a good wife to you. I'll prove it in so many ways," her glance held promise as she looked at the bed where he was sitting, "just as I did last night."

It was too bad he couldn't remember enough to credit her performance, he thought, as he watched her trying to assume a provocative pose. She had put him through such abstinence and Hell in Charleston, it was hard to believe this was the same woman.

"Jan, we have lots to talk over."

"Today my dear, all we have to do is eat breakfast, try to see a bit of this big city, and just anything else you fancy," she said in that same simpering voice.

Actually, tickets on a train and a quick trip to Nebraska were more in line with his thinking. Then he thought to himself, why let her down hard? I'll tour New York with her, then we're going to get down to the brass tacks of this impossible marriage.

"Ok, let's get going. We'll try to have a good day."

****

Thank God for train connections, John thought as he watched out the window. Nebraska hadn't changed and Crispin, the old station and the town, all looked about the same.

When the train came to a stop, John swung down and off the platform and turned to help Janice.

Temperatures were high and the humidity was higher. As he looked around, he realized there was change after all.... more people than he ever remembered seeing at this station but, of course, lots of men and women were returning from the war.

Janice's father walked toward them.

"Mr. Adams, nice to see you sir." John extended his hand and Janice ran to the elderly minister.

"Daddy, you were right. The trip to New York was just what we needed." The sly, disgusting simper was back in her voice, "Johnny and I are together again."

The man hugged his daughter tenderly, and turned towards John.

"Son, I know the two of you have had your problems, and I'm sure there will be more, but now you're home again, and I want you to know that you have the love of Janice's family to carry you through any troubles you might have." The old man turned pensive, "You know John, both of you being so far away in South Carolina with the insecurity of the war and all, well it's easy to see why the two of you had troubles."

Troubles, John thought. My troubles ended when I walked out on Janice, and damned if I want them back, family support or not.

He hadn't told her anything about Mrs. Graydon. She hadn't asked, so his new wealth, his opportunities and plans were still secret as far as Janice was concerned. He'd been pleasant with her, and now that they were in Nebraska, he could tell her that he was serious about the divorce. From the looks of it, he'd better straighten her out fast. He couldn't let her father assume they were together for good.

While Janice and her father talked, John looked around Crispin. Kate was gone. His domineering old Grandmother had died, and he hadn't had any reason to find his mother since she left him with Kate. All he had achieved this far into his life, he

The Last Magnolia

had done by himself, and now with his inheritance, he could prove more ability, more success than he had ever dreamed of. As to right here in Crispin, or in Harper, nothing meant anything to him. There were a few things from Kate's estate to be picked up. Nothing else here fit into his plans, including Janice.

She was standing by her father, a conspiratorial smile on her face.

"Have you told him about your surprise yet dear?"

Is it ready?"

"Here's the key. Why don't the two of you walk? I'll have your luggage put in the car and follow."

John was bewildered. He looked from Mr. Adams to Janice and back again. What in hell was going on?

"Come on darling, I'm going to let you in on the nicest surprise we could think of giving you for a homecoming present."

Knowlton, you've let this go too far. Your timing is lousy he thought. I have to stop it, but not here in public.

She led him down the wooden steps of the depot.

"Jan, I think there are some things we'd better get straight," he tried to slow her down, but her eagerness pulled them both forward. She took him to the sidewalk that led into town.

He remembered this street so well. A pain hit right in the pit of his stomach. He thought all of the terrible memories were gone. He had erased them effectively with bitterness, but here they were again, the fearful voids that he had suppressed so well for all of these years rose to near- recognition again. Then, as they always did, they stopped before he could find the answer to the lost frightened instability that overcame him.

Flashes of memory crossed his consciousness, but this time with pictures . . . this was the street where he had been sent, down

190

this exact road, to the third house in the next block. It was here that he, as a ten- year old boy had stood on the hard gravel packed street, crying tears of desperation as he begged his mother to leave the man she had deserted her family for. He had stood in this street, too young to understand what it was he was asking for, sobbing. She had come down the side steps.

Stop it! No more, I can't let any more in. These flashes of memory weren't to be here on this hot Nebraska afternoon. He was a grown man. He was wearing the uniform of the U.S. Army Air Force. He had attained the rank of Major, passed through years of learning, growing, forgetting. He had been through the hell of war, so memories of childhood trauma couldn't be a part of his life today, or could they? He shook his head to clear flashes of memory.

Janice was swinging along with brisk, quick steps. Her happiness was evident as she led him down this memorable block, a street that he had never come back to after one horrible day in his childhood. This was a street he had shut from his memory until now.

He was tense as he listened to her chatter.

This was her surprise and, as she continued to pull him along, he became blind to all that surrounded him. Then she stopped, and they were there. What he saw was worse than he'd expected. She had stopped in front of the horrible house of his worst memories and hate hit him. Hit him again and again. This was the house where he'd found his mother. It was too coincidental . . It couldn't be happening to him.

"See Johnny, fresh paint, the lawn trimmed, and just wait until you see how I've fixed it up inside!"

He caught her hand and pulled her back, outside the gate

leading into the yard.

"What do you mean, you fixed it up?"

The house was smaller somehow, but then he was bigger than he had been the last time he was here.

"You fixed up this old house? Why?"

He looked at it closely now. It was the same. A white clapboard house, steps of wood leading up the side to the second story.

Flash!

This is where his mother had lived with her lover.

His eyes came back down to the first floor windows. Sparkling white curtains drifted back and forth in a slight breeze.

Flash!

Someone had been watching him through those curtains.

He was numb; the strength of resistance had left him completely. Janice was leading him by the hand again, through the gate, up the front steps. She put the key in the door and he stood as if he were unconscious.

Flash!

She came down the side of the house, down those steps over there. She wiped his tears.

"Here we are Major Knowlton! Welcome to your . . . welcome to OUR new home!"

The flashes stopped and he shook his head as if he were waking from a long sleep.

"What the hell are you talking about?"

She stepped back, frightened by the tone of his voice, "John, I thought you'd be so pleased. Daddy and the rest of the family all pitched in and helped me make the down payment. It's all ours John, ours after the payments are finished," she rushed on, "we can live here, raise our family and we'll be right back in Nebraska where we belong, we'll only be a few miles from Harper where you and I grew up."

As she talked, she pulled him inside. "That's what my father meant John, when he said the family would help us." "They will and we'll all be here together."

The feeling of numbness began to leave him. Only a few moments ago he'd felt as if his entire blood supply had stopped momentarily. Now his system started to work again. There was a tingling of blood coursing through his body. He sat on the nearest thing he could find. A wooden chair. Kate's chair. My God, she'd gotten his things into this house too! He couldn't believe he had been so taken in, so stupid, so damned dumb to let this skinny woman whom he didn't even like, believe, even for these two days, he would stay with her. Any shock he received he deserved, he told himself, because he had allowed the whole farce to have a beginning.

Now it was time.

"Janice, we can't accept this house."

"But it's ours. We'll finish paying for it."

"That isn't what I mean."

"Oh John, stop being so serious. I have this house all ready for us. The sheets are on the bed, the refrigerator is well stocked, I only have to unpack your things and you'll be home."

"No, you don't understand," he kept his voice low. "Sit down."

Nervously, she sat on a chair facing him. His voice frightened her. She had never seen him like this before.

"Jan, my life has taken on some new direction, and if you're determined to continue as my wife, I have to tell you what my plans are. I can assure you right now, they don't include Crispin, Nebraska."

She gasped.

John took off his hat, unbuttoned his jacket and leaned back in his chair. He told her of his good fortune, the partnership with Hank and Barbara. He outlined the business and each detail as he saw them in his future.

"No! No!" She jumped up and her voice took on the shrillness he remembered from their last months together in Charleston. She was screaming at him, the sound shrewish and head-splitting.

"I am your wife! You didn't consult me about any of this."

She was so distraught, he was sure her screams were carried through the open door and down Crispin's streets with great clarity. He folded his arms and grinned. This was going to be a good one and, by George, he was going to win!

"Touché", Jan. Neither did you consult me about your plans. If you had, I assure you, I would have advised you in no uncertain terms exactly what we'd be doing, and where we'd be doing it."

She ran to him and began beating on his chest and he grabbed her by the arms, shook her gently and sat her down.

"Listen to me! I have no intention of remaining your husband. I wrote and told you that. You knew. Divorce is the only answer for us. You know that too. Then for some reason you cooked up this scheme to meet me in New York. What in hell did you think? Did you honestly believe I would stay in a part of the country I left years ago with no intention to return? A place that has given me only pain. You thought I'd come back to that?"

He walked away from her, then turned quickly, "I don't know

who encouraged you, or how that silly mind of yours put this together but, Jan, you've added two and two and come up with five." Voice steadily under control, he enunciated each of his next words, "There isn't any way I will live here. There isn't any way you and I can stay married. Do you understand me?"

He could have gone on, to explain about the memories he held of this house. He could have apologized for allowing her charade to last for as long as he had allowed it to. He didn't. To hell with it.

Janice was crumpled in a large wing chair. She was sobbing, little mewing sounds, but there wasn't any way he wanted to approach her or give her comfort.

The sounds of tires in the driveway were followed by footsteps as her father walked into the house.

Janice looked up and, seeing her father, straightened. Her head arched forward on its thin neck, looking like the snake she could be. Her voice fit the picture as she hissed at him grimly.

"Here's my Daddy. He'll tell you what you're going to do John Knowlton. He'll set you straight!" Her hiss increased in volume to a scream, "You deserted me. Just like your mother. Just like your father. There's a weakness in your blood line, Johnny!"

He stepped forward, as he moved toward her, his hand began to rise. No. He couldn't do that again. He jerked his hand down by his side. Slapping her wasn't the way.

Mr. Adams entered the front room, his smile fading when he heard the screaming and felt the strain of the moment. He looked at his daughter, disheveled, perspiration and tears covering her face.

"Mr. Adams, I think you had better sit down." John spoke

kindly as he gestured to the straight chair he had first used, "I have a great deal to tell you..." John explained in careful detail the facts regarding their marriage, the offered move to the west and the anticipated divorce . . . "and there you have it sir. This has been a sham, sexless, loveless marriage from its very beginning. I have carved out a future that doesn't and shouldn't include your daughter. And I'm not going to change this because it would only make for unhappiness for both of us."

John had told the old man everything, and his final words gave his decision in the matter with great clarity.

The old man listened quietly, and then stopped John. He had heard enough.

"You're absolutely right, John."

Janice gasped, "Daddy, what are you saying?" Her face registered shock and disbelief, "I'm your daughter. You have to make him see, make him do the things I want him to do."

"No, Janice, John is your husband, but he doesn't want to continue with your marriage. From what he has just told me I can only agree with him. You didn't tell me that he had explained that to you by mail. He says he's offered to let you come west with him. If you want him, then I suggest you do just that, and that you start working at being the wife he wants and deserves."

The old man was sad and very serious.

"I'd hate to have you move far away from me again my dear daughter, but you already have friends there. You have that young couple, Barbara and Hank."

She almost hated her father. He was so stupid.

"Hank and Barbara. I hate them! I never liked them, and they never liked me. They certainly aren't going to be any help because I'm not going anywhere with John Knowlton!"

The Last Magnolia

She directed her fury at John again, "Get your damned divorce! I hate you as much as I hate Hank and Barbara!"

"Janice!" Her father was shocked, and now he too was shouting. He turned to John, "She's upset and distraught now John, she'll change her mind."

John faced his father-in-law, "No sir, she's right. For Janice to go with me and try to make our marriage work would only mean more unhappiness. I don't love Janice, and she wants to be here in Nebraska with you."

He stopped to look at this woman who was his wife, "I'm sorry I've allowed Janice to believe we would live here with your family. I should have told her about my plans while we were in New York. I wrote to her from England to tell her I'd divorce her when I came home. I guess she didn't understand. I'm sorry."

The minister seemed to lose the starch that held him up. He had encouraged Janice in this reconciliation and now it had created a terrible scene of truths. They had come out. She hadn't told him of John's letters, had led him to believe that all was well with them again. He had accepted her lies as facts. Now he realized neither he nor his daughter had accepted the truth: The marriage was ended. He looked at his daughter, rumpled, sitting in the large chair, her tear-streaked shrewish face that showed so much hate . . . she had deceived him and John, but most of all, herself.

"I understand son. Stay here tonight. I'll take her home with me."

John heard the engine crank, listened as the car backed out of the driveway. He didn't go to the window to watch them leave, just listened. When the car was beyond hearing he walked out to the porch, closed the door softly behind him and picked up his bags. Retracing his steps to the station, he didn't look back at the first haunting hell in his life.

The house that Janice fixed.

Chapter 22

KNOWLTON AIR SERVICE

November 1945

Spokane, Washington

She whirled in her chair to face Hank at his desk.

"Hank! This is getting ridiculous!"

Barbara was only a matter of feet away from her husband and the filing cabinets. Less space separated her from John's desk and the book-keeper's corner. Everything was closing in around her.

"Getting a little claustrophobic honey?" Hank grinned at his beautiful flustered wife.

"You know I don't complain often, but this trailer has gotten completely out of hand. I don't know what to do with half the stuff we have in this so-called 'office'."

John listened to the conversation. How could he miss it?

Sunshine streamed through one of the little high windows onto his desk, and the rays made it difficult for him to read the material in front of him as the beams danced back and forth, up and down.

He leaned back in his old mahogany army-surplus swivel chair to survey the mess Barb was talking about.

Barbara was pregnant again, and Hank had mended nicely. They expected a third child to join the two boys they already had and John noticed that the usual cool and calm good old Barb had become a little at odds lately. She looked tired and it didn't seem right that she should be further oppressed by this tiny trailer that was all of Knowlton Air Service.

Who could have known that in the short three months since he had arrived, and in only a year of actual business, they'd be able to claim such a great success? The fact that the company had made a steady profit from its very inception showed that fast service by air was desperately needed in the Pacific Northwest.

Postwar building was booming and construction firms were setting up further and further away from Spokane, which was their main source for supplies.

John and Hank were profiting from every contractor who was building at remote sites by supplying and delivering, in their own aircraft, the parts required to keep jobs ongoing.

Knowlton Air Service was the first expediting business to form in Spokane. From the looks of its success, it had cornered the market.

From sites in Washington, Oregon, western Montana and even northern California, contractors were demanding and receiving service delivery speed by air from John and Hank. In this short amount of time in business, they were ready and needed to expand.

Still tipped back in his chair, John broke into the conversation.

"Barb, I think it's about time for us to think about firing you."

Her sharp, expected retort came quickly, "Fire me? If you let me go, you and this husband of mine can just kiss this entire company goodbye! I know more about what's going on than anyone else who cares to find a place to sit in this office . . . and I'd be the first to tell them there isn't a place to sit!"

Her quick smile made her retort a typical good-natured Barbara-ism, and John felt a warm surge of love and caring for the wife of his best friend.

"Easy girl, easy there . . .”

He got up and started toward her small typing desk, but the cramped quarters made it impossible for him to move freely, so he just turned back and sat.

"What I mean is, it's time for you to start thinking about the new baby, and time for you to have more time with the boys. I'd like you to find a couple of women to replace you."

Barbara looked smug, "It will take two, huh. Two to take my place?"

"Yeah, maybe even three."

"Well my smart Mr. Johnny, just where are you going to put three women?"

John needed to move as he tried to get his thoughts together, so he stood again and walked toward Hank, stumbling over the leg of his chair.

"Do you think you're up to helping your wife select a suite of offices downtown?"

"Boy, do you know how to treat a lady!" Hank laughed, "You know she'll be scouting out new buildings within the hour, and she sure won't need me."

"Hooray!" Barb swung around, picked up the Spokesman Review and leafed through the classified ads.

"Seriously Hank, we have hanger space enough until next year, then I want to add a couple of larger planes."

"Hey! You're really thinking big today, aren't you?"

John shook his head in wonderment, "It seems impossible that we hit the right formula, the right time and the right place,

201

but we did, and we're making big money. Things are going to keep right on expanding, and we're going to have to meet the needs of the market. It's only right to move downtown and leave the mechanical end here at Felts Field. Besides, I have other directions I think we should consider in air service in the next couple of years."

"Sounds good to me John, and old Barb will take care of it, believe me."

"Seriously Barb, how long would it take you to train a couple of women?"

She looked up from the paper, "About a month. Then of course, I could be on call, couldn't I?"

He knew she didn't want to give up complete control; she had been the key to the groundwork of this outfit, without her knowledge of business, he and Hank would have been shot down from the beginning.

"Tell you what, hire three women. I want a secretary for Hank and me to share. Get two more to replace you and when you go to look at offices, let me suggest this . . . "He jotted down a few figures, "get downtown, right in the center of the city. Find something with a private office for me, one for Hank and off that, if possible, a small director's office for you to use when you're 'on call'. Then there has to be an office for the bookkeeper, a small reception area, and a large central office where our secretary and the other girls will work." He thought a minute, "Oh, be sure there's a parking garage nearby."

"Do you need the car, Hank?"

"See, what'd I tell you John, she's already on her way."

"Take it honey, I'll use the company truck if I need to go anywhere."

The Last Magnolia

As Barbara gathered her things and headed out the door, John called after her, "You have to think about the furniture, machines, stuff like that, you know."

"I'm way ahead of you, get out the checkbook!"

"You know John, there's a little more we should discuss," Hank seemed serious, but when John had heard him out, he was pleased.

"It's time you and Barb thought about a house and I'm glad you've found one. Didn't even know you were looking. A ranch? Are you sure that's what the two of you really want?"

"It's Barb's dream. You remember, she's an old Texas girl. We'll just run a few horses for the kids. It's going to be a big old overrun farm with dogs, cats and horses. The location is great. It's easy to get into town from the Marshall area. Do you know it, down there by the creek?"

"Sounds to me as if I'm going to know it well."

Hank stopped his happy banter. John seemed so alone, so vulnerable. He knew there were other women, just dates though. Barb had fixed him up with a couple of gals, but nothing seemed to stick. John had no permanence. It was as if, except for the business and time John spent with him and Barb and the boys, he'd encased himself in a shell that no one else seemed able to penetrate.

"How about you, John? When are you going to start filling a house with family? Is your apartment still big enough for you?"

"The apartment is great and with offices in town, I'll be that much closer to the office. Of course, it's further from the hanger and the planes, but I've invested in some property out east on the river. Someday I'll build what I feel I need. For now my apartment is just fine."

Getting up, he pulled his cap from a rack and headed out the door, "Come on, let's see to the planes and the hanger."

After a brief inspection of the two company Cessna's John came back to the business of business. "I think we'd better plan a little more expansion today."

"My God, the big spender speaks. What now?"

"The two boys we have working on the planes are fine Hank, and as long as I'm here to tell them what and how to do it, they'll get it all done. One of these days I'm not going to be here, and they're going to have to make a key maintenance decision for themselves. They don't know enough about the planes to do that yet, and it could mean the loss of a plane or a life. We don't want that."

"What do you want to do?"

"There's a guy I'd like you to meet. His Dad taught him and me all we ever wanted or needed to know about flying and the maintenance of planes. I just heard the other day that some of the big boys came in and bought up the little airport in Nebraska that his family owned. I figure Er could probably use some work. He's a top aircraft mechanic, a pilot and a good friend. I'd like to offer him a partnership."

"You think we're ready for that, Johnny?"

"More than ready, actually we need him probably more than he needs us. You say the word Hank, and I'm on my way to Nebraska today."

"Go, man!"

Hank hated to interfere in John's private life, but they were as close as brothers would ever be and felt he had to ask the next question.

"Speaking of Nebraska, what's the status of Jan and your

marriage?"

John smiled, good old Hank, he thought, clearing the air with honesty and openness is so like him.

"There isn't a marriage Hank. I should never have gone along with her when she met my ship. I found out in two short days that things would never work for us. This trip to the Midwest will do double duty. I haven't done anything about divorcing her yet, so while I'm there, I'll get the paper work started. I'll be gone for a couple of weeks. There's business in Charleston too, and then I'm going to spend Christmas with Shirley and her family."

They had almost reached the parking lot when John added, "God Hank, have you ever thought that we really should have named this business after Mary Elizabeth Graydon? Without her, it would never have happened."

"She'd be proud of us John, no matter what we called it. Why, I'll bet she and that nice husband of hers are watching us right now and grinning like Cheshire cats because they left their money to the right guy."

"Do you realize, at the rate we're growing, we're going to have to add a couple of pilots at years' end. You and I won't be able to handle all of the flying anymore, even with Er to help out, there will have to be more."

Heading in opposite directions, the air was alive with their warmth, "Merry Christmas Hank. See you when I get back."

Chapter 23

ER AND GRACE

November 1945

Nebraska

The snow was frozen and crisp and it made a sharp crackling sound as he walked across the yard. The air showed white steam from his breath and this house in Bratton Falls looked like a warm answer to the cold that snapped across his face. So this was the house Erwin and Grace bought, he thought.

John hoped the offer he planned to propose would be welcome, and for his sake he hoped Er would consider the partnership in Knowlton Air Service. Lord knows, everything he knew about airplanes Er knew too. They had been friends for many years, and to include Er now in his own success was a dream that could end with satisfaction. He needed a man he could trust, who knew aircraft and maintenance.

The door opened to his sharp rap and Grace, large, ample bosomed and always full of open love, stood in the doorway.
"Johnny!" She hugged him to her, cold and all, and her warmth of spirit made it seem as if winter was already gone. This was such a good woman. She cried over her shoulder, "Er, its John!" as if John rapped at their door several times a day.

Er came into the living room, pipe in hand. He had taken shrapnel in his leg during the Pacific campaign where he flew as a Navy pilot, and he walked with a slight limp.

The Last Magnolia

"Hey friend, must be telepathy, you've been on my mind a lot this week."

John laughed, "I guess we must have some kind of mental connection because I've been counting, thinking about you, talking about you and working you into lots of projects this week. Now we can talk them all over face to face."

When the offer was laid on the table, and the talking was done, Er's response was typical of him. The way he had been since he and John first met during their first days in High School, frank, trusting and decisive.

"Well Johnny I think we can tie things up here by next month and could be in Spokane for Christmas."

John grinned and slapped his hand on the table, "That's what I wanted to hear! But no, have Christmas here with your family and head for Spokane in January. Lots of snow out there you know. I'm going to Charleston for the holidays and I'd like to be out west to welcome you when you get there and see to it that you get a good start. Shake on it, partner."

He hesitated before asking the next question. Having enough money to do anything he wanted to do was still a source of surprise, and sometimes of embarrassment to him. He didn't ever want to have any of his friends think he was flaunting his wealth.

"Er, will you need any money to settle out there?"

"No thanks John, we can sell this house easily and that will take care of us and get us into something in Spokane to start us on our way."

"Don't hesitate to call me or Hank if you need anything, OK? You're a partner and it's all a part of business expenses you know." He thought for a moment, "Hank and Barb are going to buy a ranch out there. They hope to be in by spring. I don't

207

know if having a little spread in the country appeals to you, but I'm sure he and Barb will be glad to show you what's available."

Grace interrupted, "Johnny, we don't like to be nosy, but what about Janice?"

"Why do you ask?"

Avoiding his eyes, she put her head down, "I don't like to repeat things, you know that, but there's a lot of talk. Folks say you deserted her."

"I'm sure there's talk, but Jan is going to have to handle that. I have a meeting with an attorney here in town this afternoon, and I'll start divorce proceedings then. I don't know how long a divorce takes, but our marriage is all over Grace, it's been over for a long time."

"Well, that isn't exactly what I meant John." Grace paused and Er was giving her a hard look, as if to tell her to stop, but she continued, "Jan's pregnant, John. That's what the talk is all about. Folks say you deserted her, left her pregnant..." Grace's voice drifted off.

He cursed himself silently, and anyone else remotely connected with this mess. Grace's words hit him like a pail of ice water. Pregnant. New York. Damn! He couldn't even remember being with her on that one night, and for Pete's sake, if you're going to conceive a child, it would be nice to remember something about the conception.

"Where did you hear this Grace?"

"It's all over Crispin, Harper and a part of Bratton Falls. I'm sorry John, but I thought you should know."

"Well, I guess before I see the lawyer, I'd better see Janice. I sure hadn't planned on another run in with her, but if there's a baby involved, it's mine," he thought for a minute, and said, almost to himself, " she sure as hell wouldn't tumble anyone else, not the way she feels about sex. No, the baby's mine, and damn it I'm going to have to do the right thing." He shrugged into his coat, "Grace, Er, I'll see both of you and the family in Spokane. Thanks for coming with the firm. You're going to like it there." His expression was tight and he only nodded in a preoccupied manner as they thanked him for their new opportunity.

Chapter 24

JANICE

November 1945

Crispin, Nebraska

She sat. He stood, looking down at her.

"Jan, the baby is ours. It's mine and yours. I don't want you to have to raise it alone, and I don't want you to have it alone."

She hadn't changed at all, the thrust of her snake like posture was back with all its venom.

"That's really kind of you John," she said sarcastically, "you and your damned sex. But for you this would never have happened."

She was as pinched and hateful, filled with as much spite as ever. Pregnancy, he thought, hasn't beautified Janice.

"It wouldn't have happened if you hadn't cooked up the 'big meet- the- ship- in- New York and return to Nebraska and- stay-married to John routine if you'll remember."

They were in the small den of the house Janice had bought in Crispin. The room was warm, but you could hear the roar of a cold north wind blowing across the plains into town.

John's small gun collection that had been with Kate's things was still in the case where Janice had put it for him. She brought him back to this house after she met him in New York. She'd been sure he would live here with her when he returned from the war.

"I did it because I thought you might have changed, damn you."

He was shocked at her use of profanity. She had seldom talked that way before.

"Jan, don't talk like that, it doesn't suit you."

She arched her body to fling words, "Doesn't suit me! What rights have . . . "her voice dropped, stopped, "I'll talk any way I want!"

"What do you want, Jan? What do you want me to do? How do you want me to handle this? I'm in this as much as you are, I'll help you and the baby any way I can."

She sniffed and got up from her small chair.

"I'll tell you what I want. I want to be Mrs. John Knowlton, the wife of that wealthy and successful businessman. I want to walk down the streets of Crispin and Bratton Falls and have heads turn to look at me. I want everyone to know who I am and that because you're important, I'm important. That's what I want, John Knowlton!" She stopped for only a second, to catch her breath and added, "and I want you right here walking by my side!"

He listened and observed her quietly. She didn't move him one way or another.

"You can be Mrs. Knowlton. You can have enough money to give you all the attention you want. You can walk down any of those streets with your head held high because John Knowlton is taking care of you, but damn it Jan, you can't and you won't have me living here in Nebraska with you."

He stopped to see if what he was saying was making any sort of impression, "You don't want me Jan, you never did. I wanted you and now I don't. It's as simple as that."

His words didn't stop her vindictiveness.

211

"This is your baby John, and you have to help take care of it."

"I'll do that. I intend to do that."

I can come here regularly, he thought. I can help take care of the child and certainly support is no problem. I don't want Jan in Spokane and I won't come here permanently.

"You really have to deal with facts Jan. When it comes right down to it, you really don't want me here at all, do you?"

She sat again, "I don't know what I want."

He walked over to the gun case, removed one of the guns, sighted down the barrel, turned it, checked for dust, and put it back in the case. There were two more guns that had been in the Knowlton family for many years. He repeated the routine to check the second gun.

"That's what I want, you bastard!"

"Jan!" he spoke crossly, "don't lower yourself to language like that. What do you want? I'm listening."

She hardly heard him.

"I want those damned guns out of this house. I'm scared to death of guns. You know that, and just having them here scares me."

He watched her closely and looked back at the guns, "Why did you bring them here then? Where are the other two, the revolver and the pistol?"

"There wasn't enough room in the case," she gestured toward the desk, "I put them over there." She pointed at the desk.

He walked over and opened the top drawer.

"You see?" she smiled a sly, condescending smile, "I took care of your precious guns for you. The ammunition is there too. And Mr. Superior, I brought them here because I thought you'd have the decency to be here too."

The Last Magnolia

Checking the guns, he closed the drawer and ignored her latest attack.

"I have Mr. Graydon's collection in Charleston. I don't have a home of my own yet, and I hesitate to put any of the guns in my apartment in Spokane. I'd like to leave these here for the time being, and when I move into something larger, I'll have all the guns shipped west."

He hoped she'd be reasonable. She seemed to be cooling down.

"Well, if there's going to be a baby, you don't want it to have access to guns, do you?" She sniffed as only Janice could sniff, "I want them out of here to protect my baby. I don't want any shooting accidents."

John was beginning to lose patience, but he knew he had lots of dealing to do with this crazy woman.

"Don't make a mountain out of a molehill. The guns will be of no danger to a tiny infant." I'll get them to Spokane before they're a threat. He sat down at the desk, "The problem is what's to be done about us?"

"You can do anything you please, damn you. I'm not leaving this house, nor am I leaving Nebraska."

That was a relief!

"All right. You know I won't come here. My business is in the west and that's where it's going to stay and where I'm going to be."

Sniff.

"So you're taking the Knowlton way out. You're going to desert me."

Now he understood where the stories Grace had repeated had begun. He held his temper. What else could he expect from her? "I'm not going to desert you. I have, up to now, seen to it that you receive a nice monthly income, haven't I?"

She nodded, yes.

"All right, as I see it, here's the way it's going to have to be. I'll finish paying off this house for you and the baby. I won't start any divorce action, so you can still be Mrs. John Knowlton."

"Humph!"

He could see the difficulty in dealing with her was far from over.

"You stay here.   I'll be in Spokane, but I'll get back occasionally to make you look as important as you want to be."

She smiled smugly, she was getting more than she expected.

"When the baby comes," John continued, "I want to be part of its life. Do you understand that Jan?" He watched her from across the desk, "I don't want any fighting over our child."

She couldn't let him off too easily, even though her wishes were more than being met, and she answered sharply,

"If my father wasn't a minister and this wasn't such a small town, I'd find a way to have an abortion, that's what I'd do. As far as I'm concerned, you can have the damned baby. I don't want it now, and I won't want it when it gets here. You bet your life you can have a part in raising it John Knowlton, you and your filthy sex. This was your fault and by God, you'll pay for it!"

He heaved a heavy sigh and thought,   I'll make that baby happy. I owe it that. Maybe after it's born, I can go ahead with the divorce, get custody and then this whole mistake will be all over.

"Will you accept my terms Jan? Is it enough for you to be a long distance Mrs. Knowlton?"

Like a cat she watched him, she wanted to be sure she was

getting the best side of the deal,

"You bet. I don't want you anywhere around me. You'd probably rape me, even in my condition."

She wasn't rational. He wondered how long she had been this unbalanced? Forever? He just hadn't recognized its severity before.

Distaste evident in his words, he answered, "I'm trying to do what's best for all of us, let's stick to basics. Don't worry Jan. You'll just have to make up an extra room for me," he looked around the room they were in, "Why don't you just make this den my bedroom. Replace that couch with one of those new sleep-sofas and this will be my part of the house."

"That all takes money, you know."

"There's money Jan. You will have all the money you need and there will be trusts set up for the child. I'll have my lawyers in Charleston take care of that." He thought for a minute, and decided he had better protect himself carefully from what this woman could do to him if he gave her carte blanche. "You will submit any of your expenses above what I send to you monthly to them, and they will pay the bills for me." He tried to think of anything else he could offer to make her happy.

"Now, there's something I want."

"I might have known it," she sneered.

He didn't let her stop him.

"We're having a child together and while we aren't living together as man and wife and never will, I'm agreeing to give you all the show of a marriage you seem to want, do you understand?"

She shrugged, "I understand," she snapped.

"Is that all you want, Jan?"

"Yes, that's what I want."

The Last Magnolia

"OK, then I want a truce. I don't want any more arguments, none of your spitefulness. I don't want to fight with you anymore. We'll be civil to one another and, when the baby comes, we'll decide what the next step will be in our relationship. Are you sure you understand what I'm saying?"

The snake seemed to leave her and she looked nearly relieved that she didn't have to put forth the energy to coil and attack again.

"Yes John, I'll try."

This was the first decent moment between them since he'd come up the steps of the house.

"Will you stay here tonight?"

That would be too much for now.

"No, I have tickets out of Bratton Falls and I'm headed for business in Charleston. I'll make arrangements for all I have promised you, and I'll make sure you know where I am at all times. I want you to call me, or the attorneys in Charleston if you need anything." He tried to be as kind as possible. "I'll be back when it's time for the baby to come. I won't let you be alone then."

She opened her mouth, the retort promised to be Jan-like. She looks like a fish, he smiled, it wasn't over yet Knowlton, brace yourself.

She snapped it closed. The retort her angry, sick mind wanted to throw at him was silenced as she thought better of it.

Oh God, I thought I was free, and . . . oh boy, this is going to be rough.

Chapter 25

MARY KATHERINE

March 1946

Nebraska

The nurse held the tiny moving, naked baby on an open blanket.

"Ten fingers, ten toes, and it's a baby girl, Mr. Knowlton."

Her little fists were balled together tightly, one up near her head, the other with tiny curled fingers, was under her chin. He grinned, it's almost as if she were posing for me.

He didn't believe this tiny human being was a part of him. He looked at her closely. She wasn't pretty. Matter of fact, she was ugly.

Oh no, she was beautiful!

There was still evidence of the birth canal secretions. She hadn't even been washed. Her little body was tiny and tinged with pink. A trace of fine hair on a perfectly shaped head showed a little wrinkled face and he could see on the top of her head the soft spot.

Oh, that face. Still swollen by the ravages of birth, it was tiny and perfect. The eyes were blue. At least the eye that was open was blue and staring straight at him. Someone told him once that all babies were born with blue eyes. He knew it was impossible for her to see him. She was too young. But he could swear she was assessing him, looking him over in order to see if she approved of her father or not.

With several swift movements, the nurse wrapped the baby in a tiny pink blanket.

"She's going to the nursery now. You can see her this afternoon during visiting hours."

Involuntarily, he reached for the pink bundle. He didn't want to have his daughter taken away. The greatest love affair in the life of John Knowlton had begun. He didn't want to be without this precious bundle of life for a moment. He wanted to hold her close, to protect her from everything for the rest of her days. He had never felt an emotion as strong. She was his baby, a part of him.

He watched the nurse walk down the rubber-tiled hall in her soft-soled white shoes, the creak of rubber on rubber being the only audible sound in the drama he felt as he watched his young daughter leave him for the first of many separations.

He went back to the chair he had occupied during the hours of waiting for Jan to give birth and realized he had a silly grin on his face. He didn't care, he liked it. My gosh, that baby's part of me. I helped create her. Immediately he banished that thought because it meant considering his relationship with the baby's mother, and it was a fraud. Instead, he let his thoughts swing back to the months of waiting for his child.

He'd missed all of the joy and shared anticipation a firstborn's arrival brings. For Jan, the pregnancy was a burden she complained about whenever he would listen. She left him no opportunity to think about the happiness of fatherhood.

But now, he thought, I have all the joy I can handle. This baby is mine. She's a perfect little human being. The thought of her brought swelling inner joy that churned his insides, turned his heart inside out and gave a lift to his spirit such as he had never felt before.

His daughter! He had to tell somebody.

"What do you mean, what am I going to name her, Barb? I've just seen her." Wires sputtered as Barbara asked more questions. "Just wait, I'll have pictures taken. You haven't had the joy of a girl yet. Just wait till you have a girl, Barb, then you'll feel like I do."

Barb's voice crackled across the miles again and he realized she was laughing at him.

"Aw Barb, I know you and Hank have had the same thrill with the boys, what I mean is" . . ." he smiled. Of course Barbara would understand. "You'll call Hank and tell him, and Grace and Er?" With assurances accepted, he finished the call and sat again.

Imagination painted the promise of fatherhood. There were visions of pink. Blonde little girls of various sizes passed before him, growing, growing, and the pirouette of tiny figures whirled until they became a beautiful fully grown woman. She was all his. He snapped out of his dreamlike trance. What am I doing sitting here? I feel weak and I haven't done a thing.

Barbara's question came to mind. A name.

That perfect little being had to have a special name, one that would be loved and admired for the rest of her life. He thought for a moment more, and then he knew.

The child would be called Mary Katherine Knowlton. She would be named for the two women who had shown him kindness and love. His baby girl would be named for Mary Elizabeth Graydon and for his aunt, Katherine Knowlton. If she had even the smallest attributes of these wonderful women, she'd be perfect.

219

At the same time, he felt he was giving great honor to Mary Elizabeth and to Aunt Kate. Mary Katherine was a name with dignity, one she could carry with pride.

Automatically he reached into his back pocket for a handkerchief. He was crying. It didn't matter. He was a father and an exciting future stretched before him and his child.

A nurse interrupted his reverie.

"Mrs. Knowlton is back in her room now. You can go in to see her."

Exactly as Janice had demanded, her room was the largest on the maternity ward. John had acceded to all her wishes and she was firmly ensconced as the wife of the wealthy John Knowlton. She didn't care about him, the baby or his business. All she wanted was Nebraska, money, position and her own tiny world.

As he stepped in she was sleeping. He didn't want to disturb her, so he made himself comfortable in one of the easy chairs that faced the bed.

She stirred.

"John, are you here?"

It was the first time he had heard softness in her usually high-pitched voice since she had met his ship with her sham plan.

He stood and walked over to the bedside, "Here I am, Jan."

"Have you seen the baby?"

"Yes. Just for a moment. She's . . . ," he was overcome and couldn't finish.

"I saw her too," Jan said sleepily, "She's tiny and awfully red. I don't think I'm up to handling anything that small." The whine in the voice was back.

"I'll help you."

She turned her head on the pillow, "You? You won't help. You aren't even here!"

John thought of the baby, "I'll be here more often now," he was smiling, "Oh Jan, she's a lovely baby." He couldn't contain the excitement in his voice, and she caught it.

A conspiratorial smile lit her face. This will be my hold on him, she thought. I just may end up with a resident husband after all. She had worried about keeping that personal ample allowance coming after the baby was born, and now she had him. She turned her head so he couldn't see her smug expression, but John was too excited to notice.

"I'd like to name the baby if I could."

She started to say no, then thought better of it. If I go along with him, there may be bonuses later.

"What do you want to call her, John?"

He smiled. He was pleased, more pleased than ever with his choice.

"I'd like to name her for Mrs. Graydon and Aunt Kate. Mary Katherine Knowlton. Would that be all right?"

She held her tongue. Mrs. Graydon again! Well, she supposed, that's how John had gotten his start, that's where the money was coming from. She'd always liked his Aunt Kate.

"That sounds all right. What will we call her?"

"Let's just wait and see what comes naturally."

As the months passed, John traveled to and from the Midwest more and more often. While he planned at first to be with the baby monthly, he found himself flying one of the Knowlton Air Service planes to the small field in Bratton Falls nearly every weekend. He kept a small car there so was able to drive to Crispin and his daughter.

She was six months old now, chirping, sitting alone, smiling.

221

She knew him and extended as much adoration his way as he did hers. She had captured him completely. Even Janice seemed to enjoy watching the relationship grow between father and daughter.

Jan cared for the baby with the daily help of a local lady who acted as nursemaid. This was another part of Jan's enjoyment in being the wife of a successful man. John didn't know of any other family in Crispin who used the services of a full time baby nurse, but Jan enjoyed the attention and the freedom it provided for her.

The baby was thriving. She was a healthy, chubby, good natured and adored child. Her eyes had changed from blue to violet, and then to brown. Her hair was still thin and clung to her head in loose golden ringlets. To John she was beautiful.

He was having a home built on the Spokane river and suggested that he take the baby west with him. He assured Jan that he would staff the house so the baby would be well cared for at all times.

Jan balked. With two feet firmly on the floor she delivered her ultimatum.

"Mary Katherine will stay right here in Nebraska with her mother where she belongs. She isn't going to have any of that Knowlton wanderlust drummed into her. Just remember John, she's our baby, not yours, and she'll become accustomed to seeing both of us in a normal household. I know you can always leave someone else in charge of your business. I know you and Hank have become the young wonders of Spokane. Everyone is reading about the war veteran boy who made good. It seems to me, now that you've made yourself known, there isn't any reason why you can't live permanently here with the baby and me in Crispin."

The Last Magnolia

His words were filled with disgust, "I think you realize that's impossible. Hank and I are busy all of the time. Just because our business is one of the first of its kind in the northwest doesn't mean its success will continue without effort and expansion plans."

He folded the papers he had been studying carefully. "I'm not going to go into the details of my business with you. You haven't ever shown an interest, so you aren't going to be included now. Hank and Barb, Er and Grace and I plan to expand. As we've developed our air services, we've seen other directions we can take, to serve other fields efficiently with our planes. We plan to pioneer new services too. Actually, I'm going to be busier than I've ever been."

He tapped the point of a pencil against a small notebook. "To get back to Mary Katherine, I merely was offering to help you out. You were complaining about the pressures her care puts on you."

Jan held her ground. She knew Nebraska was her trump card in possession and custody of the baby. As long as his little darling was here, he'd continue to fly back and forth. She knew if she let the child go, her demands for ever more luxury and comfort would be met with less eagerness.

As a mother, Jan's relationship with Mary Katherine was designed to favor the mother more than the baby.

The child was a picture. She was loving and responsive, and Jan was proud of her but affection and training were left to the nurse and John. Jan only used her daughter. Used her as a prop to make Jan appear the perfect wife and mother. The child was dressed perfectly, and taken to places where she could be admired by the people whom Jan considered worthwhile. "A perfect mother" was the impression Jan tried to convey at all times in her small corner of Nebraska.

She had learned the basics of baby care, and exercised that knowledge sanitarily and expertly.

Mary Katherine's father and her nurse were the sparks in the baby's life. They adored her, played with her and concentrated on the baby's growth, development and affection with their attentions. If these relationships could continue it would be greatly to Jan's benefit.

****

Months passed, the baby grew and John's visits to Crispin continued on a regular schedule. Mary Katherine's first year passed quickly.

Janice was irritated when the telephone rang. She had been comfortably curled up with a good magazine story. She threw the afghan aside and walked into the kitchen to answer.

"Jan, how's the weather out there?"

It was only John. Why was he calling on a Thursday? He usually arrived unannounced on Fridays. She tried to hide her irritation.

"It's windy and cold."

"How's the baby, our birthday girl?"

"She's had a little case of the sniffles. Not any fever but we've kept her indoors. She'll be ready for her birthday party on Sunday."

"Have you had the doctor for her?"

"No John," a tone of testiness crept into her words "as I said, there isn't any fever and no congestion. Mrs. Bryan and I both feel a little chest balm and nose drops will do the trick. As a matter of fact, she's been in bed several hours, and she's sleeping peacefully."

"Good. I called to tell you there's been a terrible blizzard here, and I may not be able to get my plane dug out until tomorrow. Right now, the big commercial jobs are the only ones flying. Don't worry though, I'll be there in time for Mary Kate's birthday. Wait until she gets a ride in the little red wagon I bought for her."

"All RIGHT John," she was anxious to get back to her story, "we'll expect you on Saturday then?"

"Well, if she's sick, maybe I should catch a commercial flight tonight. Maybe I should come ahead."

Janice was exasperated, "John that won't be necessary. The baby is cross and Mrs. Bryan and I can handle a little cold just fine by ourselves."

Doubt and impatience were discernible in his voice,

"Mrs. Bryan is off this weekend, don't you remember?"

"Oh dammit John, I am not a total imbecile. I know how to take care of my own daughter for God's sake!"

"All right, all right. I'll call you in the morning to see how she's doing."

She spoke into the telephone with great drama and accentuated resignation, "You do that."

"You'll call me if she doesn't improve, won't you?"

"Of course I will, what's the matter with you?" She was sick and tired of this conversation. I'll see you on Saturday." She put the receiver back on its hook with a resounding snap.

Walking to the refrigerator she took out a small pitcher of cream and tinted the coffee in her cup then added more sugar to the brew and sat at the kitchen table.

I'm going to have to face some facts one of these days, she

thought. After a year, I'm sick and tired of motherhood. Just like tonight. I'm stuck with a sick baby, Mrs. Bryan won't be here tomorrow and I'll probably be up with her all night.

She picked up her coffee and walked back into the living room, deep in thought.

Maybe it's time to give in to John. I'm tired of being tied to Crispin by the baby

She knew her church group was planning a bus tour to California, and she wanted to go. Yes, now would be the time to acquiesce.

I won't do it easily. I won't let him have her too quickly, but that's what I'm going to do. I don't want the responsibility anymore. She's toddling and will be into everything. I just don't want to be tied down any more.

A look of cunning crossed her face, and with a shrewd smile, she said out loud, "Yes, I think it's time for little Mary Kate to move to Washington with Daddy."

Finishing the coffee, she left it on the end of the table, turned off the lamp and carried her magazine to the bedroom. In case the baby wakened in the night, she had to get some rest. If that damned cold held, she could be tied up all weekend with a sick child. Then what would she do about the party?

John pushed the accelerator a little harder. No snow here, thank God. He had this gut feeling of urgency. He had to get into Crispin, and fast.

After Jan hung up on him, he felt a cold shudder. He didn't entertain any more thoughts of flying his own plane to Nebraska. Instead he dialed the airlines and booked the earliest possible commercial flight. He had gotten as far as Chicago, then picked up a feeder flight back to Bratton Falls. The baby and this strange feeling of urgency had been with him all the way. But Jan said the baby wasn't even feverish, why was he so worried?

The speedometer showed eighty, and he lessened the pressure on the pedal a little. No sense picking up a speeding ticket.

He tried to put his fear aside by telling himself the rush of travel had created his anxiety. But the sense of urgency was strange. He had carried this ominous, intuitive feeling of dread all the way. He tried to relax. There were only a few miles to go. He was tired, but not sleepy. He had slept on the plane.

The sky was a cloudless bright blue, and the wind swirled across the plains, picking up tumbleweeds and rolling them across the dark soil of the fields. Sunshine on the white farm buildings created a brightness that was unnatural, and John tried to concentrate on the perfectly apportioned sections of farmland as he sped down the highway.

There was a sudden jolt and a pull to the left.

"Damn!"

He righted the steering, pulled to the side of the road and got out of the car. His jack and spare were in good condition, so it shouldn't take too long to change the tire. Anyway, Jan wouldn't try to take the baby anywhere today, he'd be sure to find them at home.

He pushed the door to the house open. It was seldom, if ever locked. Leaving the cold wind of the outdoors, the heat hit him in the face like a sharp slap.

He started down the hall to the nursery, glancing into the living room as he passed. The door to his den was open, and as he walked by, a slight movement caught his eye.

Janice was sitting ramrod straight in the large chair at his

227

desk. She was staring through the door at something beyond him, just over his shoulder. She seemed to be having trouble focusing, because as he crossed her line of vision there was no reaction. She was in a sort of trance.

"I decided you'd need some help this weekend, so I caught a commercial flight last night to be with the baby while she fights this cold," he said, as he walked into the den.

Jan didn't move. There wasn't any reaction to his words.

"Jan?"

"She's dead."

His heart stopped for an instant.

"Dead? Who's dead?" He didn't want to hear the answer.

"My God!" He rushed to the nursery. The door was open, and the breath came out of him. There she was, his small darling in her little white crib. Face down. Very still.

He reached the side of her bed in two long strides and bent toward her. This wasn't right. There was something wrong. A cold intuitive dread crept up his back, across his shoulders. He reached down to touch the tiny hand. It was cold. The body was limp. She was gone. He shook her gently, picked her up and laid her over one arm. With his other hand on her head, he breathed his warm live breath into her half-open mouth and gently pushed on her chest.

He knew. No, he couldn't know. The confusion in his mind battled facts. The dread of truth fought reality.

Yes. She was gone.

He clutched his darling little cherub to his breast and turned to walk quickly to the den. He carried his little girl. His dead little girl.

"What happened?" He was screaming at Janice. "Where's

228

Mrs. Bryan? Jan! Answer me!"

Jan came out of her trance with a start. The sight of the limp dead baby in his arms brought her back to the present.

"Take her back John. I can't bear it. Take her back to bed."

In his numbness he stood, holding the child.

"Take her back? What happened? You said she was fine." He started to cry, "that was only last night for God's sake. What happened?"

She started to cry too. Small sobs as tears ran down her face.

"She was fine. She fussed last night, and I was up several times. I called Dr. Price this morning to see if she should have a shot. He stopped on his way to the office." She put her head down on her arms on the desk, "He said. He said". . . Now sobs wracked her body, and it was difficult to hear her. John stood shock still, gently cradling the body of his dead daughter . . . "He said the same thing Mrs. Bryan said. It was a bad case of the sniffles and we could give her baby aspirin if there was a fever."

She looked at him, pleading with her eyes to be understood.

"There wasn't any fever. I used the syringe in her little nose, and she had juice and mush for breakfast. She was tired, but she clapped when I sang that little song she loves so much. She was getting better."

For the first time in their marriage, Janice needed John's comfort.

"I called Mrs. Bryan to come in even though it was her day off but she had developed a cold and I changed my mind." Her voice dropped, the crying had stopped. "Mary Kate went right down for a morning nap after her breakfast. She was better."

Janice screamed, "SHE WAS BETTER! Don't you believe me, John? SHE WAS BETTER! I looked in to be sure she was sleeping and she was still awake, just chattering, playing with her toys. I knew she'd be all right and fall asleep."

John hugged the tiny body to him. His tears wet the little knit pajamas Nothing was right. Why was his beautiful baby dead?

"When did she die?"

"When she didn't wake for lunch, I went in to get her." Wracking sobs took over. "I went to get her and she was gone."

She looked at her husband, holding their child and screamed, "JOHN! Take . . . the . . . baby . . . back to her bed!"

He looked at this screaming woman, this person who was his wife in name only, possibly the murderer of his baby and felt no sympathy, no emotion what so ever for her. Cradling Mary Katherine in his arms John gazed at the tiny face, the curly blond locks with adoration. Turning gently, he carried his daughter to her crib, laid her gently on the bed, straightened her head, pushed the little curls back, and laid the dimpled arms at the sides of her tiny body.

No.

He stood back. He didn't like that. It made her look like a little dead baby.

He was overtaken with the madness of grief.

He couldn't let his darling look like a dead baby.

He turned Mary Kate on her side, pulled her little legs up at the knees and put her hands near her head. The body wouldn't stay that way.

Obsessed with his macabre actions, he started again. He couldn't stop, he had to perform this ritual. It was to honor his baby girl. He had to make her lie properly. Lie as if she were alive.

But she wasn't alive. She was dead.

Ghoulishly his motions continued as he straightened the body again. He reached for a small pink knitted blanket and placed it over the child, drawing the edge under the tiny feet and up to her chin. Satisfied, he pulled a large rocking chair nearer to the crib and watched her.

This was his vigil. He rocked back and forth, taking physical comfort from the motion. Then the sobs began. A man's sobs. Huge tearing gasps that would not, could not stop. He rocked and cried. The tears flooded from a lifetime of hurt and he could not stop the flow. There was no comfort for him as his daughter slept her soft, soundless sleep of death.

Chapter 26

JANICE AND JOHN

March 1947

Crispin, Nebraska

"Janice, John," the young doctor looked at the stricken couple with compassion as they sat before him in his office. "Someday there will be an explanation and a way to prevent what happened to your little girl." He consulted a paper he held, "There are so few statistics for me to quote for you."

John stood up and walked away from his chair. Janice sat still. She was pale, withdrawn, strangely silent.

"Doctor, you saw her less than four hours before she died. How do you explain your misdiagnosis?"

"John," the doctor spoke as firmly as compassion would allow, "your child was the victim of crib death. It is called Sudden Infant Death Syndrome. There are over ten-thousand such deaths in America today, and there hasn't been enough research for us to determine how many such deaths have occurred in the rest of the world. There isn't any explanation for it. I examined the baby with the coroner. She was a perfectly healthy child."

The Doctor realized his explanation was unsatisfactory but it was all he had to go on.

"Whose fault was it then? Was her death a result of a birth defect? Were my bloodlines or Jan's bloodlines somehow at fault?"

The Last Magnolia

"No, no. It wasn't your fault, or Jan's, not mine either. Your baby was perfect."

He looked down at the letter opener he passed from hand to hand, "I'm sorry John. There's been so little research. I can only tell you this. Your baby didn't die from suffocation. She didn't die of pneumonia or a strong case of the sniffles or some hidden virus. She didn't die from neglect. Your baby died from the most mysterious death there is today. Most babies who die this way are much younger. Mary Kate's case is even rarer because she was a full year old. "

Anger underlined his next words. "Many doctors will tell you her death was an act of God. It wasn't. Not unless it's God's will to take a beloved, normal and healthy baby from her parents for no apparent reason. There's no way I can find a medical or theological answer for you. Perhaps someone else, more understanding, less clinical, can. All I can tell you is that someday, research will come up with an answer. Now, although there are thousands of deaths of this kind, they are widely spread and isolated, so there isn't funding or enough concentration in the area to allow research. It will come eventually, and until it does I can only tell you that you must never feel guilty. Neither of you was responsible for your daughter's death in any way."

The doctor knew he wasn't succeeding in helping this couple. He couldn't give them solace, comfort or information. He felt helpless as he watched John and Janice Knowlton, knowing full well that neither would be able to face or understand this loss. The doctor silently asked himself how he could be of further help when he didn't understand this kind of unfair death either.

Janice didn't respond to anyone since she'd told John about finding the baby dead. She remained remote. Her flaring temper was gone and she seemed to just exist as she wandered through her home, arms hugged against her, saying nothing, accomplishing nothing.

John hated Janice. Somehow the entire death was on her shoulders and he saw her as an uncaring woman who had used his precious child to gain for herself only. To be in the same room with her was nearly impossible.

Jan's father, the old minister approached John and asked if he would make some effort to take the burden of guilt away from her. John wanted nothing to do with it. Grief inside of him churned with resentment, and to be kind in any way to this woman who had neglected his daughter wasn't possible.

Finally, after talking with the doctor over and over again, he agreed to bring Janice to his office to try to convince her that she was without blame.

He would never completely believe that, but agreed to take her for this session with the doctor.

In his bitterness, John was like a madman. He heaped loss upon loss with paranoia. As he reviewed his life, he realized everything he'd cherished was gone.

Previously suppressed knowledge seemed to nag at him, to tell him that he deserved these losses. Closely, once again with the fear of discovery, he pressed down on the ugliness that somewhere in his life, he had hidden from himself. Once again denying answers to the personal grievances he had suffered, he held back. Instead, John sank into a pit of self pity, allowing this new tumor of loss to grow and affect him harmfully. All of these emotions were unobserved by those around him as he went about the necessary acts to provide for the burial of his beloved child.

The Last Magnolia

Neighbors mourned with them and friends and family had come steadily and in droves to share the grief of the young Knowltons over the loss of their small child.

"Where's Janice, John?" Her father had delivered Mary Katherine's eulogy. He was still visibly affected by the effort, his eyes red rimmed, his body shaking slightly.

After the tiny white casket had been lowered into its small black crevice of earth, the family had returned to the house. Talk was subdued. The day had been a difficult one. Barbara and Hank and Grace and Er had flown in from the west, and Shirley Graydon had come up from South Carolina. Seeing the state of mind John was in they all encouraged him to return with them to Spokane. They felt hard work might be the best medicine.

John started from his own reverie at the question. Where was Janice? He really didn't care.

"I don't know sir."

"What are your plans now John? Will you stay for a while?"

This seemed to be the incentive John needed to reach a decision.

"No Mr. Adams, there's nothing left for me here now. You understand, don't you?"

The old man started to speak, stopped and shook his head sadly, "I understand, I'll see to it that Janice is well cared for the rest of her life, but I won't be back."

****

Janice sat at the desk in the den.

They all blame me. I know. I can feel it and see it by the way they look at me. It doesn't matter about the medical explanations, they think I killed her.

Her mind raged and ranted as her imagination sought out

235

accusing glances that didn't exist. She wanted everyone to respect and pity her, she needed the assurance that she was blameless. The past three days had been dreadful. She was so tired.

She tried to remember exactly what she did and what she thought when she found the baby. The details had fled her mind, but then . . . no it was coming back. Now she could think about it. Perhaps the memory would heal her.

She had watched the baby sleep, had checked on her. Mary Kate had only been dozing for an hour or so.

No! She had to stop this and couldn't bear the memories. She had to push the pictures from her mind.

The self-incrimination returned. She thought, John really has reason to hate me now. He thinks I killed his baby. I don't care. HIS baby? Indignation rose in her mind. It was MY baby too!

With her right hand, she pulled open the top right drawer of John's desk. The pistol and the revolver still lay there. She hated these guns, but, curiously, she picked up the revolver, and turned it over, end to end in her hand. Holding it flat in the palm of her left hand, she pushed hard enough to move the cylinder to one side, as if to load the gun.

Strange, she thought, and dropped the cocked gun in her lap as her attitude changed from curiosity to fear and disgust.

The box of bullets remained in the drawer. Idly, she pulled the end flap of the box open and removed one of the elongated pieces of lead and metal. Holding the bullet, she picked up the gun and pushed the bullet into one of the little holes of the chamber. Pushing the cylinder, she tried to force it back into place. It wouldn't go.

She looked at the gun closely and saw that she needed to push the bullet flush with the chamber's edge. As she did that, the cylinder slipped easily into place.

Pleased with herself, she half-smiled at the gun and spun the cylinder again with her finger.

Now what will happen with my life, she wondered? She felt a guilt she didn't deserve. That's right. They all think I murdered my own child.

Well damn them. Let them think what they want. I'll show them.

GOD DAMN THEM!

She lifted the gun to the right side of her head.

Janice pulled the trigger three times before the one bullet in the cylinder registered a sharp, exploding report.

Chapter 27

JOHN

September 1957

Pacific Northwest

She follows the road as if she knows it by heart, he thought as he navigated the late model white Cadillac along Highway 99 between Portland and Seattle. He drove with a relaxed and easy manner. The car had made this trip so many times John felt it could navigate the road by itself and that he was nothing more than a legal necessity behind the wheel.

For more years than he cared to count, he had been traveling between Portland, Seattle-Tacoma and Spokane. In those years he had come to know the roads well.

Hank and Barb and Er and Grace continued to handle the headquarters of Knowlton Air Service from Spokane. John had spent the past years traveling, researching, and developing new services that the largely expanded air service company could deliver.

Because of this, new offices had been opened in key northwest locations and John traveled easily from one to the other, guiding, and exploring the quality of the work their firm delivered. Branch offices had been established with accompanying aircraft and additional flight crews in Portland and Seattle.

At the same time, branches for communication and service

had sprung up in Montana. Kalispell and Billings were on tap to serve customers in western and eastern parts of that state. In Southern Idaho agricultural needs had been assessed and parts delivery to large farms was developed through Knowlton Air Service. Oregon locations were served from the Portland headquarters and now Northern California loomed on the horizon as potential for Knowlton Air Services. John and his team had grown, and in growing had produced services to every part of the northwest.

Pioneers in the expediting business, they were still the leaders, at the top with the development and addition of new services. There was crop dusting and other farm related service. Emergency health lifts provided health and accident evacuations by air in state of the art medically equipped Knowlton Air Service planes. Small towns and remote areas had been given access to large city hospitals.

John had just negotiated an airlift program throughout the northwest. This would provide small package delivery service to create express delivery that would be far superior to the limited city to city rural postal service.

Through all of its successes and progress, Knowlton Air Service and its directors had maintained a reliable and compassionate interest in every community they served. For this reason they were in constant demand.

John, Hank and Er had become wealthy with the profits from the company, yet each of them still held an active position in its operations.

It was 1957, a long time since we launched operations with two small planes from the rented space at Felts Field in Spokane, he thought as he maneuvered through a sudden influx of heavy traffic. So much has happened.

John Knowlton was still a handsome man. Thirty-seven years had brought a touch of premature white hair to his temples, adding distinction to his appearance. His lean body was in excellent shape and he dressed the part. His clothing reflected quality and style, a gentlemanly sportsman look. Woolens and tweeds were tailored to perfection. He hadn't married again. His life seemed full with his relationship with his partners and their families, and Shirley Graydon Knight and her family in Charleston. Essentially he belonged to three families, none of his making.

Hunting and fishing were his two major recreational pursuits. He spent leisure time on his favorite lake or in the mountains angling or hunting for the seasonal wildlife he could find in the Northwest Territory he had adopted as his home.

A small cabin along the south fork of the Flathead River in Montana was where he entertained fellow hunting and fishing companions.

John dated but seldom saw the same woman more than once. His life seemed to follow the direction of business or sports, and he made little room for romance.

The early years in Spokane had been spent choosing the ideal plan for his large, open home before he had it built along the Spokane River.   He kept a competent couple to manage the property so he was able to come and go as he pleased.

Between the house, the cabin and Charleston, John was busy. He surrounded himself with friends and business associates, and if possible, was never alone.   His life was personally arranged to avoid any emotional pain.

Pushing on toward Tacoma, he passed Fort Lewis, Lakewood

and Gravelly Lake. All familiar territory. He planned to pick up a bite to eat and stop at the company apartment in this area and then after a good night's sleep, finish the trip to Spokane.

Using the car phone, he put through a call to Barb at the ranch near Spokane.

"Hey 'Mam', how about that nice afternoon of relaxing around the pool and enjoying cocktails and the dinner that we're going to have?"

"Johnny! You devil!" Barb was the same good sport, "You never mentioned anything about a party."

"I'm mentioning it right now. Will you join me tomorrow? Bring the boys. You and Hank come and get hold of Grace and Er. Tell them to bring their kids too. We'll consider it a write-off . . . a board of directors meeting or something like that."

"As if we needed an excuse to get together," she replied.

"You know the pool's nice and warm and this is a great time for all of us to get caught up again. How are the boys? Are they in school yet?"

"If you'd stick around home more, you'd know they're all back in school. It happens every September, you know," Barb answered sarcastically. "They'll be thrilled to have a final swim before you close it for the winter. I assume you still have the heater on," then with the weather-watch prowess of a good pilot's wife, she added, "the weather's good for the whole weekend."

"I know. That's why we're going for a swim"

"Want me to bring anything, John?"

"Well, if you can swing it, why don't you bring Hank and the boys?"

"OK, enough John."

"Well, we're all fixed up then and if you'll be good enough to

241

hang up, I'll call Annie at the house and tell her to get everything ready for us on Sunday."

"See you then old dear."

He made the second call and slowed to swing off the ramp that exited the highway and led to his apartment. It was beginning to mist, the light was dimming and evening shadows monopolized the landscape. He was tired, happy he had split the drive. It meant the trip across Snoqualmie pass would be a cinch tomorrow morning.

Chapter 28

SUSAN

September 1957

Pacific Northwest

She slammed on her brakes. When the car skidded to the right, she reacted instinctively by turning the wheel in the same direction as the skid to bring the car to a stop.

The small terrier sleeping on the passenger seat slid onto the floor of the car with a rush when it stopped.

"Stay here!" She ordered as she opened the door and started to run.

Ahead, lights were pushing up into the evening haze crazily. They weren't klieg lights. She could see that. But where were they coming from?

Moving forward, never stopping, she ran toward them. As she came closer to the scene, she realized what she was seeing. Her throat closed with horror for a moment. Good Lord!

A school bus was lying on its side, tires still spinning. As she swung her head around, she saw that the lights came from a small sports car whose headlights speared into the murky mist at angles that were all wrong.

How can anything that smashed still show light, she wondered?

Fear of what she would find ahead filled her with horror but she continued to run, unable to turn away from what she knew was more than she wanted to deal with. Her breath came in heavy gasps as she reached the intersection. Suddenly her feet skidded and she fell into a depression in the asphalt that was filled with a damp, sticky substance. Then she was down and skidding through warm, red blood. She continued to slide crazily towards the twisted mass of metal that had been a sports car until somehow she stopped herself and crawled away on her knees, the retch of vomit in her throat.

Why blood? She wondered. From where?

Then she heard the screams of small children accompanied by moans and groans, coming at her from all directions.

She pulled herself to her feet and looked into what was left of the car. There was someone sitting in the seat. She ran to the car and her intake of breath when she saw the corpse was filled with terror as her lungs were violated to create a piercing pain that crept down to her intestines, painfully turning them into a tight, writhing, heaving mass.

It was a corpse. He didn't have a head!

Blood still oozed from the torso and the intersection was filled with it as a lifeless body, a piece of flesh that had housed a person simply oozed blood onto itself as it spilled onto the road.

This was the same sticky wetness she had slid into.

Turning in shock and revulsion, she watched her steps carefully as the need to help those small crying children who were still alive and screaming and moaning became primary.

She ran to the left bank of the large intersection and saw other cars stopping, other people running as fast as she was.

I must have been the first to arrive, she thought as she

shouted at a man headed in her direction,

"Get to a phone! There's a school bus involved. Get help fast!"

The man turned, looking nearly relieved that he didn't have to continue into the blood-filled horror engulfing this filthy screaming woman.

She ran on, up the bank and through the dusk, saw a little girl. The child was crumpled and still. She bent over her. Blood was streaming into the child's eyes from a deep scalp wound. She picked up a limp wrist. There was only a faint pulse. Now she was confused, as if at a loss as to what to do. She picked up the little body and carried it to the edge of the road. There was so much blood from the head wound that she couldn't decide where it was coming from. Ripping off her jacket, she covered the child and used her handkerchief to try to stop the bleeding. She spotted an elderly woman moving in a walk-run gait toward the bus.

"Here . . . come here," she motioned to the woman, "take care of this child, stop the bleeding if you can and stay with her until you see an ambulance. Please, please help me. There are so many others. Watch for the medics!"

The older woman changed direction and immediately was with the child, "Bring me more. I'll watch them. Hurry . . . hurry . . . get back to the other children . . . hurry . . . I can hear them."

The woman in the bloodstained clothing retraced her path. Night was coming on fast and placing the cries was difficult.

There. A small boy sat with his head down, crying softly, holding a badly broken right arm.

"Here son, it's all right," she said, "I'll help you."

She reached his side and his whimpers became screams. He

bawled as he tried to lift his arm to show her where it hurt. The pain was too much and its pressures drove themselves into his body so he simply held the badly twisted, torn arm and cried softly.

"I'll help you. What's your name?"

"Brad," he said, sobbing. He bit his lip, "It hurts so bad."

"Stay there Brad, that's a boy. Don't move." She could hear sirens in the distance and, by the eerie light of the cars that had stopped and emergency vehicles, she could see passersby's carrying injured children. They seemed to be collecting them and placing them near the vicinity where she had carried the unconscious little girl.

"Can you walk? Come on Brad. Doctors are coming now, and they'll help you." She took his other arm and led him to the spot where medics and ambulances were attending the injured.

Other children were walking to the ambulance. Some were helping friends, many were crying openly. There seemed to be many with cuts and scratches, while others, thank heavens, were unscathed. Still, she thought as she looked around her, there have to be more. She ran in the direction of the bus.

As she swerved around the back of the overturned bus, she heard a faint cry. Squinting to peer through the darkness, she saw a man climbing up over a small grassy embankment and ran to him.

Sweat glistened on his gray face as he crawled through the wet grass dragging a leg behind him.

She reached him and he looked up at her with eyes glazed over with shock, "Lady, can you please help me...help me find my foot?"

Horrified, she took a closer look and saw that his left foot was missing. He was bleeding heavily, was in severe shock, but still remarkably conscious.

"Stop! I'll help you."

Screaming back towards the ambulance area for a doctor, she reached under her skirt and tore her slip down over her hips. Balling the soft material, she held it against the stump where the ankle used to be. She tried to staunch the flow of blood with pressure.

"Be still now, we'll find your foot, don't worry."

A young emergency attendant reached them.

"He's in shock. His foot's gone."

"Help me get him to the wagon."

Between them, they pulled and carried the man to the ambulance.

"Thanks, lady."

She smiled, but didn't take the time to reply. The insane intent to help, to save, totally invaded her consciousness and again she ran toward the bus.

There were many helping now. Police medics and passersby's. Others simply had parked their cars and were watching the grotesque scene. She wanted to shout at them to do something. She wanted them to see the horror, and pain. She resented their comfort behind the shatterproof windows of their cars and somehow wanted them to share the revulsion of the past moments. Moving forward, she realized she didn't have time for resentment. Too many needed help. The thought propelled her forward to find more victims.

Once more, she returned to the overturned bus.

Coming up and over the same embankment where she had found the footless man, she spotted a tall figure. It was a man, carrying the limp, seemingly unconscious body of a little girl.

Yellow curls, matted with blood hung over his arm and the man held the child close to him, sobbing. Sobbing and saying nothing, but the picture of grief was poignant, and she caught her breath, watching his agony.

She moved toward him. "Can I take her? Is she unconscious? Is this your daughter?" With yet another victim to help, she became inwardly calm. He didn't acknowledge her presence, just continued to cry so she put her hand on his arm.

"Let me help you sir, I'll take the little girl. Perhaps it would be better."

He clutched the small body closer to him as if to fend her off.

"Why do you want her? She's dead. I have to hold her just this one more time. Hold her just as I held my own little Mary Katherine."

He looked down at the child's face with an expression of grief and suffering such as she had never seen before. Suddenly, as if he remembered where he was, he relaxed his hold on the child's body and what had seemed to be confused association quickly disappeared.

"The child is dead." His tone was flat, without expression. His crying stopped.

The woman moved toward him.

"May I take her?"

He stepped away from her, "No! I'll carry her over to the ambulances."

He walked ahead, carrying the child and she followed him closely with a feeling of suspicion. In seconds, nearly mid-sentence, how could this man go from emotional involvement with the dead child to become so self-assured and capable? She forgot the horror of the past minutes as she caught up and walked alongside him until they met a medic.

"Here sir, let me take her."

The man took one last tender look at the small girl. He brushed back her hair with his free hand, and gave the lifeless body to the waiting attendant.

Lights of every color were turning and shining. Darkness was total now, and the road glistened with what at any other time would seem festive as the brightness of the colors combined with the shiny moisture of the softly falling light rain on the pavement. Reflections magnified the surrounding areas of light as red lights flashed. Sirens approaching could still be heard as their noise created a crescendo, while the sound of departing ambulances diminished as they gained distance moving their burdens of pain toward hospitals. In the background, voices hummed as people dealt with the terrible necessities this accident had created. Shouts and cries, screams, agonizing moans, commands and verbal instructions mingled to become sonorous humming decibels that created a background for the activity they supported. Yellow lights whirled in unbroken arcs and blue lights zipped across the tops of official cars. The headlights of onlookers' cars held steady on the wet pavement and the business of rescue continued.

The woman's eyes moved to the center of the intersection. There it was. Thick and coagulated now. A dark, deep red pool of blood. The same blood she fell and skidded in. How long had she been here? She looked down at her skirt, her legs, shoes and reached for the arm of the man standing beside her. The sight of her bloodiness, and the smell of it, pervaded her senses.

"Help me. Oh my God, I'm going to be sick."

The Last Magnolia

He grabbed her and held her at the waist as she bent over to vomit, retching over and over again until there was nothing left but the ache from the heaves of her body. The memory of what she had just been through horrified her system over and over again.

With one hand he reached into his pocket and pulled out a handkerchief to wipe her forehead, eyes and her mouth. When the surges were over, he cleaned her face gently.

The taste in her mouth was of gall, and she was embarrassed. "Thank you."

"You have blood all over you. Were you in the accident?"

"No."

"Where's your car?"

"Over there," she pointed, then turned around, "No . . . there I'm all turned around. I think I was one of the first people here."

She kept her back to the intersection so she didn't have to see it, but the pictures returned anyway and she felt lightheaded, almost giddy with the memory evoking images.

"The man driving that little car . . . I guess he must have hit the bus. He lost his head."

She giggled and then the horror of what had to have happened in these last hours or minutes came back to her. There wasn't any humor here. Why was she giggling? This kind man must think I'm out of my mind. She tried to explain but he didn't seem to notice. As a matter of fact, it looked as if he had removed himself totally from the scene again, acting mechanically as he continued to dab at her face, still holding her. He was muttering.

"I had to hold her again. I had to know she was dead again and hold her. Oh God, will it never go away?" His cry was impassioned, as if he were asking for help.

"You had to hold whom?"

He answered in a monotone, "My daughter. My baby. Mary Katherine. She's dead too." His voice was far away and his eyes were narrowed as if to see clearly, to pierce the darkness and see something in the past.

"She was so tiny. If she had lived, she would have been about the age of that little girl. I had to hold her again. I had to know she was gone." Light tears began to show on his face as they coursed down his cheeks. He took a deep, gut wrenching breath, "Oh God, she's gone. I had put it all away and here it is again," he cried softly. "It's as if she died all over again."

She put her arms around the stranger and held him tightly. The sticky blood on her clothing stuck to his sport coat and slacks as she held him, patting him gently on the back as he cried. She tried to comfort him with all of her being.

His cries turned to sobs. Taking a deep breath, he tried to stop but the crying wouldn't abate. He leaned into her solace and she held, hugged and patted him, giving him as much comfort as she could.

A state patrolman walked over to them.

"Was either of you in this accident?"

The man straightened, and she spoke, "We were among the first on the scene, officer. We're all right, just horrified, dirty and . . ."

"Can I help you ma'am? Can the two of you get back to your car?"

The man had calmed himself, "We'll be all right officer. Just let us catch our breath."

"Sir, before you leave, could you stop by one of the patrol

The Last Magnolia

cars to give us your names?"

"Yes, we'll do that." She felt as if she were the stronger of the two of them and turned to the man, "Are you all right now?"

"All right. Thank you. I'm sorry. So much came back to me. Thank you for your concern."

"The thanks should come from me," she said stepping back to survey him, "I'm afraid I've messed you up pretty badly."

"It's all right, come on, let me help you to your car." Arms around each other's waists, they walked together, nearly as if they had known one another for a long time.

As they reached her car, the man stood back to look at her. "For some reason, you look familiar to me." He stuck out his hand. "My name is John Knowlton."

"John Knowlton? From Spokane?"
Now she could relate to his break-down at the scene of the accident. She knew about this man, knew what a terrible loss he had suffered.

"Yes, have we met?"

"No, not formally," she said. "My name is Susan Marshall. I'm a Spokanite too."

"The plot thickens," John said, "Now I think your name seems familiar. Are you driving to Spokane tonight?"

Susan laughed, "I was, but . . . what time is it?"

He checked his watch, "About 9:30."

"My gosh! I think I got here about five o'clock! No! I'll find a hotel, it's too late to drive home now." She turned, as if to return to her car, then added, "You bet the plot thickens. John Knowlton you and I have been near neighbors for years!"

John was perplexed, he really liked the frank manner this woman exhibited, and appreciated the compassion she had shown

252

when he had allowed himself to go to pieces, but he couldn't seem to put any other association between them together. "OK. Your name is Susan Marshall, but neighbors? I'd remember you!"

The smile on Susan's face turned into a grin as the horror of the scene they had just shared was replaced with an 'almost' familiar face.

"Our neighborhood is really related to business. Do you ever use commercial food services in Spokane?"

"Yeah, Marshalls.....well I'll be darned! Your family owns Marshalls! We're practically next door neighbors at the field!"

"Well John, we finally meet. Barbara Bailey has been trying to get us together for years, did you know that?"

John was shaking his head, "That darned Barb, always trying to fix me up with someone, but if I'd known it was you . . . well, I apologize, but if she mentioned it, I forgot." He looked her over carefully, shaking his head, "What a way to meet," he indicated the scene they had just come from, then seemed to realize with the recall, what they had just been through together.

"Susan, we're both a mess, and it's late. I keep a company apartment to use when I'm in this area on business. It's about a mile from here. I was just on my way there when I came on the accident. From the looks of us, we'd do well to go to the apartment for some serious cleaning up. You don't have to bother with a hotel. After all, we're from the same neighborhood . . . Would that suit you?"

She looked down at herself, bloodstained and disheveled and without a moment's hesitation answered, "It's either that or a motel for me and if you have a place nearby, I'll take you up on it. I can't drive home looking like this and the fact that we practically know one another makes accepting your offer completely legit."

She laughed, "Wait until Barb hears about this! My car's right over there, I could follow you."

"Just come with me, and I'll bring you back to pick it up."

"Oh no! Muffin, my dog is with me, and where I go, Muffin goes . . . may I bring her?"

"Sure you can," he turned her from the gruesome, still eerily lit accident scene. Holding her by the arm he guided her in the direction of the parked cars, "I'll put you in your car and you can wait for me . . . then follow me to the apartment."

As he led her along the grassy incline he said, "A clean up and a good cup of coffee is what we both need."

"Cup of coffee my foot, I'll settle for a strong scotch and soda, and if you don't have any, I do. Right in the trunk of my car. Besides that, I'm famished!"

She stopped short, "That is, if you . . ."

John threw his head back and laughed out loud, this was some woman!

"I can fill your order, and lady, you're right on target . . . scotch . . . food . . . let's go!"

Chapter 29

SUSAN MARSHALL

September 1957

Pacific Northwest

She looked small curled up in the corner of the sofa. Actually she was rather a large woman, not overweight, not thin, but large framed and well proportioned with long legs and arms. Her hands were long and tapered, adding a grace to her words as they helped to project her thoughts. The elongated shape of her head was a compliment to handsome features. Dark brown hair was pulled back casually and hooked behind her ears with the twist of a chignon at the base of her neck.

Sitting next to her was a small perfectly groomed Silky terrier. The dog was nearly, but not quite on her lap, and showed a positively possessive attitude towards her mistress.

Susan cradled a highball glass in her right hand. She looked refreshed, neat and comfortable.

John was more than impressed when she returned from her shower in sleek clean slacks topped by a soft, cashmere sweater in a muted shade of pink that complimented her coloring. His masculinity asserted itself as he took the time to appreciate her well proportioned figure, the smooth way she had of carrying herself and her complete assurance in each of her moves. She was a woman of purpose, he decided.

"Time flies. It's eleven-thirty already," she lifted her empty

255

glass to be refilled, "I usually don't drink this fast, but tonight is a little different. It seems to help wash it all away."

"You know, we've talked on the phone," John mused. I always liked your efficiency and the sound of your voice . . . meant to walk down the flight line to meet you, but there was never enough time. I should have recognized you, but there was so much happening at the accident, so much horror. I just didn't connect.

Taking another sip from her drink Susan watched him over the rim of her glass, "You know, Barb's right, I do like you."

"If Barb mentioned you, I'm sorry to say, I don't remember," he shook his head in wonder.

"I'm sure she mentioned me, she probably said something like, 'John, I have this old maid friend I think you could do a little life-brightening for.' That's probably what she said."

This woman is great company he thought, too bad they had missed one another for so long.

"I'm not going to qualify the old maid statement. You don't look like an old maid to me, but that's not important right now. Aren't you hungry?"

"Boy am I . . . and my dog! My gosh, I have her food in the trunk of the car. I didn't even think about her," she jumped up from the sofa, "I'll run down for it. Do you suppose you could lend me a dish?"

"I think a dish is just about all there is here. I don't keep food in the apartment, I seldom eat here. It's just a stopping off place between the Portland and Spokane offices. Go ahead, get your dog food while I figure out something brilliant for dinner while you're gone."

Muffin's tail wagged as she tackled the kibbled dog food and

The Last Magnolia

John and Susan watched with amusement.

"We could go out for dinner . . . Johnny's Dock is close, but it's probably closing by now. I'm not sure what we can find open this late during the week."

"Let's not even to think about going out, we've had a tough night and it's too late," she looked apologetic.

John picked up a light raincoat, "You're a gal after my own heart ma'am. There's an all- night diner down the road a bit, and if hamburgers will solve your famine problem, I'll be on my way."

"Pick up some French fries too. Muffin and I will wait here."

Susan was thirty-five years old. She'd graduated from the University of Washington and entered the family catering concern in Spokane. When airline service became popular, the feeding of passengers offered a new opportunity for them. Susan and her brother developed a freeze-quick procedure that had been accepted and put into use by the small feeder airlines that served the Pacific Northwest. The Marshalls had expanded to contract for all catering services, and now provided most of the in-flight food used for trips in and out of Spokane, Seattle, Tacoma, Portland, Missoula, Kalispell and eastern Montana as far east as Minneapolis. Their central dispensing department was still located in Spokane, but SEATAC Airport in Seattle was growing by leaps and bounds and Susan found herself involved in a rapidly growing expansion at that location.

As the Marshall concern had branched into other cities with yet more catering services, Susan had assumed the leadership of the northwestern branch and now functioned as its corporate head.

She came from a large family and her life revolved around them and the business. Whenever she felt the need for company, she called someone in Spokane who was related to her and there was instant entertainment.

There had been one long affair with a banking official. A man she thought she loved. She ended the liaison when she discovered he had been seeing other women. Deciding that she was a one-man woman, she didn't look further for a mate. However, she assured her family, if ever a man came along who shared her feelings of morality then perhaps she would think about marrying. Until then she was content with her life as it was.

Muffin was a constant companion. The dog traveled in Susan's private plane and all the car trips. The dog had special quarters in the Spokane office, and her presence was accepted by all, employees and family alike, as, "Susan's idiosyncrasy."

The waste of extra driving time irked Susan. She loved her small MG, but preferred it for local use only. The rest of her traveling, and there was a lot of it, was done in her private plane, a yellow Beechcraft Bonanza. She was an excellent pilot, and had flown for ten years, logging many hours with capability. Only when the weather forecast was dangerous for flying, as it had been for this trip, did she travel by car.

"Hey, I hope these hamburgers are still warm, I wouldn't want to serve the caterer anything shoddy."

"It looks as if you've brought enough for six of us."

They ate voraciously and, when the meal was finished, Susan cleared away papers and trash.

"You could spend the night here you know, Susan."

She turned quickly to look at him and appraise the invitation. He was a gentleman. She felt she didn't have to worry about a thing.

"If that sofa makes into a bed, I'm going to take you up on

the invitation. I'm exhausted, and tomorrow I can deal with getting to Spokane."

"You're the guest, so you take the bedroom, I'll sleep out here."

"That's fine, but there's one thing I hope you understand. Muffin shares a bed with me."

"Well that just proves my point, if you let a dog set one foot in the door, it's bound to be in bed with you." John's slow grin teased her, "Darned good protection if you ask me!"

Susan laughed, it was so easy to be with this man.

"You know, I haven't had a dog since I was a kid, but from the looks of Muffin, canine styles have changed. That's the damnedest looking dog I've ever seen. Her hair looks like a grass skirt and when she walks you'd swear she originated in Hawaii and was doing the hula."

"Don't you make fun of her! Susan laughed and bent to pick up the little bundle of fur, "To be my friend is to be Muffin's friend. If she wants to do the hula, that's just fine, just as long as she does it well." She picked up her overnight bag.

"Night John, we'll see you in the morning, and I'll buy your breakfast."

Chapter 30

SUSAN AND JOHN

Spokane

October 1957

She wasn't kidding when she said she lived on the top of a building John thought as he climbed the third flight of stairs. What kind of charm could a place that took so long to reach hold, he wondered?

The staircase narrowed and his steps slowed. Reaching the top, he found himself in a narrow, dead-ended hallway that led to only one door. It was beautiful. Large, heavy and framed ornately by woodwork that curled with the carved expertise of an artisan from another generation. The wood was probably oak and comprising four panels that were duplicated. It was the sort of barrier you would expect to find outside an old Victorian mansion.

It would be interesting to know the history of this building, he thought as he checked for some evidence that this was indeed the door to Susan's apartment. Then he spotted her card above a square, antiquated bell that had to be twisted to ring.

On the second twist of the bell, the door opened and Susan stood with the light of the room behind her. She was wearing a soft blue dress scooped deeply at the neck, cinched in at the waist to fall into gentle soft pleats that tamed the full skirt. Her elegant dark hair was twisted in its usual knot at the base of her neck and she was stunning.

Damn! She's a good-looking woman.

"John!" She put her hand out to greet him and her smile let him know he was welcome. "You're early."

"If you're not ready for me, I'll sit on these little steps here and wait for you to give me the signal. I'd have to sit here because I don't think I have the energy to walk up again."

Her low spontaneous laugh warmed him, and she stepped aside to hold the door open.

"Don't be silly. I'm ready and anxious to show off my apartment."

He thrust a small bouquet toward her.

"My Aunt Katie always told me that daisies were the best flowers to give because they last longer than any other cut flower," he grinned, "and Miss Marshall, during the time we've known one another, I've come to the conclusion that this relationship should last a long time. From here on, it's daisies for you from me."

She accepted the bunch of yellow-centered flowers and held them to her face.

"Thanks, I'm glad we're finally getting together for dinner at my house."

"I'm expecting the best you know. You have a reputation to live up to."

The moment he stepped across the threshold, the charm of her home overwhelmed him.

They stood on a side balcony that squared and surrounded the entire apartment. The balcony was surrounded by a rail of the same dark oak with the identical intricacies in carved work that had framed the door. To their right, a flight of about ten steps led

261

down to the sunken portion of the room below. On the level where they stood were three doors. Carved and slightly open, he decided they must be bedrooms and a bath.

The walls of the entire balcony were filled with paintings, water colors, etchings, and framed art works hung in a bright happy profusion of colors and shapes. Indirect lighting illuminated the works of art and, at the same time, created shadows to add yet another level for visual pleasure.

Susan led him down the stairs and he noted the antique furniture conversationally grouped on a thick, white oriental rug. French, he guessed, as he thought back to some of the pieces in the Graydon home.

"This is a stunning room." She smiled and he continued to turn, to take in the room that was obviously designed for the warmth of welcome and total comfort.

Down here, on what seemed to be the living level, the outer walls were soft white. Paintings of obvious worth had been placed to add complimentary color. Soft lemon fabric that covered chairs, settees and other furniture in groupings, was enhanced by lighting achieved with free-standing torchieres arranged to keep the room tinted in soft light. The total effect was regal yet charming.

Louvered white swinging doors lead, he assumed, to a kitchen. Against the main wall, near the steps, was a high credenza, nearly all of glass. The interior of this cabinet was illuminated softly to show strategically placed pieces of sparkling crystal.

A small table, set for formal dining for two, was to the right of the steps.

"Now I can appreciate what can be done with one of these

old square stucco buildings," he said with admiration, "This is one of the most elegant homes I've ever been in. Someday I'll tell you about the Graydon home. It was the other truly grand home in my experience. But let me assure you, you've achieved the same beauty as that lovely old Charleston mansion has right here in your bird's-nest in Spokane."

He stepped away from her and gave her a mock salute. "You've done a fantastic job."

"My gosh John. I knew I liked it, and had a wonderful time doing it, but until you stepped in, with your gift for flattery, I didn't know how much."

"What's below on the other two levels?"

"When I bought the property, I decided I simply had to live up here in, my bird's-nest, so I had two apartments done below. They're large and I don't have any trouble keeping the original tenants."

She led him to one of the comfortable living room chairs and turned toward the kitchen.

"There you go. You get me in a beautiful spot and then you take off. I thought you said you were ready for me to arrive."

"For your information, I'm headed for a vase for the daisies. They may be as long lasting as your Aunt Katie says, but they aren't going to last long without some water."

When Susan pushed the kitchen doors open, Muffin ran through them quickly, suddenly free to be with the company. Curiosity and a sharp nose led her to John's feet and she came to a skidding stop just an inch short of hitting the toe of his shoe. She sniffed carefully, then with a little wiggle, arranged her richly lustrous hula skirt and sat gazing up at him expectantly, her little cowlick held in a pony tail by a yellow ribbon.

The Last Magnolia

"Hi Muffin, I'm John, remember me?"

The dog shivered expectantly, never taking her eyes from him, watching as if she wanted to have a conversation.

"If you invite her, she'll sit on your lap."

Susan settled the daisies on a small table, and sat opposite John.

He patted his leg, "OK Muffin, come on up." The silky dog jumped and settled herself comfortably.

Both he and Susan started talking at the same time, stopped, laughed and pointed each to the other, "You first."

"Seeing Barb and meeting Hank and Grace and Er and their families was so nice, John. I'm sorry we haven't been able to get together sooner."

He had tried many times during the past weeks to reach her, and it bothered him that she was unavailable. He wanted to see more of her and the fact that she wasn't around all of the time irked him.

"We'll do it again Susan. The bunch of us get together often and you fit in nicely."

"Hey! I'm neglecting my duties as a hostess. The bar's over there and, if you don't mind, I'll let you do the honors."

"Will you be in town next week? I picked up tickets for one of the shows coming in and I'd like to take you to dinner as well."

"As far as I can remember, I'll be here all week."

Smiling, he pulled the tickets from his pocket, "Wednesday, OK?"

"Sounds great."

Dinner over, they found they'd covered lots of common ground. Their enjoyment of one another was evident as their conversation and easy banter flew from one subject to another.

"I'm driving up to my cabin in Montana this weekend to close it for the winter. Want to come with me? Could you give me a weekend?"

Slowly she sipped her liqueur and her easygoing attitude changed rapidly. She was suddenly tense, almost cool as she answered quickly with an expression that was businesslike, "Sorry John, my weekend's filled. Your little trip sounds nice, but I'll take a rain check."

Boy! That was a putdown if he'd ever heard one. She was so crisp and efficient, it was as if she were wrapping up a business deal so she could get him out of the way as quickly as possible. The gracious charm she displayed could turn cold quickly and disappear totally.

He suddenly realized she had interpreted his invitation the wrong way, and began to appreciate her morality.

"Hey, wait a minute. I didn't mean" . . . Look Susan, Barb and Hank are coming along with the boys. "It's not just you and I." He felt like a clumsy high school boy. "I told you the first time we met that I didn't want to risk impressing you with the fact that I could be a Don Juan."

She relaxed with a smile and laughed, "I've been approached in so many ways . . . you have no idea! When you put your invitation on the line, I thought I'd made a mistake about you . . . no more Mr. Nice Guy from just down the flight line. If you were making a long pass, I wasn't about to catch it." She got up to refresh his drink. "You know John, I've been around a few years and, if you hadn't noticed, I'm too old to say, 'I'm not that kind of a girl', so I usually just toss the passes back, lightly and finally."

He lifted himself out of his chair and came to sit beside her on the sofa.

265

The Last Magnolia

"Mark up one mistake up for me. I'm sorry. I'm sure glad I didn't have to catch a return pass." Feeling anxious about this relationship, he knew he liked Susan, and wanted to know her better. And he knew he would have to be careful not to offend her, but was that a good beginning for a relationship? He had been stung too many times to jump into anything and now he reassessed his feelings for her.

She watched him closely. He seemed uncharacteristically anxious. About their relationship maybe? She hoped so. Here was a man, not a boy. A successful man with whom she could laugh, and perhaps there could be more. She hoped so and wanted to know him better.

"We need to get to know one another John, and if the invitation to the cabin with Barb and Hank is still open, maybe that would be a good way to start."

His heart jumped. My God, I'm like a kid. She's affecting me differently than any woman. "I'll pick you up Saturday morning with Barb, Hank and the boys. Dress warmly and be prepared for beautiful scenery and a lively weekend with those kids."

"I'll be ready."

"Now," he stood, as if to stretch, "how long has it been since you took a drive up to the Rimrock to look over the top of the city?"

"Ages and ages, but you know, High Drive is a spectacular view too, and that's just a short walk from here. I used to drive up there with my boyfriends and smooch a little," she threw him a little sidelong glance and sang, "My Johnnie and I remember still, the night we spent on the Spokane hill . . ."

He grinned, "The proper Miss Marshall! I was under the

266

impression, after the conversation of a few minutes ago, that you didn't do things like that."

She's just as warm as I knew she would be, he thought, and so much fun.

"Come on," she laughed, heading toward a closet, "let's walk some of this food off and breathe in some of the good crisp air. It's just around the corner and up the hill."

"My God another hill after all these steps? You're going to kill me, woman!"

The lights of the city were clear in the chilly fall air. Main streets were easily identified by name from their vantage point near a large rock at the edge of the cliff. The lights of cars below seemed to be the size of pinpoints as they moved in all directions, up Washington Street, down Division, across Riverside and over the Monroe Street Bridge to the north side of town.

They were a handsome couple, tall, with equal strides and they seemed perfectly matched as they held hands and walked along the drive, stopping occasionally to point out another familiar landmark in the view that stretched out below them.

The only incongruity in the picture they projected was the small, very feminine terrier held on a leash by the man. She skirted along with them, so tiny it seemed she was more suited to people who were smaller in stature.

There didn't seem to be any need for constant talk between Susan and John. The mutual enjoyment of being together was all each of them needed.

The small dog tugged at the leash and they stopped occasionally to let her sniff at a bush along the walk.

"Do you know what a Natatorium is?"

"Sure, it's an amusement park over on the north side of

town."

Susan hung her coat back in the closet,

"Right and wrong. A natatorium is a swimming pool, as well as our biggest fun place here in town."

"Does the park have a big swimming pool?"

"I don't know. I've been going there all of my life, even when I was a teenager. That's where the big bands played. We tried to hear all the music, dance to all of the wonderful band leaders, Goodman, James . . . all of them. Really though, I don't know if there's a swimming pool there or not. Tell you what John, before the Nat closes, if it hasn't already, let's go. Have you ever been there?"

"Nope. That's for kids."

"Aw come on John. Let's be kids. I'll treat you to the best Pronto Pup you've ever tasted."

"Pronto Pup? What's that? I thought this little silky character called Muffin was a pretty prompt puppy."

"Oh, come on. You'll see!" She began to brighten and warm up to her subject and John loved the sparkle in her eyes, and her natural happiness. She made him feel warm, included and a part of her life. He'd never had an experience with a woman like this before.

"We'll ride the Jack Rabbit, and oh, John, wait until you see the merry-go-round. It's probably the most beautiful one in the world. Will you ride the merry-go round with me, and help me catch the brass ring?"

John was enchanted. She was like a young girl, all the happiness of good memories showing on her slightly flushed face. He pulled her to him and unexpectedly held her tightly as he kissed her.

Her response was instant, and they held each other warmly as the kiss lingered, as they explored each other and their bodies moved against each other. Then they parted.

"What was that for?" She was a little short of breath.

"That my dear proper Miss Marshall was for you to hang onto until our next date which will be at Natatorium Park. I'll go. I'll ride on anything you want me to ride on. I'll feel like a fool, but I'll do it, because, for some reason you are beginning to hold some sort of power over me. Don't get overconfident but you know, where I grew up we didn't have merry- go-rounds, or Big Bands, or even Pronto Pups. So keep telling me about them, and show me . . . I think I'm going to like it. All of it. And I know I like you."

"The feeling is mutual . . . but, oh you're going to love the park. Just wait. I'll even get a brass ring for you!"

****

"John, what in hell are you waiting for?"

Hank was on the other end of the line, his voice raised, "Barb and I think you've finally found the right woman, and you can't tell me you don't feel the same way."

John grinned into the mouthpiece. Hank was right, but he wouldn't let him get a word in edgewise.

"You two are so damned compatible. Lord knows, you've become sort of a thing in town. You know when the Spokane matrons start inviting the two of you together to the social events, you darned well have been marked and filed as a couple."

The weeks had grown into months and Susan and John were together as much as their time would allow. Their relationship was warm and mature and they had begun to include themselves in each other's worlds exclusively. They were in love.

The Last Magnolia

Hank stopped talking long enough for John to get in a word.

"I'm gun shy, you know that Hank. For that matter, so is Susan." He rubbed the stubble of a five o'clock beard on his chin, "I haven't had the pleasure of a long courtship before. Let me take my time and enjoy it."

"Well, just a piece of advice from old Hank here, don't let this one get away."

They got back to business discussions and finally John was able to hang up. Continuing to rub his chin he thought, I'm probably in love for the first time in my life. Susan was something like he had never known before.

During the past fall and through the cold winter they had been together. The things they had done alone, before they met, they did as a couple now and their relationship had become nearly exclusive. They were companions. They learned from one another, laughed together and there was affection between the two of them, but there was a problem.

A physical relationship seemed impossible. He wanted her, but her attitude kept him from making anything more than the lightest of proposals. She really had been burned and was so overly careful that the rejection was beginning to disturb him. She was too damned careful and he didn't want to wait any longer. Then again, he had been married to one frigid woman. He didn't ever want to have that experience again.

Well, spring is here. There are new things we can do together. Maybe warm weather will heat things up a bit. He reached for the telephone and dialed her number.

When she came on the line he offered his invitation, "Tomorrow's the opening day of fishing, and if we start early, we might pull some nice ones out of Williams Lake. Are you on?"

270

"How early?"

"Four a.m."

"Oh my God." Then with mock resignation, "OK John, I'll bring the lunch, you make the coffee."

When they had finished their arrangements for the early morning trip, he hung up and paced the floor. There's only one way to complete this relationship. She has to be my wife. As he left his office, fierce determination was written on his face.

****

"Set the hook!" He shut off the outboard motor, "Hold up the tip of your rod!"

"OK. OK." She was cranking the reel as fast as she could, and his voice was getting louder with each command.

"Don't let the line go slack!" He stayed in a crouch, but moved toward her, "Reel in, don't stop, keep on reeling!"

She was handling the light rod as well as she could.

"Damn it John, shut up!"

She continued to turn the crank and her concentration stopped her from realizing she'd spoken sharply to him.

"I can't turn it anymore. Look, he's pulling the line right out of the reel."

"You can do it, let him go a little," John lowered his voice as if whispering would catch the fish faster.

"There! Start to pull him in again. Keep the tip of that rod up!"

She kept reeling, the line slipped a little, out toward the very large fish that was bouncing the tip of the rod.

Continuing to speak softly he said, "That's it honey. Pull him back. All right, lower your rod, pull!" His excitement increased and so did his voice.

271

"John, I can't do this . . . you take it."

"Yes you can!"

They were shouting at one another now, and it was a happy noise.

"Go on, pull him in!"

"I'm going to fall out of this boat!"

"No you won't, play him. Play him darling. Keep a taut line, that's it. Pull him in!"

She was standing in the boat now,

"John, he's going to get away. Get the net!"

The line was coming in fast now, as the monster on the end rested before its last effort to rid itself of the irritating hook in its mouth.

John reached down for the small hand net, expecting to have her pull in a trout about a pound or so. The fish broke water.

"Oh John, he's huge!"

She swung the pole around, the fish rose out of the water doing a little tail-walk. The sun shone on its twisting body and shots of silver flashed from its scales. The drops of water shaking from the silver fish reflected to create a momentary picture of glitter. Susan swung her rod, horsing the big fish into the boat. The fish flew in and with a wet resounding smack, hit John in the face. He rolled back in shock to the deck and the fish pounded and flopped on his chest.

Still holding the rod in her hand, Susan shouted with laughter.

He grabbed the line and held it firm as he got to his knees and then gave the fish two smart whacks on the head with a heavy stick. The fish stilled, to lie on the bottom of the boat.

Muffin, not at all happy with her boat ride, stirred herself to wiggle over for a sniff and satisfied that this was not a competitor, with a look of disdain, returned to her blanket in the prow.

John was roaring with laughter.

"You! You're some fisherman! You've caught the biggest fish of the day, and then you add insult to injury by hitting me in the face with it."

Susan was doubled up in the back of the boat, tears ran down her face and she gasped through the laughter,

"Oh John you looked so funny. So surprised."

Carefully he lifted himself to his knees and moved toward her. Still on his knees when he reached her, he put his arms around her.

"You get a kiss for the best fish."

He tried to brush her lips with his, but suddenly she started to laugh again, then stopped, getting herself under control.

"OK, now," she leaned toward him, offering her face and her lips for a kiss and then shuddered again into peals of laughter. Reaching out, she put her arms around his neck.

"Darling, this is the best day I can remember."

He kissed her lightly, but her arms tightened, she held him to her, pressing her body tightly into his.

"John, oh John."

The embrace was more than they or the boat could handle, so they parted.

Breathlessly she said, "Ask me to go to the mountains again."

He held her away from him, his voice breathless with passion too.

"What?"

"Ask me John. Ask me to come to the mountains. To the cabin. And don't ask Barb and Hank." She pushed herself into his body. He reached down to kiss her and her response was instantaneous. Frigid? He didn't think so.

"The only way you're going to come to that cabin is," she pulled away from him as if he were rejecting her and he pulled her back, roughly against his chest, "Let me finish. The only way you're coming to that cabin with me, and without the Baileys, is as Mrs. John Knowlton. Will you marry me?"

"When?"

"My God, you've held me at your arms length for so long . . . Now!"

"Yes. Let's go. Hurry!"

****

A squirrel hit the high-pitched metal roof and thundered across it. The sound was more elephant-like. It was cold and the sheets smelled faintly of musty pine.

There were gentle breezes in the top of the pine trees, nearly like a song, and that quiet harmony other than the recent activity of the squirrel on the roof was the only sound.

He rolled to his side, toward her. She began to stir, and he reached up and gently pushed the hair from her face, then lifted himself up on one elbow to watch as she wakened slowly.

"Good morning, Mrs. Knowlton."

Her arms came up from under the blankets. They stretched toward the head of the bed.

"Good morning my darling, I love you."

"Why did we wait so long?"

"It had to be just right. It had to be . . . "she smiled, remembering, "and it was!"

She snuggled her arms and shoulders back under the covers, "It's so cold!"

He pulled her to him.

"Do you want me to get you some pajamas? It's awfully early to be up here in the mountains."

"No, I want to feel all of you. Oh my darling, you're so gentle, so loving. I'm glad we waited. Glad and a little sad. We're so good together, we should have been doing this since the day we met. I thought we would be good together and now we both know. We're compatible in every way."

There was a small movement on Susan's side of the bed as Muffin made an attempt to get closer to her mistress.

"See, even Muffin likes the extra person in bed with her."

"My God, who'd ever have thought I'd share my wedding night with a dancing hula dog?"

"What do you suppose that Justice of the Peace thought when we showed up in fishing clothes with only Muffin for a witness?"

"Boy, talk about informal," John said, "I really don't think he was any more shocked than the jeweler when we walked in paid the price he asked for your ring."

"Oh John, it's so beautiful, I hope we didn't pay too much for it."

"Not for you. Not for us. The sky's the limit. I like it as much as you do."

"The only things we missed were the daisies."

"I'll see to it that you have daisies every day of your life from now on."

"Better wait for the first ones to fade."

"Well," John chuckled, "we probably had one of the most informal weddings anyone has ever had in the Black Bear Hotel in Thompson Falls, Montana. It's a good thing there's no waiting period for a license in Montana, if there had been, you'd have been a fallen woman."

"It's a good thing we got to the court house before it closed!" She pulled herself closer to him, "I don't care. Formal, informal, license, anything. I have just what I want. Do you have any idea how long I have wanted you?"

"Hey wife, you only had to say the word, the feeling was mutual."

With her closeness, he could feel every curve of her body, and he bent to kiss her breasts.

"I think you're a naughty lady . . . now what is it you're getting so close to me for, what is it you want here ma'am?" He stopped, was quiet and still for a moment, deep in serious thought.

"No, Susan, you aren't naughty. You are the most passionate woman, the most complete woman I have ever known."

"I've wanted you for so long. Am I really naughty? Am I bad?"

"You're wonderful . . . just a little slow to pick up on that want, honey . . . I thought we'd never get together. I had almost decided you were frigid, and boy I'm glad I hung around."

He began to caress the inside of her legs.

"I want you. Now." Her words were demanding, and then, "Oh please darling, come to me."

Without any further foreplay he entered her, and the tenderness, the pressure, the beginnings of knives that shot between them built as if a symphony of horns were blending. Up, on...the brassy pitch screamed, 'make it last, stay with me, make me feel more and more . . . It was as if they had been making love only to each other, as if they had been rehearsing their own private music all their lives.

The Last Magnolia

Their rhythm became slower, andante. The tones muted, then again the pace accelerated to allegretto as it pressed upwards, raising the strains of their composition to an even higher plane. With the horns their bodies rose and fell, met the crescendo, then dropped to the deeper mellow tones of a cello. Their timing was perfect, and the pressure climbed from the pianissimo of a soft, low-toned, subdued coronet to the forte of loud brassy trumpets setting mutual unison of play. They were their own conductors and their rhythm continued to fluctuate, becoming longer, smoother, as they were one note, rocking upwards toward the climax of their musical union. Up . . . up. . . ! Cymbals silenced the horns with a clanging, shocking resonance and the deafening crash punctuated the totality of their composed act as they collapsed into clutching. Breathing. Catching. Releasing.

"John, I love you. Oh my John."

Their music had died momentarily, but the cherished concert memories were still with them as they lay breathless, held in each other's arms.

"You are mine. You are the first, the last. Oh Sue, I've needed you for so many years."

All of his grief, fear, hate and loss were gone. This woman who lay exhausted from their mutual act of love had filled his past months, and he could hardly believe she was his for the rest of their lives.

He touched her gently,

"How can I thank you for being you? For being mine?"

"Just hold me my dear, keep me."

They slept.

Sunshine flooded the small flag-stoned patio where they sat, dressed in warm clothing, drinking their coffee. The peaceful quiet was shattered by an occasional squawk from a mountain Jay. Spectacular pines growing from a needled forest floor completely surrounded them in their retreat. The only evidence of the outside world was their car parked in the driveway. Otherwise they were alone. There was no telephone, no one knew where they were. This honeymoon filled, as it should, only their needs.

"I'd really like to continue with my business."

He took a sip of the hot coffee. "If you want that, then you should have it, but I'd like to do some traveling. You have to come to Charleston with me. I don't want to go anywhere without you."

"Nor me without you. I'll build the office staff. My secretary knows enough about the business to handle things if I'm away."

"Why don't you give her a share of the corporation? Make her the manager and then you'll have the freedom you need, and she'll have owner-incentive to insure good management."

She grinned at him,

"There you go, showing off. Now I know why you were such a fast-rising executive." She looked at him with the pride of ownership, ownership that had occurred just the night before. Hers was a possession that was firmly cemented for their lives together.

The two young executives, now acting toward the singular goal of love and a good marriage, plotted their future.

Chapter 31

FAMILY

Spokane

October 1959

She tried to quiet him, but he was laughing so hard as they left the front porch and headed for their car she was afraid her family would think he was laughing at them. They stepped down into autumn's fallen leaves, and the crisp crackle of their feet as they walked to their car matched the crispness of the fall air.

"You know, I've never known a family like yours before." Susan's large happy family had become a pleasant addition to their marriage. Their acceptance of John as one of them was another good part of their lives together.

He kept laughing,

"Your father keeps telling me the only reason he's glad to have me for another son is that he thought for sure he had an old maid on his hands."

Susan turned to her husband with a look of disgust tinged with good-natured amusement.

"That old monster," she laughed, "for years he'd dig up some old crony's son or nephew or grandson for me to look over. Why he held open market on me, his own daughter!"

Holding the car door open for her, John watched as she slid into the passenger seat.

"If he only knew how lucky I feel after these two years of

marriage to that old maid daughter of his," he reached over and kissed her lightly, "he'd know his worries are over. You're set for life my dear . . . with me!"

She returned his kiss, "John, get yourself over around to the other side of this car and stop lolly-gagging," she patted him affectionately, "come on honey, let's go home. Tomorrow's going to be a busy day if I'm going to get to the office in Tacoma and back for the bon voyage party."

John was still on the subject of the Marshall family and he chuckled, "So help me," he started the car, "there's not a family anywhere in this world like yours. Are you sure you don't want me to go with you? The forecast looks good, but there can always be an unexpected early storm in the Cascades."

"You said yourself that you have lots to wrap up. I'll spin right over. If I leave early," she slid over closer to him on the front seat of the car, "I can be there before noon and the business with Bob can be cleared up in a couple of hours. I'm giving him Power of Attorney so he can complete the necessary work on the merger while we're gone. Then I'll head right back for home."

She assumed what John called her "organizing" look and began to tick off items of concern.

"We have our reservations for the day after tomorrow, right? Let's see, you've taken care of the passports and visas, the bags are nearly packed, Annie can finish that , and . . . who's going to take us to the plane?"

"Hank and Barb are taking us to Geiger because they insist they have to give us a proper champagne sendoff."

She rested her hand on his knee, "Just think. You and me. You showing me parts of Great Britain that you knew and then the two of us learning about Europe together. Three months to tour. I can't believe it. Can we really be completely free from all of our business for three months?"

"By golly, we did it honey. As sure as I'm driving this car, all's well. The Knowltons are on the way to their first European trip." He grinned with pride, "Who would ever have thought that John Knowlton, lately of Harper, Nebraska, would be leaving with his handsome, gorgeous, beloved," a lump came into his throat and he swallowed it, "wife of two years for a trip on the continent?" He turned the car onto East Sprague Avenue, "We've made it babe."

"Oh come on John, you'd made it before we ever met."

"Not in happiness, my love. Not in happiness."

As they traveled through the night-lit streets, she kept making verbal lists.

"How about Muffin? Do you really think Barb and the boys will give her the love she needs?"

"Probably more than she'll be able to stand. Her hula skirt might be dirty when we get back, ranch life being what it is, but we'll take care of that."

"If it's all right, I guess we'll take her out there when we go for the party tomorrow night. Let's see, Barb said nine o'clock would be early enough. I guess it's going to be a pretty big sendoff. More than just the folks and Grace and Er. They're really going all out for us, did you know that?"

Susan yawned, "I'm tired. I hope I can get back tomorrow in time to catch a little nap before our party."

"You've been tired a lot lately. You're feeling OK, aren't you? The overseas shots didn't take too much out of you, did they?"

"Oh now," her voice drifted and they rode in silence as the street lights began to be spaced themselves further apart as the city was left behind.

She laid her head on his shoulder to doze, but came awake as they turned through the gates to go up the long winding drive. She nuzzled closer to him.

"I have a little surprise for you. No, I guess you could call it a big surprise."

He laughed, "Now what did you buy to add to my traveling wardrobe, my little fashion coordinator? At the rate you've been buying, we're going to be overweight in the baggage department with my clothes alone."

"No, nothing like that, but you know, it's a good thing we're going now. Good that we'll be back in three months," she tilted her head provocatively, "home for Christmas. I'll be growing by that time."

He slowed to take the last curve before the garage, "What do you mean, growing? Is Marshalls planning more expansion?"

"No, but Knowltons are. I'm going to have a baby."

The words were calm, nearly whispered, but he slammed on the brakes as if she had screamed them at him. The car came to a jarring stop and the engine died.

"A baby!" He was pushed back against the seat by the sudden stop, and he simply rested there, "My God Sue! We're too old!"

"Come on, old man, we're still in our thirties and we're going to have a baby!" She threw her arms around his neck. "Just think, our baby!"

Choked with emotion, he held her closely. Memories flooded back and he clutched her to him more tightly.

"Are you all right? It's all right for you to make this trip isn't it?"

The Last Magnolia

She hugged him, a short happy hug.

"I'm perfect, and in answer to your other question, yes. I have this wonderful Doctor who assures me that I am a healthy house for this infant to grow in and you and I are going to have a perfect baby." She put her head on his shoulder.

"You know darling," her words were reflective, "everything about our marriage has been so good. Each time we've made love, I've wanted to say, thank you. We've always seemed so complete, so wonderful together."

"It's me who should say thanks over and over . . ."

"No, let me finish. Now I feel, as a result of those many complete unions, that I can say, thank you the way God created me to. Do I make sense?"

"Yes, oh yes."

His mind leapt ahead, but she kept talking, "God let me love you, he gave us a complete love and then he added a special privilege by letting me carry our baby." She was crying now, happily.

"Thank you John. Thank you God."

He held her.

"A baby. Another chance. Another little girl."

She pulled away from him,

"No my dear, you and I aren't going to have a girl. Not this time. I can tell you right now, we're going to have a fine healthy baby boy. Any man who enjoys doing all the manly things you do needs a son to teach, and I'm going to give you that son. Forget about girls honey, you and I are going to produce boys!"

"What do you mean, boys?"

"You bet your life old man. I mean we've gotten this thing turned on, we seem to mate like jack rabbits, and now we're going to do our share toward finishing Barb and Hank's baseball team." She hugged him to her again, "Oh John," her voice was soft and loving, "you and I. I really thought we had everything, but now we, the two of us have added the ultimate in coupling, a child! I love you, darling."

"I love you. You've given me so much. You. Your fine, happy family. Your love. I have so much. How can there be more? How can I ever begin to repay you for this? Oh my love . . . but if you're going to keep it turned on, couldn't we maybe have just one girl?"

She laughed, "Never satisfied are you? Of course my dear . . . we're going to have a family! A family for you and for us John. What a fortunate meeting ours was."

She straightened, moving his head from her shoulder, "Now let's drive into the garage, park this car and go to bed."

As they walked into the house John said thoughtfully, "You know honey, Hank's flying over to Tacoma tomorrow. Why don't you ride with him? He's just there for the day. I'd feel better if you came back with him."

"I've been flying between here and our little drop point for more years than you have. Don't worry. I'll be fine." She put her coat on the back of a chair and walked across the living room, "Don't worry, if there's any trouble, it's nice to know Hank will be there, but I don't anticipate a problem. I'll call you when I get there, and I'll call you just before I leave to fly back home."

"I'll wait for you at the hanger."

"All right! Come to bed!"

John just shook his head. Her stubbornness was more than he cared to deal with this late at night.

284

Chapter 32

YELLOWBIRD

Tacoma, Washington

October 1959

She checked her watch. It was just three o'clock, so her timing was perfect.

"Muffin, it looks as if you and I are going to get that little nap before the party after all." she looked at the little ball of silky fur curled up in the seat next to her. "We'll be in Spokane in a couple of hours."

Her preflight checks were all perfect, and now she sat at the end of the short runway at Valley Field, near Tacoma in her private plane.

She followed the safety rule of thumb that all cautious, experienced pilots use, as she did a second pre-take-off check.

Fuel selector, on main. Flaps, one quarter. Prop, high RPM. Mixture, rich. Carburetor heat, off. Throttle friction, off. OK, ready to go.

Achieving a three hundred and sixty degree turn to ensure that the runway was clear of any incoming traffic, Susan aligned her plane with the runway, pushed the throttle forward to wide open and set the friction lock.

Seconds later the bright yellow Beechcraft Bonanza, with its butterfly tail, broke ground.

The gears retracted, and a severe vibration shook the aircraft.

285

The door to the plane flew open.

A massive pull of suction jerked at Muffin, and the little dog, as if she were going to get off of the plane, jumped from her seat to head out the door.

"Muffin!"

With one hand still on her control wheel, Susan turned to the right, throwing her right arm with her entire body, to catch the dog.

The plane's engine stopped. At a rapid descent, it crashed through high power lines beyond the runway. Fire shot from the left wing, and the little plane dug into the green carpet of the grassy valley.

All that was left of the yellow bird was the scorched, flared yellow butterfly tail.

Chapter 33

JOHN

Spokane

October 1959

He was the only one remaining in the small old trailer left over from the early business days of Knowlton Air Service. They had retained this first set of quarters for the company as a maintenance office after they moved the main offices into town John felt closer to the Air Service activity here than in the posh center city offices.

Sitting at his desk, he watched the lights play on the wet runway. Rain had come unexpectedly about four o'clock. The weather man hadn't seen it in his forecast, so John assumed it was just a local storm.

He looked at the clock. It was nearly five-thirty; Susan should be in any time now. She had called just before taking off and planned to be in between five and six. Any of the planes taxiing up to the hanger could be hers, and when she got here the two of them could be on their way.

He thought of the child. Susan's child excited him more than anything that happened to him since they were married. Finally, complete happiness was his. It was hard to fathom after so many years of hurt and heartache.

Susan had taught him to laugh all over again, and to trust. She had proven that true love could and did exist. With her he had gained stability. Togetherness was theirs, as was mutuality. This was the relationship he had been seeking since he was ten years old.

Susan had made him deal with his past. At her insistence, he had hired someone to find his mother. He hadn't wanted to deal with it, but she forced the issue and when, after many months, the agency they hired called with news of Mildred, he felt threatened, yet released to some extent.

His sister Donna was married, living in San Luis Obispo, California, and it was she who was able to tell Susan and John about his mother's life.

After going through a divorce, and taking the two youngest children, Mildred had gone with her new husband Fred, to California. Her life had been good. They settled permanently and lived comfortably. Her husband died several years ago and then John's brother, who had been a baby when Mildred left him, was killed in a highway crash.

Donna explained that the purpose for living seemed to go out of their mother at that time. Stricken with a massive stroke, she was confined to a nursing home, unable to move, speak or realize her surroundings.

John and Susan visited California and he renewed his relationship with his sister and visited his mother. She was as Donna had described. John knew he wanted to provide the best care for her. It was then he felt he had come almost full circle. He allowed other memories from his tragedy-ridden life to recede as his love for Susan filled his new life.

Ironically, during this time, John was notified by an attorney from Nebraska that his Grandmother, Francis Meiner, had died intestate. Survivors were being contacted as to the inheritance of her considerable fortune.

She never admitted, even to herself, John mused, that she would lose her power to death. Now all the people she treated with such cruelty would inherit what she denied them as long as she lived. It was fitting somehow.

As one of the heirs, John felt he was comfortable with his own successes and the portion of the Graydon estate that he held. He saw to it that his sister Donna and her children would receive his considerable part of his cruel grandmother's estate.

His thoughts returned to the present as he watched from his window when another small plane came in.

That's it. Yes. The Bonanza taxied toward their hanger through the damp dusk.

He shuffled papers he'd been working on, slipped them into his desk and locked it.

When he looked again at the incoming plane, disappointment crowded out the excitement he always felt when he was going to see his wife again. The plane that had come to a stop was Hank's.

Shrugging on his jacket, he headed for his partner and arrived at the side of the plane just as Hank jumped down.

"Hey friend, I thought you were giving a party tonight, shouldn't you be at home helping your wife?"

Hank didn't answer, just continued toward him, head down.

"John, come into the office with me."

Sobered, a quick jab of fear cutting into his gut, John followed Hank.

"That's not possible!" John paled.

"Come on Hank, she's too good a pilot, that couldn't happen to her." He grabbed his heavy flight jacket, "Come on, take me to her. We can fly back in good time man, come on. Come with me."

"She's gone, John."

Hank was crying openly. He cradled Muffin in the crook of one arm. Her usually glossy coat was covered with grease, oil, mud and blood. She shivered violently as Hank held her close.

"We don't know how Muffin survived. They found her wandering near the end of the flight line."

John watched Hank's face. Comprehension turned his expression to horror as he surveyed the dirty little dog. He crumpled to the floor as the awful shock and final acceptance of his tragic loss caused him to lose consciousness.

This was the only way life could continue for John on this night.

Chapter 34

JOHN KNOWLTON SENIOR

Kiawah Island, South Carolina

May 1960

The spring evening was clear and the salt smell of the air carried in with each wave.

A receding tide defied a beach walker's guess by overlapping the last wave, rather than sinking below the previous water's level. Little curls of foam washed over his feet and grains of sand stuck to his instep as they found their way between his toes.

It was still difficult for him to stay alert. Eight months had passed since Susan's death, and he couldn't find his way back into the mainstream of life.

He didn't care, nor did he want to care.

Hank, Barb, Grace and Er, Shirley and Susan's family had been so caring, but they wouldn't talk about her. They wouldn't keep her alive by reliving his relationship with her through verbal memories.

He wanted to hear her name. Wanted to remember every moment, her every word. There had been so many precious times together, he wanted to share them with those who had known her, but no one would talk about her. When he mentioned her, or something they had shared, eyes lowered, and no one would carry the ball to bring her back if only for a few brief moments.

Her mother and father hardly seemed to realize she was gone, their grief was so great.

Hank and Barbara avoided her name in their quest for something new for him to think about, to do.

Susan's brothers and sisters avoided any connection he might make between them and their eldest sister.

He knew they were all trying to help, but it wasn't the way he wanted to be helped.

He had always heard that grief caused pain, now he knew it was true. This pain, the isolated pain of anguish, found somewhere in the center of him always came unexpectedly and was physically terrible. It was a huge red-hot ache that seemed to grow and move from the center of his body, through his lungs, into his throat, and it throbbed with an intensity of fierceness that sapped all his strength. At times, it was difficult to recognize and then, as it throbbed to become agony, he realized it was grief that attacked physically and then joined in a mental awareness that was nearly impossible to bear. Yet, strange as it might seem, he welcomed the distress for somehow it helped him show his loyalty, his love for Susan. He wanted to grieve, to be able to cry. He wanted someone to hold him. Oh God. He wanted Susan to hold him. His body, his mind and his entire being screamed inside of him silently, screamed for someone. But he was alone.

He had come to Charleston, making every attempt to put grief behind him. He had come because Susan and he had never been together here. This was foreign terrain for them as a pair and perhaps here he could get back to life without her, to the empty life he had before they met. He rationalized that he had been able to function before Susan entered his life, so perhaps he could regain that nothingness by staying here for a while.

His first stop had been with Shirley and her family in the

lovely old Graydon mansion. She had been attentive and understanding as always, and she had heard him out. Too many times, he supposed.

It was Shirley's husband who suggested that John come out here to the old beach house on Kiawah Island where there were no Susan memories, where he could fish and perhaps find himself. He snapped up the idea.

The cottage hadn't been opened for the season yet and he threw himself into fierce activity as he took down shutters, replaced them with screens, painted and pounded. He had worked, cooking for himself only when hunger sent urgent signals to the rest of his body and then when he was exhausted, he finally slept.

The memories and pain came when he walked the beach, following the foamy paths of waves for miles, only to return to the cottage to take up some menial task to keep occupied.

As he walked today, he noted that the beach was relatively deserted for this time of year. In only a few weeks though, the crowds would be here. Children would be laughing, splashing and rolling in the sand.

Children.

He couldn't think about children.

Oh God, if he could hear her voice. Would he recognize it if he heard it? Where was she? Could she hear him when he called to her, talked to her, shared some part of his day with her? Why was death such a mystery? Wouldn't it be easier to grieve if we knew what happened after you died? If he could just hear her voice.

A few fishermen were casting lines. That's what he'd do! He was pleased to drop his maudlin speculations and gained purpose as he headed through the soft sand to the cottage to get a surf rod from the shed.

Arming himself with a medium-weight casting rod, he got into the tackle box and realized there wasn't any live bait to cut. Damn. He should have thought about that before he came on the island. Well, there was bacon in the refrigerator and, unorthodox as it was, he'd give it a try.

Sitting in a chair on the sand with the rod in a spike, John watched the waves as they shimmered against the sun as it began its drop in the west, out there in back of him. It was still early, but slowly, daylight was departing and in the beginning dusk he could just discern the beating pulsation of his pole. Back and forth, it was gently alive with the sea's action; he concentrated on the rod, and wondered if the crazy bacon bait was still hanging onto the shiny Hopkins spoon he had attached it to.

Suddenly the reel clicked and the line whizzed out to sea with a screaming whine.

"I'll be damned!"

He jumped to grab the pole and set the hook. Speaking to the dusky pink-orange waves, reflecting the beauty of the afterglow, he said laughing at the incongruity of fish eating bacon,

"I may have come across the perfect bait for this beach!"

He checked the line's output and little by little began to reel it in. Whatever was on was a fighter. It felt almost like a bass. My gosh could he have a bass on this late in the season? Whatever it was, it was a big boy, and it was playing rough.

John reeled and the line remained taut, but refused to be wound any further. He fought and whatever mystery lay at the end of the line, fought back.

Here then, was catharsis as the inconsolable man pitted

himself against an unrelenting fish. They pulled at one another, the fish and the man. They struggled. John lifted the weight of the pole, turning the reel quickly to keep the line tight. There was another strong pull. The line moved from side to side with the direction the fish took in the froth of the big waves offshore.

Pull.

Wind quickly.

Let the pole down.

Raise it slowly, reeling in all the time.

The fish stops to rest, and there's a slack period a time when the rapid turning of the reel brings in yards and yards of line.

The action is reversed as once again the creature in the sea gains strength and fights back, pulling line behind him as he heads for deeper water.

The fisherman's work is cut out for him. There is no time for self pity. No time for wishes and dreams or for grief.

As John reeled and fought his catch, his thoughts were only involved with bringing in the fish, on bringing this strong adversary held on the end of a fine line to the beach.

How in hell was he going to horse the damned thing up here on the sand without losing it in the surf? This fish was larger than any he had ever caught surf fishing.

To the south, a lone walker appeared in the dusk, striding quickly. The figure gained size and shape as it approached the area of John's struggle.

It was a woman.

Damn.

She probably didn't know the first thing about surf fishing or landing a fish.

The fish, nearer now, gave another strong pull away and into the sea.

My God, how long had he been fighting this baby?

The lone figure, sensing the struggle, stepped up her pace and then started to run.

"What do you have there?" She ran toward him.

He didn't look at her, he was reaching the end of the battle, and he was determined to be the victor.

"Get that gaff over there. Help me. I'm going to try to bring it up on the beach. Can you get the gaff in the gills?"

He was shouting over his shoulder as the surf and the reel continued to bring in his trophy. "I don't know what it is, but it's a big one!"

The woman stopped, picked up the gaff and headed for the surf.

"You're not even supposed to gaff a surf fish, but don't worry, I'll get it for you!"

She strode into the surf, carrying the unorthodox gaff. A breaker hit her waist high, but she stood her ground.

He continued to reel as the fish tired.

There he was! The fish's back began to show between rollers. It was black and shiny. It was a bass, lost to seasonal fishing and now lost to a fisherman.

At precisely the right moment, the woman spotted it and swung the hook of the gaff under the gills. She started to pull with the wooden handle, against the big fish in the foamy surf. It had to weigh nearly fifty pounds, judging from the size.

John put his pole down and ran into the surf.

The dumb woman had gaffed it too soon. She was still in water too deep to pull it with the short-handled hook.

"Here! Let me help!"

The Last Magnolia

The slight woman's body exerted surprising strength as he grabbed the handle to help her pull the flopping fish up and out of the breakers.

"My God Mister, don't lay that pole down!"

Letting her grip on the gaff go, she headed for the beach. A wave knocked both of them over. They came up, breathing fast. Another breaker hit them, but he hung onto the gaff.

"You're going to lose him, you fool!"

She ran out of the ocean for the discarded pole, picked it up and rapidly reeled in the excess line.

It was totally dark now and she yelled into the evening sea breeze, "We've got him now! Bring him on up. I've still got him on the line. Get him up here on the beach and out of that surf."

John was aware of two things in all of the excitement. This tiny woman had a southern accent you couldn't cut with a knife. She had obviously done quite a bit of surf fishing and she was as strong as a man.

He rushed forward with the push of a breaker and gave one last lurching pull on the gaff. The fish was free, flopping on the sand, headed back toward the water.

"Hit him man! Hit him on the head! Hit him with the handle. Good. That's the way!"

He had crushed the skull of the big bass. The flopping stopped and the woman placed the rod in the spike and came walking triumphantly it seemed, dripping wet, toward him.

Her voice changed from the excited yelling of only moments ago to the soft gentility of a southern lady.

"My goodness, you probably think I'm just awful, but really, when I saw you bringing in that fish . . . why that's the dream of every surf fisherman! And you and I caught him . . . " her voice faltered . . . she was even with him now, and she looked up through the darkness into his face. "Johnny?"

"Honey!"

His heart stopped for an instant. He rubbed his eyes as if to remove a film from them.

"Honey Bascomb! How in hell can a beautiful, delicate little southern magnolia blossom handle a fish the way you just did?"

****

She cradled the glass of bourbon carefully between her hands, as though to warm it. The ice popped and she took a small sip, looking over the rim of the glass at John as he sat on the opposite side of the kitchen table facing her.

"It's just not humanly possible that you're here, Johnny. You can't imagine how long I've been thinking about you. I've needed to talk to you," she watched him, looking for the effect she might be having on him. "We could always talk. You listened to me and straightened out so much of my thinking for me."

"Is that why you left before I could get back to you in London?"

His question showed no bitterness, only curiosity.

"Knowing what I know now, I should never have mailed that box," she twirled the now half-empty glass, rattling the ice, and then said, defensively, "Johnny, I never meant to lead you to believe we'd be together forever. I told you I had expectations to live up to. I was born to those awful expectations."

Her words were bitter now. "As I grew up, it was Bobby who they matched me to. I had to fit the pattern our families had cut out for us. You might think arranged marriages are from cultures in other lands, away from us, but they exist, and I am an example of one."

The Last Magnolia

Her eyes, wide, still beautiful, held the same little girls' innocence of years ago. "I don't fool myself anymore."

That would be a change, he thought.

"I can rationalize evenly now. I know now, most of the patterns I've followed, most of the expectations I lived up to were wrong, but you have to understand in our way down here in the south, it was right. I did exactly as I should have, exactly what was expected of me."

She rattled the remaining ice cubes again, "Another please?"

He took her glass, and keeping his back to her while he prepared the refill, smiled to himself. She was still delightful with her immature little girl ways. Here they were, approaching middle age and they could still drink each other in, size one another up, and continue a completely candid relationship as long as she was the primary subject, just as they had done nearly twenty years ago.

Handing her the filled glass, he returned to sit facing her.

"Tell me about your life, Honey."

"Well," she inhaled deeply and then let the air back out again in one long, deep sigh, "I've done everything exactly to fit the Charleston pattern, to satisfy my parents and the society we live in," she frowned, "and I'm still doing it. Now I want out."

"I thought you were rational in your assessment of your situation, Honey."

"What do you mean?"

"Haven't you lived exactly as you indicated you wanted to live? Why do you want out? I don't understand."

She looked at him with surprise.

"Oh, I'm rational. It's Charleston and its damned old requirements of me that aren't levelheaded."

She stopped talking and seemed to be resting, seemed to be

299

putting things in order verbally before she continued.

"I came home with Bobby and we had the wedding of the year. Everything was done right. Oh Johnny, I was such a beautiful bride!""

He smiled knowingly, "I can well imagine," he noted dryly.

She didn't catch the sarcasm or she ignored him, she was too far into her tale to reflect on his reactions.

"Bobby went with the family bank, and he's still there. He's the president now. Of course that's no surprise," a look of anger crossed her face, "I delivered the exact number of acceptable children, just as I told you I would, and in the prescribed necessary time, of course." She smiled as if she had pleased the entire world. "Two years after the wedding, I had little Bobby and exactly two years later, little Honoria came along."

"A God-damned fairy tale as I live and breathe, and just think Honey, you're living it."

"Oh Johnny, stop talking that way! I've raised two fine, healthy children. They fit the pattern and Bobby is just like his daddy, while my little girl is trying awfully hard these days to be like my mother. Can you imagine?"

It was difficult to think of her as a mother, a matron. He still saw too many of the little-girl qualities he had found enchanting so many years ago.

"Of course, its better she be like Mama than me. I wouldn't want my little girl to do anything wild, anything like I did." Eyelashes lowered over blue eyes. "But then what I can do, and what I did, well, that's our secret, isn't it?"

He took a long swallow and the raw whiskey burned as it went down. There had been lots of burning on the way down since Susan died. He had been drinking too much. He stopped the thought. He wasn't going to remember Susan now. To relate her in any way to this selfish, over-sexed little woman would be wrong. For some reason, watching Honey and listening to her made it possible for him to achieve the total detachment he needed as he listened to her rattle on about her family, her social connections and achievements, and things that were important to her and of no concern to him. Finally he interrupted.

"If you are so busy and important, so well placed, why are you at your folk's beach house all alone before the season starts? Where are your children? Why are you alone?"

Tears pooled and spilled over her lower lids to run down her cheeks.

"Johnny dear, I can be perfectly free with you can't I? Like I used to?"

"You know you can."

"Bobby has another woman. He wants a divorce. He doesn't want me anymore."

The eyes opened wide, the cheeks were covered with the dampness of her tears now, "And after all I've done for him!"

"What about the position, family, that sort of thing? Aren't they important to him anymore?"

"He doesn't care, and then, he knows."

"Knows what?"

"He knows I've had a number of tiny little indiscretions over the years. He never knew about you and me, Johnny. My God if he had, he wouldn't ever have married me, but there were others."

The truth will out.

Of course there had been other 'indiscretions'; Honey couldn't change. She wasn't built for monogamy.

"He says," she continued, "if I let him go, he'll keep all of my

301

little, what he calls, 'arrangements' out of the divorce action. He'll let me keep the children, and he'll support all of us in the style I'm accustomed to." She started to cry.

"Well Honey, you said you wanted out. It seems to me he's giving you a pretty easy way to go."

She wailed, "Oh Johnny, I don't know what I want. That's why I'm down here, to sort everything out. I'm not sure I want to be a middle-aged grass widow with two children. You just can't know how bleak life is for a single woman in Charleston."

"So you want to stay married, no matter how he feels about you. What if you don't agree to his terms? How is he going to take that?"

"He says he'll expose all he knows, take the children and leave me without one thing."

"Well Honey, just how much does he know? How much is there for him to know?"

"Don't judge me. I don't need that." She wasn't crying anymore, her tears were replaced with a guarded look. "There was plenty...Well, let's just say he's sure to know things I didn't ever expect him to find out."

She shook the ice in the glass again, "give me another drink will you? I can't tell you how good it is to have you back, back for me to talk to just when I needed you so badly."

Then in typical Honey fashion, she switched gears, "Oh my goodness, I'm doing all the talking. Johnny, what are you doing in Charleston? The last time I talked with Shirley, she said you'd only been down once since your last marriage. Tell me about your wife. You old devil you, married again!"

"You mean Susan?" It was difficult to say her name in front of Honey for some reason.

The Last Magnolia

"Yes. Does she make you happy Johnny? Is she a good wife? My goodness I know how very successful you've been, Shirley Graydon has kept me up to date on your wonderful company." She leaned across the table and reached for his hand, "Oh my, I surely have talked too much about myself. Tell me about Susan."

He drained his drink with unsteady hands and poured another long stream of whiskey over the half melted ice in his glass. The gut pain tightened.

"Susan was killed in a plane crash nearly a year ago, Honey."

"Oh Johnny, can you talk about it?"

"I'm not sure I can, but I want to. Can you understand that? I need to talk about Susan, about the wonderful life we had together. Oh God, there's so much."

He moved to the refrigerator, dropped more ice in his glass and then absently poured more liquor into it before he took the seat opposite her again.

"Go on, tell me about her."

He began, but the tale wandered, it flitted as he talked like a slightly confused madman about each of the women in his life. Susan, his mother, his grandmother, Katie, the baby, Janice, Honey herself and then Susan again, back full circle to the love of his life.

Overcome with compassion, Honey got up and took his hand to lead him to the couch in the living room. Probably for the first time in her life, Honey realized she had to think of someone other than herself, and she rose to the occasion as a grand southern matriarch would, with dignity and compassion.

He didn't cry as the words came. He spoke evenly and steadily, painting a perfect portrait of the beautiful woman who'd

The Last Magnolia

given him all there was in life. The story was a tribute and, when he finished, the room was still. He felt deep pride and great pleasure because he had been able to characterize Susan so completely for someone else, just as she must be remembered.

"Oh my dear John, I'm so sorry. What a wonderful woman she was. The two of you were so lucky to have those years together, do you know that?"

"Yes. Now that the talking is done, yes Honey. Thank you for letting me talk about her. I guess I needed you."

They sat, bonded together by an understanding and compassion for one another that kept all other forces outside. Good friends.

****

The morning sunlight filtered through the venetian blinds and he turned over to get the light out of his eyes. His mouth felt like gravel and his body ached. The fish fight had used muscles he hadn't exercised in years.

A slight movement beside him made him open his eyes.

Honey rolled towards him. They were both naked. They touched each other.

"I'm glad it happened this way, Johnny. We needed each other."

He was silent.

She laid her head on his outstretched arm. Her hair was brittle now, her body showed the beginning ravages of age. Yet with cosmetic aid, she was still a beautiful woman.

"Did we ever gut out that damned fish?"

"No it's still lying out there on the porch. I guess the sport of catching it was enough."

She stroked his chest, "It was like it used to be for us wasn't it

304

The Last Magnolia

Johnny? Good. Remember?"

"I remember." He really didn't count those memories for much and wondered why the two of them were here now.

"Honey, when do you have to be home?"

"Not till this afternoon. We have the rest of the day. The best news is, I've decided what to do about Bobby."

John sat up and propped his head with a pillow.

"As I see it, you don't have much choice."

She matched his position by twisting her pillow and elevating her head to his level.

"Well, you're right about that, but now I've found you, it really doesn't matter."

She jumped from the bed like a girl and headed for the bathroom. When she returned she was showered and wrapped in Turkish towels. One wrapped her head in a turban, the other was tubed around her.

Picking up the slacks she had worn the evening before, she dressed systematically, and smiling, leaned down to kiss him.

"I'm going to my place now Johnny, there's something I have to get you."

"What?"

"I'm going to get MY 'come back' toothbrush for you darling. Do you remember?"

He nodded.

"This time it's going to mean what you said it meant. I'm going to leave my toothbrush with you. That way you'll know I'm coming back. When all this is over with Bobby, I'm going to be yours. The way it should have been years ago. We belong together. You need me and I need you. I should have known it years ago."

She headed out the bedroom door.

"All right Johnny?"

She was still moving, out the door and away from him, so it was difficult to know whether she heard his reply or not. He answered her sadly,

"No, not any more Honey."

He turned his back to the sounds of her departure by rolling over on his side.

The loneliness, the madness came back to him. He was awake now. Sober and alone. His eyes focused on the bedroom wall as if someone were there that he was able to speak to.

"God", he said, "am I being punished by having everything taken away from me? Why?"

The wall seemed to open and the scene he had suppressed since he was only ten years old revealed itself. The memory hit him like lightening! It came so fast he couldn't push the pictures of that August night so long ago away, as he had done of all of the past years.

****

There was a light in the barn. When he saw it, he knew there was trouble. He put on his pants, slipped down the back stairs and out the door. Before he even got to the barnyard, he heard the voices.

"I told you to get the hell out of here, you son of a bitch. You didn't take the chance I gave you, so now I'll help you leave. You're better off dead, you God-damned wife stealer. You won't take my wife again, or anybody else's. I'll see to that!"

"John!"

It was his mother's voice, crying, pleading with his father.

"John, let us go. We won't come back. Please don't do this."

"Shut up you slut. You common whore. Get yourself back up to the house. I'll take care of this no good drifter. Now get up there!"

"John, for God's sakes don't do this. Let him go. I'll stay. Think of the scandal."

"Scandal! You're the scandal of the county, you bitch. Go on . . . get out of here!"

Johnny reached the door to the barn. What he saw scared him so badly, his sharp intake of breath made his throat feel raw. Momentarily, he froze.

In the soft glow of the kerosene lantern, he saw Fred, backed up, tied against one of the stall walls. His mother was beside him, weeping softly and his father faced them. He was holding a shotgun, waving it irrationally and moving ominously closer to Fred and his mother.

She saw her son.

"Johnny! Go back to the house, son," she screamed.

"Let him stay, Mildred. He may as well know now what a tramp you are, the kind of mother you really are and he may as well learn what we do to wife stealers."

"No, John, don't do this. Please don't do this." She was sobbing, dry, gasping terrified sounds.

Johnny didn't know what to do. He had never seen his father act crazy like this before.

"Get over here son, I'm going to kill a wife-stealer. You can help me bury him. Come to think of it, he's a mother-stealer too." The old man laughed hysterically. "You may's well get in on it."

Fred said nothing. His eyes rolled back in fear as he watched the old man with the gun.

"Dad, don't do this."

307

How could a ten-year-old tell his father what to do?

His father swung around momentarily pointing his gun at Johnny.

"I'll do what should've been done a long time ago. Now get over here," he waved the gun to signal which way he wanted the boy to move.

Johnny lunged without any plan. He tried to grab the gun. His father fell to the floor cursing, and dropped the weapon.

Johnny dove for it and picked it up from the dirt floor. He rolled to the side as his father threw his heavy body at him.

"Give me that gun, damn it."

The old man wrestled with the little boy, and Johnny could hear his mother's screams.

"John! Stop it! Johnny! Fred! Stop them!"

Johnny held onto the gun, and swung to run from the barn with it when his father got to his feet and charged him.

The gun went off.

A dark red blotch crept across the front of his father's overalls. As the old man fell back, his insane expression was replaced by a mild look of surprise.

Mildred ran and knelt by her husband.

"My God! He's dead!"

Johnny was sweating. The scuffle, the humidity of the August night and the fear made him feel slick.

And sick.

What had he done? He had killed his own father!

He stood with the gun in his hands. His mother stared at it, a look of horror on her face.

"Cut me loose, Mildred."

She rose and helped Fred cut his bindings. Then she came to

her son.

"Johnny, Johnny, don't worry," she held him, stroked him, making tools of comfort and assurance with her hands, "What you did was right, you tried to save me. The gun went off accidentally. He was crazy. When he went for you, he tripped the trigger on that gun, and it shot him instead of us. He was going to kill us, and he ended up killing himself."

Fred put his arms around the boy's shoulders. "Don't worry. It will be all right. We'll fix it."

Johnny was too horrified, too scared to cry, and he wondered who was right.

"What are we going to do?" He looked at the crumpled, bleeding body of his father.

"Help me."

Fred moved into the stall next to Wind, picked up a pick and started to drive it into the hard packed floor of the barn.

In a daze, not sure what was right, Johnny picked up a shovel and helped to make the grave. They worked together, hard and fast, his mother digging too, and when the hole was deep enough, they moved the still warm body of his father into it.

Dirt was shoveled over him. As it reached the level of the floor, it was tamped heavily as they stamped on it over and over again with their feet. When there was no depression, Fred, in charge now, directed Mildred.

"Sweep the dirt now. John, go to your grandmother's and tell her your folks are gone. When you come back, put Wind in this stall," he pointed to the space where the grave had been dug.
"Oh no, Fred, we can't do that." Johnny's mother started to cry again.

"It's the only way." Fred's voice was tight, frightened.

The Last Magnolia

Johnny watched his mother. Was she going to leave them again? She didn't have to. His father was dead now. No one ever had to know. She could stay. He reasoned as a child looking for happy endings. Erasing the night's wrongs made it possible for him to rewrite life the way he felt it ought to be.

His mother hugged him. She was still crying.

"Johnny, oh Johnny, you must never believe this was your fault. It was an accident, but you have to understand, we can't tell anyone, ever."

"I understand Mom." He was crying, but he wanted to show her how grown up he was. "It's all right. Will you stay now that he's dead?"

She shuddered and hugged him closer to her. Then she straightened, and her voice was strong and steady as she looked directly at him, "Yes."

His heart skipped a beat as happiness flooded his being.

"You go get your grandmother. Remember, never a word. You and Fred and I know what happened, and we all know it was an accident. You must never forget that."

When he came back, his mother was gone.

He never forgot her lie.

Sunshine flooded the bedroom and drenched the glisten of sweat on John's body. The horror, the shame and the memory all flooded in as he reconstructed that gruesome night for the first time and a joyful revelation hit him.

He hadn't murdered his father! It was an accident! The tragedies of his life had not been a series of punishments for that long hidden horror. God didn't hate him.

No, he thought, my life has been lived with joy, hate, the power of knowledge, regret, experience, strength, love and loss. It has been no different from any other man's life.

From this epiphany, John realized that those same aspects of life would be his future.

He reached down and patted the small silky body of fur pressed against his thigh and a transformation occurred.

The old John, a strong, capable, vibrant man emerged from the shell of the one who had come here beaten by grief.

He pushed the sheet aside and sat up, moving swiftly with a positive sense of renewal, he laughed, picked the little pup up and walked to the swing on the porch. He sat, still holding her.

"By God, I still have you, Muffin!" The little dog recognized the change and roused herself to sit up with ears cocked, head tilted in question.

The Magnolia tree in front of the house was beginning to drop its waxy petals, the beautiful blossoms were edged with soft brown rot, and the older yellowing leaves drooped, soon to drop between the large and still beautiful waxy evergreen leaves to the ground. Those blossoms of beauty would be become now sharp brackets on the remaining bud. Dead sharp brackets that showed age and deterioration. Red berries would show themselves later in the year between the now ugly brackets; but now, for the next months, the magnolia blossoms were gone and what they left in their aged departure was old and ugly.

"We can wallow in grief here and watch those magnolia blossoms flourish and fade for the rest of our lives," John said more to himself than to the dog as he sat still naked, his strong body reflecting virility and power, as he pushed the swing forward and backward with his bare feet, "but we would wither too, and I'm not ready for that."

He strode with determination into the house and toward the

closet and started to pull things from the hangers. "Let's go home Muffin. They need us at home."

He grinned. It was the old familiar John grin. His eyes were bright with purpose as he examined his face in the mirror. The strength that had carried him through life asserted itself once more, and this man who had survived every obstacle thrown in his path with the force of sheer will, began his next move toward what life optimistically would give him.

He could face it all now without the fear of recrimination for an event he had kept buried for most of his life.

He did not kill his father! Watch out Spokane...Here we come!

THE END

The Author

Dixie Lee Anderson is published internationally as a newspaper and magazine columnist, children's author and freelance writer.

Born in Cheney, Washington she attended Sacred Heart School of Nursing in Spokane, Washington, worked as a nurse and married an Air Force Officer with whom she travelled through most of the world.

As the Women's Editor for the Pacific Broadcasting Company in Agana, Guam (Station KUAM) she wrote, directed, produced and performed as hostess for radio and television.

She has been the Food Columnist for Family Magazine for over 30 years. The author of fiction and non-fiction stories and children's books. She co-wrote with Dr. William F. Damitz (Charlie) The Giant Egg, published for the My Weekly Reader Children's book club. They received an author's citation from the New Jersey Institute of Technology for that work. She is remembered by many as "The Egg Lady" as she travelled at Easter-time to many of the schools in New Jersey sharing her extensive collection of decorated eggs and shared the holiday book with the younger students.

As a resident of New Jersey she writes for a number of organizations and spends time in her garden at the Jersey Shore.

The Last Magnolia is created from her observations on life, history, fascinating people and the world over her years of traveling and learning.